GIRL IN
TRANSLATION

**Center Point
Large Print**

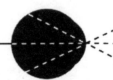

**This Large Print Book carries the
Seal of Approval of N.A.V.H.**

GIRL IN TRANSLATION

JEAN KWOK

CENTER POINT PUBLISHING
THORNDIKE, MAINE

This Center Point Large Print edition
is published in the year 2010 by arrangement with
Riverhead Books,
a member of Penguin Group (USA) Inc.

The text of this Large Print edition is unabridged.
In other aspects, this book may vary
from the original edition.
Printed in the United States of America
on permanent paper.
Set in 16-point Times New Roman type.

ISBN: 978-1-60285-887-9

Library of Congress Cataloging-in-Publication Data

Kwok, Jean.
  Girl in translation / Jean Kwok. — Center Point large print ed.
    p. cm.
  ISBN 978-1-60285-887-9 (library binding : alk. paper)
  1. Chinese—New York (State)—New York—Fiction. 2. Women immigrants—Fiction.
   3. Chinese American teenagers—Fiction. 4. Mothers and daughters—Fiction.
   5. Large type books. I. Title.
  PS3611.W65G57 2010b
  813′.6—dc22

                                                          2010021032

For Erwin,
Stefan and Milan,
and to the memory of my brother
Kwan S. Kwok

PROLOGUE

I was born with a talent. Not for dance, or comedy, or anything so delightful. I've always had a knack for school. Everything that was taught there, I could learn: quickly and without too much effort. It was as if school were a vast machine and I a cog perfectly formed to fit in it. This is not to say that my education was always easy for me. When Ma and I moved to the U.S., I spoke only a few words of English, and for a very long time, I struggled.

There's a Chinese saying that the fates are winds that blow through our lives from every angle, urging us along the paths of time. Those who are strong-willed may fight the storm and possibly choose their own road, while the weak must go where they are blown. I say I have not been so much pushed by winds as pulled forward by the force of my decisions. And all the while, I have longed for that which I could not have. At the time when it seemed that everything I'd ever wanted was finally within reach, I made a decision that changed the trajectory of the rest of my life.

From my position outside the window of the bridal shop now, I can see the little girl sitting quietly at the mannequin's feet, eyes shut, the heavy folds of falling fabric closing her in, and I think, *This isn't the life I wanted for my child.* I know how it will go: she already spends all of her time after school at the shop, helping with small tasks like sorting beads; later, she will learn to sew by hand and then on the machines until, finally, she can take over some of the embroidery and finishing work, and then she too will spend her days and weekends bent over the unending yards of fabric. For her, there will be no playing at friends' houses, no swimming lessons, no summers at the beach, not much of anything at all except for the unrelenting rhythm of the sewing needle.

But then we both look up as her father walks in and after all these years and all that's passed, my heart stirs like a wounded animal in my chest.

Was I ever as beautiful as she? There are almost no pictures of me as a child. We couldn't afford a camera. The first snapshot taken of me in the U.S. was a school photo, from the year I came to America. I was eleven. There came a moment later in my life when I wanted to move on, and I ripped this picture up. But instead of discarding the pieces, I tucked them away in an envelope.

Recently, I found that envelope and brushed off the dust. I broke open the seal and touched the torn bits of paper inside: here was the tip of an ear, a part of the jaw. My hair had been cut by my mother, unevenly and too short, parted far to the right and swept over my forehead in a boy's hairstyle. The word PROOF covers much of my face and a part of my blue polyester shirt. We hadn't been able to pay for the actual photo, so we'd kept this sample they'd sent home.

But when I join the ripped pieces of the photo and put together the puzzle, my eyes still gaze directly at the camera, their hope and ambition clear to all who care to look. If only I'd known.

ONE

A sheet of melting ice lay over the concrete. I watched my rubber boots closely, the way the toes slid on the ice, the way the heels splintered it. Ice was something I had known only in the form of small pieces in red bean drinks. This ice was wild ice, ice that defied streets and buildings.

"We are so lucky that a spot in one of Mr. N.'s buildings opened up," Aunt Paula had said as we drove to our new neighborhood. "You will have to fix it up, of course, but real estate in New York is so expensive! This is very cheap for what you're getting."

I could hardly sit still in the car and kept twisting my head, looking for skyscrapers. I didn't find any. I longed to see the New York I had heard about in school: Min-hat-ton, glistening department stores, and most of all, the Liberty Goddess, standing proud in New York Harbor. As we drove, the highways turned into impossibly broad avenues, stretching out into the distance. The buildings became dirtier, with broken windows and English writing spray-painted over the walls. We made a few more turns, passing people who were waiting in a long line, despite the early hour, and then Uncle Bob parked next to a three-story building with a boarded-up storefront. I thought he was stopping to make a pickup of some sort, but then everyone had gotten out of the car onto the icy pavement.

The people in line were waiting to go into the doorway to our right, with a sign that said "Department of Social Services." I wasn't sure what that was. Almost everyone was black. I'd never seen black people before, and a woman near the front, whom I could observe most clearly, had skin as dark as coal and gold beads gleaming in her cloudlike hair. Despite the frayed coat she wore, she was breathtaking. Some people were dressed in regular clothes but some looked exhausted and unkempt, with glazed eyes and unwashed hair.

"Don't stare," Aunt Paula hissed at me. "You might attract their attention."

I turned around and the adults had already unloaded our few possessions, which were now piled by the boarded-up storefront. We had three tweed suitcases, Ma's violin case, a few bulky packages wrapped in brown paper, and a broom. There was a large wet spot at the bottom of the front door.

"What is that, Ma?"

She bent close and peered at it.

"Don't touch that," Uncle Bob said from behind us. "It's pee."

We both sprang backward.

Aunt Paula laid a gloved hand on our shoulders. "Don't worry," she said, although I didn't find her expression reassuring. She looked uncomfortable and a bit embarrassed. "The people in your apartment moved out recently so I haven't had a chance to look at it yet, but remember, if there are any problems, we will fix them. Together. Because we are family."

Ma sighed and put her hand on top of Aunt Paula's. "Good."

"And I have a surprise for you. Here." Aunt Paula went to the car and took out a cardboard box with a few items in it: a digital radio alarm clock, a few sheets and a small black-and-white television.

"Thank you," Ma said.

"No, no," Aunt Paula replied. "Now we have to go. We're already late for the factory."

I heard them drive away and Ma struggled with the keys in front of the looming door. When she finally cracked the door open, the weight of it seemed to resist her until finally it gaped wide to reveal a bare lightbulb glowing like a tooth in its black mouth. The air smelled dank and filled with dust.

"Ma," I whispered, "is it safe?"

"Aunt Paula wouldn't send us anywhere unsafe," she said, but her low voice was laced with a thread of doubt. Although Ma's Cantonese was usually very clear, the sound of her country roots grew more pronounced when she was nervous. "Give me the broom."

While I brought our things inside the narrow

entryway, Ma started up the stairs first, wielding the broom.

"Stay here and keep the door open," she said. I knew that was so I could run for help.

My pulse pounded in my throat as I watched her climb the wooden stairs. They had been worn by years of use and each step warped, slanting sharply downward to the banister. I worried that a step would give way and Ma would fall through. When she turned the corner on the landing, I lost sight of her and I could only hear the stairs creaking one by one. I scanned our luggage to see if there was anything I could use as a weapon. I would scream and then run upstairs to help her. Images of the tough kids at my old school in Hong Kong flashed through my mind: Fat Boy Wong and Tall Guy Lam. Why wasn't I big like them? There was some scuffling upstairs, a door clicked open and a few floorboards groaned. Was that Ma or someone else? I strained my ears, listening for a gasp or a thud. There was silence.

"Come up," she called. "You can close the door now."

I felt my limbs loosen as if they'd been deflated. I ran up the stairs to see our new apartment.

"Don't brush against anything," Ma said.

I was standing in the kitchen. The wind whistled through the two windows on the wall to the right of me, and I wondered why Ma had opened them. Then I saw that they were still closed. It was only that most of the windowpanes were missing or cracked, with filthy shards of glass protruding from the wooden frame. A thick layer of dust covered the small kitchen table and wide sink, which was white and pitted. As I walked, I tried to avoid the brittle bodies of the dead roaches scattered here and there. They were huge, the thick legs delineated by the harsh shadows.

The bathroom was in the kitchen and its door directly faced the stove, which any child knows is terrible *feng shui*. A section of the dark yellow linoleum floor near the sink and refrigerator had been torn away, revealing the misshapen floorboards underneath. The walls were cracked, bulging in places as if they had swallowed something, and in some spots, the paint layer had flaked off altogether, exposing the bare plaster like flesh under the skin.

The kitchen was attached to one other room, with no door in between. Out of the corner of my eye, I saw a scattering of brown slowly recede into the walls as we walked into the next room: live roaches. There could also be rats and mice hiding in the walls. I took Ma's broom, which she was still holding, inverted it and slammed the handle hard against the floor.

"*Ah*-Kim," Ma said, "you'll disturb the neighbors."

I stopped banging and said nothing, even though I suspected we were the only tenants in the building.

The windows of this room faced the street, and their windowpanes were intact. I realized that Aunt Paula would have fixed the ones that other people could see. Despite its bareness, this room stank of old sweat. In the corner, a double mattress lay on the floor. It had blue and green stripes and was stained. There was also a low coffee table with one leg that didn't match, on which I would later do my homework, and a dresser that was shedding its lime paint like dandruff. That was all.

What Aunt Paula had said couldn't be true, I thought, no one has lived in this apartment for a long time. I realized the truth. She'd done it all on purpose: letting us move on a weekday instead of during the weekend, giving us the presents at the last moment. She wanted to drop us here and have the factory as an excuse to leave fast, to get out when we were still thanking her for her kindness. Aunt Paula wasn't going to help us. We were alone.

I hugged myself with my arms. "Ma, I want to go home," I said.

Ma bent down and touched her forehead to mine. She could hardly bring herself to smile but her eyes were intense. "It will be all right. You and me, mother and cub." The two of us as a family.

But what Ma really thought of it all, I didn't know: Ma, who wiped off all the cups and chopsticks in a restaurant with her napkin whenever we went out because she wasn't sure they were clean enough. For Ma too, something must have been exposed in her relationship with Aunt Paula when she saw the apartment, something naked and throbbing under the skin of polite talk.

In our first week in the U.S., Ma and I had stayed in the short, square house of my aunt Paula and her family on Staten Island. The night we arrived from Hong Kong it was cold outside, and the heated air inside the house felt dry in my throat. Ma hadn't seen Aunt Paula, her oldest sister, in thirteen years, not since Aunt Paula left Hong Kong to marry Uncle Bob, who had moved to America as a child. I'd been told about the big factory Uncle Bob managed and always wondered why such a rich man would have had to go back to Hong Kong to find a wife. Now I saw the way that he leaned on his walking stick to get around and understood that there was something wrong with his leg.

"Ma, can we eat now?" My cousin Nelson's Chinese was awkward, the tones not quite right. He must have been told to speak the language because of us.

"Soon. Give your cousin a kiss first. Welcome her to America," Aunt Paula said. She took three-year-old Godfrey's hand and nudged Nelson toward me. Nelson was eleven years old like me, and I'd been told he would become my closest friend here. I studied him: a fat boy with skinny legs.

Nelson rolled his eyes. "Welcome to America," he said loudly for the adults' benefit. He leaned in to pretend to kiss my cheek and said softly, "You're a rake filled with dirt." A stupid country bumpkin. This time, his tones were perfect.

I flashed my eyes at Ma, who had not heard. For a moment, I was stunned by his lack of manners. I felt a flush crawl up my neck, then I smiled and pretended to kiss him back. "At least I'm not a potato with incense sticks for legs," I whispered.

The adults beamed.

We were given a tour. Ma had told me that in our new life in America, we would be living with Aunt Paula and taking care of Nelson and Godfrey. Their house seemed luxurious to me, with orange wall-to-wall carpeting instead of the plain concrete floors I was used to. Following the adults around the house, I saw how large Aunt Paula was, nearly the same height as her husband. Ma, thinner after her recent illness, seemed small and fragile by comparison, but it was hard to think too much about it. I'd never been allowed to walk on bare feet before and I was amazed by the prickly feel of the carpet.

Aunt Paula showed us all her furniture and a closet full of linens but what impressed me most was the hot water that came out of the taps. I'd never seen such a thing. In Hong Kong, the water was rationed. It was always cold and had to be boiled to make it drinkable.

Then Aunt Paula opened her cupboards to show us the shiny tins and pots inside. "We have some very fine white tea," she said proudly. "The leaves unfurl to become as long as your finger. Very delicate aroma. Please, feel free to drink as much as you like. And here are the pans. Best-quality steel, wonderful for frying and steaming."

When Ma and I woke from our night sleeping on the couches, Aunt Paula and Uncle Bob had left to take their kids to school and attend to their work managing the clothing factory, but a note said Aunt Paula would be home at noon to arrange things with us.

"Shall we try that special white tea?" I asked Ma.

Ma gestured at the counter. It was bare except for an old ceramic pot and a box of inexpensive green tea. "My heart stem, do you think that those things were left out by accident?"

I stared at the floor, embarrassed by my stupidity.

Ma continued. "It is not easy to understand Chinese. Certain things are not said directly. But we must not be annoyed by small things. Everyone has their faults." She put her hand on my shoulder. When I looked up, her face was calm and she meant what she said. "Never forget, we owe Aunt Paula and Uncle Bob a great debt. Because they got us out of Hong Kong and brought us here to America, the Golden Mountain."

I nodded. Every single kid at my old school had

19

been openly envious when they heard we were moving to the U.S. It was difficult for anyone to escape from Hong Kong before its scheduled return from British to Communist Chinese rule in 1997. There was almost no way out in those days unless you were a woman, beautiful or charming enough to marry one of the Chinese American men who returned to Hong Kong in search of a wife. This was what Aunt Paula had done. And now, she had been kind enough to allow us to share in her good fortune.

When Aunt Paula returned to the house that first morning in America, she suggested that Ma and I join her at the kitchen table.

"So, Kimberly," Aunt Paula said, tapping her fingers on the vinyl tablecloth. She smelled of perfume and had a mole on her upper lip. "I've heard about what a bright child you are." Ma smiled and nodded; I'd always been at the head of my class in Hong Kong. "You will be such a great help to your mother here," Aunt Paula went on. "And I'm sure Nelson can learn so much from your example."

"Nelson is a smart boy too," Ma said.

"Yes, yes, he is doing quite well in school, and his teacher told me he would make a wonderful lawyer someday, he's so good at arguing. But now he will really have a reason to work hard, won't he? To keep up with his brilliant cousin?"

20

"You are putting the tall hat of flattery on her head, older sister! It will not be easy for her here. *Ah*-Kim hardly speaks any English at all."

"Yes, that *is* a problem. Nelson's Chinese needs help as well—those American-born kids! But little sister, you should call her by her American name now: Kimberly. It's very important to have a name that is as American as possible. Otherwise, they might think you were fresh off the boat!" Aunt Paula laughed.

"You're always thinking of us," Ma said politely. "We want to start helping you too, as soon as we can. Should I start Nelson's Chinese lessons soon?"

Aunt Paula hesitated. "Well, that's what I wanted to talk about. It's not actually necessary any longer."

Ma raised her eyebrows. "I thought you wanted Nelson to learn better Chinese? What about taking care of little Godfrey and picking Nelson up from school? You said their babysitter was so expensive, and careless too. Will you be staying home to take care of them yourself?" Ma was bumbling in her confusion. I wished she'd just let Aunt Paula speak.

"No, no." Aunt Paula scratched the side of her neck, something I'd seen her doing before. "I wish I could. I'm so busy now with all my responsibilities. The factory, all of Mr. N.'s buildings. I have a lot of head pains." Aunt Paula had already let us know that she was very important, managing the clothing factory and a number of buildings for a distant relative of Uncle Bob's, a businessman in Taiwan she called "Mr. N."

Ma nodded. "You must take care of your health." Her tone was searching. I too wondered where this was leading.

Aunt Paula spread her hands wide. "Everybody wants more money, everything has to make a profit. Every single building, every shipment . . ." She looked at Ma, and I could not make out her expression. "I imagined that bringing you here would help with the children. But then you had a few problems."

Ma had been diagnosed with tuberculosis about a year earlier, after all of the paperwork to bring us here had already been finalized. She'd had to choke down huge pills for months. I remembered her lying in bed in Hong Kong, flushed with fever, but at least the antibiotics had put an end to the coughing and handkerchiefs tinged with blood. The date for our journey to America had been postponed twice before she got clearance from the doctors and the immigration department.

"I'm cured now," Ma said.

"Of course. I am so glad you are well again, little sister. We must be certain that you do not relapse. Taking care of two active boys like Nelson and Godfrey, that will be too much for you. Boys are not like girls."

"I am sure I can manage," Ma said. She gave me an affectionate look. "*Ah*-Kim was also a monkey."

"I'm sure. But we wouldn't want the boys to catch anything either. Their health has always been delicate."

I was trying hard to truly understand Chinese now, like Ma was teaching me. In the awkward silence that followed, I understood this was not about illness. For whatever reason, Aunt Paula was not comfortable with Ma caring for her children.

"We are grateful you brought us over anyway," Ma finally said, breaking the tension. "But we cannot be a burden to you. I must work."

Aunt Paula's posture relaxed, as if she'd stepped into a new role. "You are my family!" She laughed. "Did you not think I could provide for you?" She stood up, walked over to me and wrapped an arm around my shoulders. "I've gone to great lengths and gotten you a job at the clothing factory. I even fired the old worker to make space for you. You see? Your older sister will take care of you. The job is picking up a dead chicken, you'll see." Aunt Paula was saying that she'd gotten Ma a sweet deal, like a free chicken dinner.

Ma swallowed, taking it in. "I will try my hardest, big sister, but nothing ever comes out straight when I sew. I'll practice."

Aunt Paula was still smiling. "I remember!" Her eyes flicked across my homemade shirt with its uneven red trimming. "I always laughed at those little dresses you tried to make. You could practice ten thousand years and never be fast enough. That's why I've given you a job hanging dresses— doing the finishing work. You don't need any skills for that, just to work hard."

Ma's face was pale and strained, but she said, "Thank you, older sister."

After that, Ma seemed lost in her own thoughts and she didn't play her violin at all, not even once. A few times Aunt Paula took her out without me to show Ma the factory and subway system. When Ma and I were alone, we mostly watched television in color, which was exciting even if we couldn't follow it. Once, though, Ma wrapped her arms around me and held me tight throughout an episode of *I Love Lucy*, as if she was the one seeking comfort from me, and I wished harder than ever that Pa were here to help.

Pa had died of a stroke when I was three, and now we had left him behind in Hong Kong. I didn't remember him at all but I missed him just the same. He'd been the principal of the elementary school where Ma taught music. Even though she had been supposed to marry an American Chinese like Aunt Paula had, and even though Pa had been sixteen years older than Ma, they had fallen in love and gotten married.

Pa, I thought hard, *Pa*. There was so much I wanted here in America and so much I was afraid of, I had no other words left. I willed his spirit to travel from Hong Kong, where he lay, to cross the ocean to join us here.

Ma and I spent several days cleaning that apartment in Brooklyn. We sealed the windows in the kitchen with garbage bags so that we had a bit more protection from the elements, even though this meant that the kitchen was always dark. When the wind gusted, the bags inflated and struggled against the industrial tape that held them in place. According to *feng shui* principles, the door to the bathroom cast a ray of unclean energy into the kitchen. We moved the stove a few inches, as far away from the bathroom's pathway as possible.

The second day into our cleaning we needed more supplies and roach spray, and Ma decided to make the trip to the convenience store a bit of a celebration, for all the work we had accomplished. From the affectionate way she ruffled my hair, I could tell she wanted to do something extra nice for me. We would buy some ice cream, she announced, a rare treat.

Inside, the store was tiny and crowded, and we stood on line with supplies until we got to the front, where there was a dingy glass display behind the counter.

"What does it say?" Ma asked me, nodding at one of the cartons. I could make out a picture of strawberries and the words "Made with real fruit" and another word, beginning with a "yo," that I didn't know.

The man behind the counter said in English, "I *ask* got all day. You gonna buy something or not?" His tone was aggressive enough that Ma understood what he meant without translation.

"Sorry, sir," Ma said in English. "Very sorry." That was about the limit of her English, so then she glanced at me.

"That," I said, pointing to the strawberry cartons. "Two."

"About time," he said. When he rang up the price, it was three times more than it said on the carton. I saw Ma glance at the price tag, but she averted her gaze quickly. I didn't know if I should speak up or how you complained about prices in English, so I kept silent as well. Ma paid without looking at the man or me, and we left. The ice cream tasted terrible: thin and sour, and it wasn't until we got to the bottom that we found the fruit, jellified and in one lump.

On the way home from the store, I didn't see any other Chinese people on the street, only blacks and a very few whites. It was quite busy, with some mothers and working people, but mostly groups of young men who swaggered as they walked. I overheard one of them calling a young woman on the street a "box." The girl didn't seem so boxlike to me. Ma kept her eyes averted and pulled me closer. Garbage was strewn everywhere: broken glass by doorways, old newspapers floating down the sidewalk, carried by the wind. The painted English writing was illegible and looked like swirls of pure anger and frenzy. It covered almost everything, even the cars parked on the street. There were a few large industrial buildings on the next block.

We saw an older black man sitting on a lawn chair in front of the used-furniture store beside our building. His face was turned up to the sun and his eyes were closed. His hair was a silver poof around his head. I gazed at him, thinking that no Chinese person I knew from home would deliberately try to make themselves tanner in the sun, especially if they were already as dark as this man was.

Suddenly, he leaped up in front of us and sprang into a one-legged martial arts pose with his arms outstretched. "Hi-yah!" he yelled.

Ma and I both screamed.

He burst into laughter, then started speaking English. "I got *cha moves*, don't I? I'm sorry *forscaring* you ladies. I just love kung fu. My name is Al."

Ma, who hadn't understood a word he'd said, grabbed my jacket and said to me in Chinese, "This is a crazy person. Don't speak to him, we'll just tiptoe away."

"Hey, that's Chinese, right? You have *anthn* you can teach me?" he asked.

I had recovered enough to nod.

"So, there's this very fat guy who comes into my store. What can I call him—he's a real whale?"

"Whale," I said in Cantonese. Now Ma looked at me like I had gone insane.

"*Kung yu*," he repeated, with the tones all wrong.

"Whale," I said again.

"*King yu*," he said. He was really trying. Still gibberish but it was closer.

"That is better," I said in English.

Ma actually giggled. I think she had never heard a non-Chinese person trying to speak our language before. "May your business be good," she said in Chinese.

"*Ho sang yee*," he repeated. "What does that mean?"

I told him in English, "It is to wish your store much money."

His face broke out in the biggest, whitest smile I had ever seen. "Now I need that. Thank you."

"You welcome," Ma said in English.

Aside from Mr. Al's store, many of the storefronts we could see were empty. We lived across the street from a huge lot filled with trash and rubble. There was a leaning apartment building sunken into the back of the lot, as if someone had forgotten to demolish it. I had seen black children clambering in the rubble, searching out bits and pieces of old toys and bottles to play with. I knew Ma would never let me join them.

On our side of the street, a few shops were open: a store with hair combs and incense in the window, a hardware store.

Even with the spray, the roaches were impossible to exterminate. We sprayed all the cracks and corners with roach spray, scattered mothballs through all our clothes and in a thick ring around our mattress. Still, the brown heads with wiggling antennae appeared out of every crack. As soon as we left an area or became too quiet, they approached. We were the only source of food in the entire building.

It was impossible to get used to them. I'd seen them in Hong Kong, of course, but not in our apartment. We'd had a nice simple place. Like most people in Hong Kong then, we didn't have luxuries like a refrigerator, but Ma had kept our leftovers in a steel-mesh cage underneath the table and cooked every meal with fresh meat and vegetables just bought at the street market. I missed our neat little living room with its red couch and piano, on which Ma used to give lessons to kids after school. The piano had been a gift from Pa when they got married. We'd had to sell it when we came here.

Now I was learning to do everything noisily, thumping around in hopes of keeping them away. Ma often hurried to the rescue, clutching a bit of toilet paper to kill the roaches near me, but I screamed when I looked down at the sweater I was wearing and found a big one clinging to my chest. I don't like to think about what happened when we slept.

I know that that was when the mice and rats came. Our first night I'd been aware of something running over me in my sleep and quickly developed the habit of sleeping burrowed deep in the covers. I wasn't as afraid of rodents as I was of roaches, because mice are at least warm-blooded. I understood they were small living things. Ma was terrified of them. In Hong Kong, she'd refused to have a cat because she was afraid that they would bring her offerings of their prey. It didn't matter that a cat actually reduced the number of live rodents. None was allowed in our house. After that night I told Ma I should sleep on the side of the mattress away from the wall because I needed to pee sometimes. I wanted to protect her from having to sleep closer to where the mice and rats were likely to be active. These were the small graces we bestowed upon each other then. They were all we had to give.

We set out a handful of mousetraps and quickly caught a few. Ma shrank back when she saw the limp bodies, and I wished desperately that Pa were alive so I wouldn't have to do this. I knew I should have removed the dead mice and reused the mousetraps, but I couldn't handle touching the dull flesh, and Ma made no complaint when I used a pair of chopsticks to pick up the traps, an act I immediately recognized as extremely unhygienic. I threw the traps, mice and chopsticks away, and after that, we put out no more mousetraps. That was Ma and me: two squeamish Buddhists in the apartment from hell.

We put the *Tong Sing*, the Chinese Almanac, at the head of the mattress. There are many *phu* in these books, words of power written by ancient masters that can pin a white bone demon under a mountain or repel wild fox spirits. In Brooklyn, we hoped they would keep any thieves away. I slept badly in that apartment and was jolted out of sleep by cars rumbling over potholes in the street. Ma whispered, "It's all right." Then she tweaked my ears to bring my sleeping soul back to my body and brushed my forehead three times with her left hand to ward off evil spirits.

Finally, my hands no longer came away covered with dust when I touched the walls. When we knew the apartment was as clean as we could get it, we set up five altars in the kitchen: to the earth god, the ancestors, the heavens, the kitchen god and Kuan Yin. Kuan Yin is the goddess of compassion who cares for all of us. We lit incense and poured tea and rice wine before the altars. We prayed to the local earth god of the building and apartment to grant us permission to live there in peace, to the ancestors and heavens to keep away troubles and evil people, to the kitchen god to keep us from starving and to Kuan Yin to bring us our hearts' desires.

The next day, I would start school. Ma would begin her job at the factory. That evening, she sat down with me on the mattress.

"*Ah*-Kim, I have been thinking about something since visiting the factory, and I realize I have no choice," Ma said.

"What is it?"

"After you get out of school, I want you to come join me at the factory. I don't want you here in this apartment by yourself, waiting for me every afternoon and evening. And I'm worried I won't be able to do the finishing at the factory alone. The last woman who had my job had two sons who came to work with her. I have to ask you to come to the factory with me after school and help me there."

"Of course, Ma. I always help you." I put my hand on hers and smiled. In Hong Kong, I'd always dried the dishes and folded our laundry.

To my surprise, Ma's face flushed, as if she were about to cry. "I know," she said. "But this is something different. I've been to the factory." She took me in her arms and squeezed so hard that I gasped, but by the time she pulled away, she had recovered control. She spoke softly, as if to herself. "The road we could follow in Hong Kong was a dead one. The only future I could see for us, for you, was here, where you could become whatever you wanted. Even though this isn't what we'd imagined back home, we will be all right."

"Mother and cub."

Ma smiled. She started tucking the thin cotton blanket we'd brought from Hong Kong around me. Then she laid both of our jackets and her sweater over the blanket to keep me warm.

"Ma? Are we going to stay in this apartment?"

"I'll talk to Aunt Paula tomorrow." Ma got up and brought her violin case over to the mattress. She stood in the middle of that darkened living room with the cracked walls behind her, lifted her violin to her chin and began to play a Chinese lullaby.

I sighed. It seemed so long since I had heard Ma play, even though we'd been in America for only a week and a half. In Hong Kong, I'd heard her teaching music at school or giving private violin or piano lessons in our apartment, but she was usually too tired to play in the evenings when I went to bed. Now Ma was here and her music was just for me.

TWO

In that third week of November, I started school. Ma and I had a hard time finding it because it was many blocks away, beyond the area we had explored so far. This new neighborhood was cleaner than the vacant lots and empty storefronts that I had seen closer to our apartment. Aunt Paula had explained with pride that my official address would be different from the one where I actually lived. I should use this other address whenever anyone asked me.

"Why?" I'd asked.

"This is another of Mr. N.'s buildings. It's one you wouldn't be able to afford to live in, but using this address will allow you to go to a better school. Don't you want that?"

"What's the problem with the one I would go to normally?"

"Nothing!" Aunt Paula shook her head, clearly frustrated by my lack of gratitude for what she had done for me. "Go see if your ma needs you."

Now, trying to find this better school, Ma and I walked across several big avenues and then past a number of governmental buildings with statues in front of them. Most of the people on the street were still black, but I saw more whites and lighter shades of black people, possibly Hispanics or other nationalities I couldn't identify yet. I was shivering in my thin jacket. Ma had bought me the warmest one she could find in Hong Kong, but it was still made of acrylic, not wool.

We passed an apartment complex and a park. Finally, we found the school. It was a square concrete building with a large school yard and a flagpole waving the American flag. It was obvious I was late—the yard was empty of people—and we rushed up a broad flight of stairs and pushed open the heavy wooden door.

A black woman in a police uniform sat behind a desk, reading a book. She wore a tag that said "Security."

We showed her the letter from the school. "Go *downda* hall, two *fights up*, classroom's *firsdur left*," she said, pointing. Then she picked up her book again.

I understood only that I had to go that way and so I started slowly down the long hallway. I saw Ma hesitate, unsure whether she was allowed to follow me. She glanced at the security guard, but Ma couldn't say anything in English. I kept going, and at the staircase, I looked back to see Ma in the distance, a thin, uncertain figure, still standing by the guard's desk. I hadn't wished her good luck for her first day at the factory. I hadn't even said good-bye. I wanted to run back and beg her to take me with her, but instead, I turned and made my way up the stairs.

After a bit of searching, I found the classroom and knocked weakly on the door.

A deep, muffled voice came from behind the door. "You're late! Come in."

I pushed it open. The teacher was a man. I learned later his name was Mr. Bogart. He was extremely tall, so that his forehead was level with the top of the blackboard, with a raspberry nose and a head bald as an egg. His green eyes seemed unnaturally light to me in his wide face and his stomach stuck out from under his shirt. He was writing English words on the blackboard, from left to right.

"Our new student *eye-prezoom*?" He gave a strange smile that made his lips disappear, then he looked at his watch and his lips reappeared. "You're very late. What's your *exsu*?"

I knew I had to answer so I guessed. "Kim Chang."

He stared at me for a second. "I know what your name is," he said, enunciating each word. "What's your *exshus*?"

A few of the kids snickered. I took a quick look around: almost all black with two or three white kids. No other Chinese at all, no help in sight.

"Can't you speak English? They said that you did." This came out as a kind of grumbled whine. Who was he talking about? He took a breath. "Why are you late?"

This, I understood. "I sorry, sir," I said. "We not find school."

He frowned, then nodded and waved at an empty desk. "Go sit down. There."

I sat down in the seat he had indicated, next to a chubby white girl with frizzy hair that stuck out in all directions. My fingers were shaking so much that I fumbled with my pencil case. It opened and everything in it clattered on the floor. Now most of the class laughed and I scrambled to pick up my things. I was so flushed I could feel the heat not only in my face but in my neck and chest. The white girl also bent down and picked up a pen and a pencil sharpener for me.

Mr. Bogart continued writing on the blackboard. I sat up straight and folded my hands behind my back to listen even though I couldn't follow it at all.

He glanced at me. "Why are you *see something that*?"

"I sorry, sir," I said, but I had no idea what I'd done wrong this time. I looked around at the other students. Most of them were sprawled in their chairs. Some had sunk so low that they were practically lying down, some were leaning on their elbows, a few were chewing gum. In Hong Kong, students must fold their hands behind their backs when the teacher is talking, to show respect. Slowly, I loosened my arms and placed my hands on the desk in front of me.

Shaking his head, Mr. Bogart turned back to the blackboard.

Our class went to the school cafeteria for lunch. I had never seen children behave the way these Americans did. They seemed to be hanging from the beams on the ceilings, shrieking. The lunch-room ladies roamed from table to table, yelling instructions no one heard. I had followed the other children and slid a tray across a long counter. Different ladies asked me questions and when I only nodded, they plopped foil-covered packages on my plate. I wound up with this: minced meat in the form of a saucer, potatoes that were not round but had been crushed into a pastelike substance, a sauce similar to soy sauce but less dark and salty, a roll and milk. I had hardly ever drunk cow's milk before and it gave me a stomachache. The rest of the food was interesting, although there was no rice, so I felt as if I hadn't really eaten.

After lunch, Mr. Bogart gave out sheets of paper with a drawing of a map.

"This is a pop *quick*," he said. "Fill in *allde captal see T's*."

The other kids groaned but many of them started writing. I looked at my piece of paper and then, in desperation, glanced at the white girl's sheet to try to see what we were supposed to do. Suddenly, the sheet of paper slid out from under my fingers. Mr. Bogart was standing next to me with my test in his hands.

"No *cheap pen*!" he said. His nose and cheeks were flushed as if he were getting a rash. "You a *hero*!"

"I sorry, sir—" I began. I knew he wasn't calling me a hero, like Superman. What had he said? Although I'd had basic English classes in school in Hong Kong, my old teacher's accent did not in any way resemble what I now heard in Brooklyn.

" 'I'mmm,' " he said, pressing his lips together. " 'I'm sorry.' "

"I'm sorry," I said. My English mistakes clearly annoyed him, although I wasn't sure why.

Mr. Bogart wrote a large "0" on my paper and gave it back to me. I felt as if the zero were fluorescent, blinking in neon to the rest of the class. What would Ma say? I'd never gotten a zero before, and now everyone thought I was a cheat too. My only hope was to impress Mr. Bogart with my industry when we cleaned the classrooms after school. If I'd lost any claim to intelligence here, I could at least show him I was a hard worker.

But when the last bell finally rang, all of the other kids ran out of the room. No one stayed behind to mop and sweep the floors, put up the chairs or clean the blackboards.

Mr. Bogart saw me hesitating and asked, "Can I help you?"

I didn't answer and hurried from the classroom.

Ma was waiting for me outside. I was so happy to see her that when I took her hand, my eyes became hot.

"What is it?" she said, turning my face to her. "Did the other children tease you?"

"No." I wiped my cheeks with the back of my hand. "It's nothing."

Ma looked at me intently. "Did some child hit you?"

"No, Ma," I said. I didn't want to worry her

when there was so little she could do. "Everything is different here, that's all."

"I know," she said, still looking concerned. "What did you do today?"

"I don't remember."

Ma sighed, then gave up and started teaching me how to get to the factory by myself. She went through a long list of things for me to be careful of: strange men, homeless people, pickpockets, touching the dirty railing, standing too close to the edge of the platform, etc.

Once we passed the entrance of the subway, the roar of an incoming train blocked out her words. Behind the grimy windows, we could see the walls of the tunnels speed by in a blur. There was so much noise that Ma and I could speak little on the subway ride there. There were two boys about my age sitting across from us. As the taller one got up, a bulky knife fell out of his pocket. It was sheathed in leather, the black handle grooved to fit a large hand. I pretended I wasn't looking and willed myself to be invisible. The other boy gestured, the first one picked it up, and then they left the train. I peeked at Ma and she had her eyes closed. I huddled closer to her and concentrated on learning the stops and transfers so I wouldn't get lost by myself.

When we got out of the train station, Ma turned to me and said, "I wish you didn't have to take the subway by yourself."

That was the first time. Going to the factory after school would become something so automatic that sometimes, even when I needed to go someplace else years later, I would find myself on the trains to the factory by accident, as if that were the place to which all roads led.

Chinatown looked very much like Hong Kong, although the streets were less cramped. The fish store was piled high with sea bass and baskets of crabs; grocery store shelves were stocked with canned papayas, lichee nuts and star fruit; peddlers on the street sold fried tofu and rice gruel. I felt like skipping beside Ma as we passed restaurants with soy sauce chickens hanging in the window and jewelry stores that glittered with yellow gold. I could understand everyone without any effort: "No, I want your best winter melons," one woman said; "That's much too expensive," said a man in a puffy jacket.

Ma brought us to a doorway that led to a freight elevator. We took the elevator upstairs and exited. When Ma pushed open the metal door of the factory, the heat rushed out and wrapped itself around me like a fist. The air was thick and tasted of metal. I was deafened by the roar of a hundred Singer sewing machines. Dark heads were bent over each one. No one looked up; they only fed reams of cloth through the machines, racing from piece to piece without pausing to cut off the connecting thread.

Almost all the seamstresses had their hair up, although some strands had escaped and were plastered to the sides of their necks and cheeks by the sweat. They wore air filters over their mouths. There was a film of dirty red dust on the filters, the color of meat exposed to air for too long.

The factory took up the entire floor of a massive industrial building on Canal Street. It was a cavernous hall bulging with exposed beams and rusting bolts covered in ever-thickening layers of filth. There were mountains of fabric on the floor next to the workers, enormous carts piled high with half-finished pieces, long metal racks hung with the pressed and finished clothes. Ten-year-old boys rushed across the floor dragging carts and racks from section to section. The fluorescent light swirled down to us through the clouds of fabric dust, bathing the tops of the women's heads in a halo of white light.

"There's Aunt Paula," Ma said. "She was out collecting rent earlier."

Aunt Paula strode across the factory floor with a load of red fabric in her arms, distributing work to the seamstresses. The ones to whom she gave the bigger loads seemed grateful, nodding repeatedly to show their thanks.

Now she had seen us and she came over.

"There you are," she said. "The factory is impressive, isn't it?"

"Older sister, can I talk to you?"

I could see this wasn't the response she wanted. Her face seemed to tighten, and then she said, "Let's go to the office."

Although no one dared to stare openly, the workers' eyes followed us as we walked with Aunt Paula to Uncle Bob's office at the front of the factory. We passed women using machines I had never seen before to hem pants and sew on buttons. Everyone worked at a frantic pace.

Through the window of the office door, we could see Uncle Bob sitting behind a desk. His walking stick leaned against the wall next to him. We entered and Aunt Paula closed the door behind us.

"First day, eh?" Uncle Bob said.

Before we had a chance to reply, Aunt Paula spoke. "I'm sorry, but we don't have much time," she said. "I can't let the other workers think I'm showing you any favoritism, just because you're family."

Ma said, "Of course not. I know you're both very busy and you haven't seen the apartment we're in, but it is not very clean." Ma meant that it was below acceptable living standards. "And I don't believe it is a safe place for *ah*-Kim."

"Oh, little sister, don't worry," Aunt Paula said, with such warmth and reassurance in her voice that I believed her despite myself. "It is only temporary. There was no place else available that you would be able to afford, not with the many

expenses you have. But Mr. N. has many buildings, and as soon as another place opens up that
you can pay for, we will move you there."

Ma visibly relaxed, and I could feel myself
beginning to smile again.

"Now, come," Aunt Paula continued, "we'd
better all get back to work before the employees
think we're having a family party in here."

"Good luck," Uncle Bob called as we left.

Aunt Paula walked us to our workstation,
passing an enormous table I hadn't seen earlier. A
combination of very old ladies and young children
were crowded around it, clipping all the extra-
neous threads off the sewn garments. This seemed
to be the easiest job.

"They enter at this table as children and they
leave from it as grandmas," Aunt Paula said with a
wink. "The circle of factory life."

From there, we walked into an enormous cloud
of steam. I could hardly see but I realized that this
was where most of the heat was coming from. Four
massive steaming stations were connected to a
central boiler that made a loud hissing sound every
few minutes as air escaped from it. One man stood
in front of each station, placing garments on the
surface of the steamers, then slamming the lid
shut, expelling huge gusts of steam. Each man had
a large sawhorse where he piled the pressed pieces
for "finishing," which was Ma's job. The piles
were already growing.

Finally, we reached our work area at the back of the factory. It was larger than our entire apartment. There was a long table and a towering stack of pressed clothing, which we were to hang, sort, belt or sash, tag and then bag in a sheath of plastic. Aunt Paula left us with the warning that the shipment was going out in a few days, and Ma and I were expected to get everything done on time.

Ma hurried to start hanging up the pants and she asked me to sort by size an enormous rack filled with pants already on hangers. She gave me an air filter as well, a rectangular piece of white cloth tied behind the ears, but we were next to the steamer section. The heat was stifling. I felt as if I couldn't breathe and took it off after a few minutes. Ma didn't wear hers either.

I spotted a wrinkled piece of Chinese newspaper in the industrial trash can and stealthily took it. It gave me heart to see the familiar characters. I spread it out on an empty stool next to me as I began my sorting.

After less than an hour in the factory, my pores were clotted with fabric dust. A net of red strands spread themselves across my arms so that when I tried to sweep myself clean with my hand, I created rolls of grime that tugged against the fine hairs on my skin. Ma constantly wiped off the table where she was working, but within a few minutes, a layer would descend, thick enough for me to draw stick figures in if I'd had the time. Even the ground was slick with dust, and whenever I walked, the motion displaced rolls of filth that tumbled and floated by my feet, lost.

Something mingled with the stink of polyester in my nostrils. I turned around. A boy was standing next to me. He was about my size, dressed in an old white T-shirt, but there was a tension in his shoulders and arms that told me he was a fighter. His eyebrows were thick, crossing his face in one line, and underneath them, his eyes were a surprising golden brown. He was munching on a roasted pork bun. The crisp crust glistened and I could almost taste the sweet and luscious meat in my mouth.

"You can still read Chinese," he said, cocking his head at the newspaper.

I nodded. I didn't mention that it was all I could read.

"I forgot everything. We've already been in America for five years." He was showing off now. "You must be smart, reading and all." This wasn't a compliment, it was a question.

I decided to be honest. "I used to be."

He thought about this a second. "Eat a bite?"

I hesitated. It isn't Chinese to eat from someone else's food. No kid in Hong Kong had ever offered any to me.

The boy waved the bun under my nose. "Come

46

on," he said. He ripped off a clean piece and held it out.

"Thanks," I said, and popped it in my mouth. It was as delicious as it had smelled.

"You can't tell though." He spoke with his mouth full. "I swiped it from Dog Flea Mama's station."

I stared at him, confused and appalled. "Who?" I'd already swallowed my part of the theft.

"The Sergeant." A sergeant is any cruel person in a position of authority.

I must have still looked confused.

He sighed. "Dog. Flea. Mama. You must have seen her." Then he scratched himself on the neck, a perfect imitation of Aunt Paula's habit.

I gasped. "That's my aunt!"

"Ay yah!" His eyes were wide.

Then I started to laugh and he did too.

"I don't normally take things, you know. I just like bothering her. Come find me at the thread-cutters' when you take a break. My name's Matt," he said.

When Ma urged me to take a break later, I edged up to the thread-cutters' counter. The tiny old ladies and kids were busy examining the garments in their hands, snipping off the excess threads with special scissors that spring back open after each cut. Some of the children were as young as five years old. I spotted Matt working with fast hands next to a younger boy in glasses. A woman who

47

must have been their mother sat next to the smaller boy. She wore large rose-tinted glasses that barely covered the enormous bags under her eyes.

When the mother saw me, she squinted through her thick lenses.

"Are you a boy or a girl?" she asked. Matt stifled a laugh.

I knew I looked like a boy, completely flat-chested, with my hair cut short by Ma because of the Hong Kong heat. I wished I could disappear.

The other boy next to Mrs. Wu was slight, with glasses that dangled from his protruding ears. He didn't look up. He only kept working on the same skirt. As I watched, he turned it over again and again, looking for threads he had missed. On the table next to him was a toy motorcycle with a color picture of an American Indian printed on the gas tank. It looked worn, as if it had been chewed upon.

"Hello," I said to him.

When the boy didn't respond, Matt leaned over and gently waved his hand in front of the boy's face. He made some gestures with his hand that looked like a kind of sign language. The boy looked up and then immediately turned his gaze downward again. In that brief glance, I saw that his eyes seemed unfocused behind the glasses.

"Park doesn't hear so well," Mrs. Wu said.

"Ma, I'm taking a break," Matt said, and he jumped off his stool. He turned to Park and made

48

a few more gestures. I thought probably he was asking if Park wanted to come with us.

When Park didn't react at all, Matt turned to me and said, "He's shy."

"Don't be too long," Mrs. Wu said. "There's a lot of work that needs to be done."

Some of the other kids gravitated to us when they saw that we were free, and we all moved toward the soda machine by the entrance. It cost twenty cents per bottle and I learned later that few people actually purchased from it because of the expense, but the idea of getting a cold soda in the sweltering factory was so attractive that the soda machine was a popular hangout anyway.

I suspected that most of the other kids were at the factory for the same reasons I was. They weren't officially employed by the factory, but there was no place else for them to go, and their parents needed their help. As Ma had explained earlier, all employees were secretly paid by the piece; this meant that the work the children did was essential to the family income. When I was in high school, I learned that piece payment was illegal, but those rules were for white people, not for us.

Leaning against the humming soda machine, I could see Matt was the leader of the factory kids. They seemed to range in age from about four to teens. To save money, Ma made many of my clothes herself, even though she couldn't do it very well, so I had on a home-sewn shirt while the other kids were wearing cool T-shirts with English say-ings like "Remember to Vote." They interspersed their Chinese with English to show off how Americanized they were and everyone apparently knew I was fresh off the boat. There was some whispering when they found out Dog Flea Mama was my aunt, but Matt seemed to have taken me under his wing and no one dared tease me. Despite the hard work, I was relieved to be among Chinese kids again.

After ten minutes, though, everyone started wandering back to the work they knew awaited them if they ever wanted to leave. I returned to Ma and resumed work but I was exhausted. I'd been there for three hours. I kept waiting for Ma to say it was time to go home. Instead, she pulled out a container of rice cooked with carrots and a bit of ham: we would have dinner at the fin-isher's table. I couldn't complain. She'd been there much longer than I had. We ate standing up and as fast as we could so we could get enough work done to stay on schedule. That first night, we left at nine o'clock. Later, I discovered that this was considered early.

The next morning, I stayed in the tiny bathroom a long time.

"Kim," Ma said. "We'll be late for school."

I reluctantly opened the door, clutching my thin towel. "I don't feel well."

She looked concerned and placed her hand on my forehead. "What is it?"

"I have a stomachache," I said. "I think I should stay home today."

Ma studied me, then smiled. "Silly girl, why are you talking the big words?" She was asking why I was lying. "You have to go to school." Ma believed in the absolute sanctity of education.

"I can't," I said. My eyes started tearing up again, even though I tried to hide it by rubbing my face with the towel.

"Are the other children mean to you?" she asked kindly.

"It's not the kids," I said. I stared at the splintered threshold of the bathroom. "It's the teacher."

Now she looked skeptical. Teachers are highly respected in Hong Kong. "What are you talking about?"

I told her the whole story, the way Mr. Bogart had corrected my accent yesterday, the way he'd been angry at the things I hadn't understood, that he'd thought I'd been cheating and given me a zero. I couldn't stop them now, I let the tears brim over but kept myself from breaking into full sobs.

When I was finished, Ma was silent. She had to work her mouth a moment before she was able to speak. Then she said haltingly, "Maybe I could talk to him and tell him what a good student you are."

For a moment, my heart caught flight but then I pictured Ma talking to Mr. Bogart with the few

English words she knew. It would only make him despise me more. "No, Ma, I will try harder."

"I am sure that if you work the way you always do, he will give you another chance." She reached out and pulled me to her. She laid her cheek against the top of my head.

I was surprised and grateful Ma hadn't automatically taken the teacher's side against me. Leaning against her, I closed my eyes and pretended for just a moment that everything would be all right.

After my talk with Ma about Mr. Bogart, I did what any sensible kid would: I started playing hooky. Ma had no choice but to leave me to walk to school alone because she had to get to the factory as early as possible in order to have any hope of finishing our work on time. She couldn't afford the luxury of escorting me again.

"Are you sure you know the way?" Ma asked. "Do you have your token for the subway after school?"

Ma was afraid to leave me alone but now that I'd done it before, the route to school was actually simple. The distance was long but it required few turns. We arrived at her subway station first. Ma hesitated at the entrance, but I nodded as confidently as I could, then headed off in the direction of the school. As soon as she was out of sight, I ducked around the corner and circled home.

Despite the cold, I was sweating. What if I ran

into Mr. Bogart or one of the kids from my class recognized me? I'd never done anything similar before. Like any good Chinese girl, I'd always followed the rules and been glad to be praised by the teachers. But the only alternative was going into Mr. Bogart's classroom again. I was learning about desperation.

It was with a sick feeling that I pulled open the heavy door to our building and entered into that dark mouth. I huddled in the dirty living room, still in my jacket, with the weak sun's rays clogged in the murky windows. I hadn't ever really been alone before. I felt a bit safer sitting in the center of the mattress where I could at least see any roaches coming before they got to me. Anything could materialize in the emptiness beyond the shadowy doorway. When the garbage bags covering the windows in the kitchen rustled, I thought about how easy it would be for a burglar to rip off the tape and step inside. I would jump out of the window on the street side if someone broke in. If I hung from the windowsill by my fingers before dropping, I would probably live. That became my solution for all the contingencies that flashed across my mind: if the stove caught on fire, if a ghost appeared in the bathroom, if a rat attacked, if Ma walked through the door looking for something she'd forgotten.

The apartment air felt damp and raw. It was November of what would turn out to be one of the most bitter winters in New York's history. To keep myself from becoming too chilled and scared, I flicked on the small television. Its busy chatter brought me into the world of dishes and lemon-scented sprays. There were a lot of shows about hospitals: doctors kissing nurses, nurses kissing patients; there were films about cowboys and Indians; shows with people sitting in squares with flashing lights. In particular, the commercials mystified me: "Raise your arms to be sure," the voice boomed, showing men and women thrusting their arms into the air. Why should you do this? Was it something to do with the Liberty Goddess?

"Triple your vocabulary in thirty days," the authoritative male voice promised. "*Impess* your friends. Show your boss who's boss." I sat up straighter. I imagined myself going back to class, using words even Mr. Bogart didn't know. Then came a commercial for alphabet soup, the concept of which fascinated me, as all things in letter form did. I realized it was almost lunchtime and I was hungry.

I braved the darkened kitchen to peek into the small refrigerator. Ma wasn't used to having one and it was mostly empty. I found only a few small pieces of leftover chicken, the bones protruding from under the fatty skin, some yellowing vegetables with cold rice, and a shallow container of oyster sauce. I didn't dare touch anything. I'd been taught that everything had to be thoroughly heated.

The kids in a commercial I'd just seen were eating cheese sandwiches with apples and milk, but there was no bread here, let alone anything to put on it. I was afraid even to get a glass of water by myself; back home, I'd gotten such bad diarrhea from drinking unboiled tap water that I'd almost died. Ma had always made a warm snack for me when we came home from school together: steamed mackerel in black beans, roasted pork skins, winter melon soup, fried rice with scallions.

My stomach rumbled as I continued to watch TV. Gleaming toy kitchens, bouncing balls large enough for kids to sit on, kids eating cookies in tree houses. There was a commercial with a family at a long table laden with food. I longed for the room in the background of that table. It was so clean there you could have lain down on the floor. In our apartment, I didn't dare to touch much. Even after our rigorous cleaning, everything seemed shrouded with the dust of dead insects and mice. I indulged in one of my favorite fantasies, that Pa had stayed alive. If he were here, maybe we wouldn't have had to work at the factory at all. Maybe he'd have been able to get a regular job and help us build up a life like those people on TV.

Even with the television, the day stretched out long and gray through the empty hours, and I kept thinking about Ma working alone at the factory. I could see her neat hands moving slowly over the pressed clothes. I imagined how tired she must be but I couldn't go to join her yet because I had to pretend to be at school. I jumped when a mouse ran across the floorboards and disappeared into the kitchen. I kept the broom by me, for both intruders and roaches, and when roaches started scurrying across the wall by the mattress, I made noise with the broom to keep them at a distance, careful not to squash them. This was partly due to my Buddhist training to care for all life, but it was mostly because I didn't want to see them smeared across the wall.

Out of boredom, I started looking through Ma's things. In her suitcase, I found a square piece of cardboard carefully bound with twine. I could tell it was an old 78 rpm record, the kind that played only one song per side. It must have held great emotional value for her. There was no other reason for her to keep it; we didn't even have a record player here. I opened the case carefully, expecting something from a Chinese opera, and was surprised to find an Italian one instead. I read the label: it was Caruso singing Cavaradossi's aria "E lucevan le stelle," from *Tosca*. A photograph fluttered to the floor. Then I remembered:

Our apartment in Hong Kong, the ceiling fan humming as I lay on the sofa, Ma playing a record for me before bedtime. That had been our nightly routine, one song and then bed. Usually she chose Chinese music, but this one night she had put on a man singing with sorrow in another language, the words escaping him in gasps of regret. She had turned away then. When I could see her face again, she had composed herself and showed me no more of her feelings.

I had gone to bed that night, and many nights since, thinking about Ma's life and the grief that connected her to that music. I knew her parents had been landowners and intellectuals, and for that, they'd been unfairly sentenced to death during the Cultural Revolution. Before they died, they had spent all the wealth they had left to get Ma and Aunt Paula out of China and into Hong Kong before it was too late. And then Ma's true love, my pa, had been taken from her far too young, only in his early forties, going to bed with a headache one evening to die of a massive stroke later that night.

I picked up the photograph that had fallen from the record album. It was the one Ma had framed and kept on the piano in our living room in Hong Kong. Like many people in Hong Kong then, we didn't have a camera because it was too expensive, and so this was the only photo I'd seen of the three of us. Despite the stiffness of the pose, the three heads were slightly inclined toward one another, like a true family. Ma looked lovely, with her small neat features and pale skin stretched tight over her bones, and Pa was the perfect accompaniment: dark luminous eyes, handsome and sculpted, like a movie star. I looked at the size of his hands, one of which was tenderly—it seemed to me—cupping the child's elbow, my elbow. That was a heroic hand, a hand that would take over a heavy plow, a hand to save you from demons and muggers. And me, balanced on Pa's knee, about two years old, and peering curiously at the camera. I was wearing a sailor's outfit and my hand was raised to my forehead in a military salute, no doubt the photographer's idea. Lucky child: had I really been so cute, had I ever been so happy?

A few characters had been scrawled on the back. Our names and the date. I knew it wasn't Ma's handwriting, so it had to be his. I ran my finger over the impressions the pen had made in the thick paper. This was my pa, his hand had written these words.

This was all I had to take the place of memory. However, no matter how great my loss, Ma's was even greater. She had actually known and loved him, and his death had left her alone to raise and support me. I carefully put the record and the photograph back. I wanted more than ever to be by Ma's side, helping her in any way I could.

Finally, I could leave for the factory. I passed by a street cart with a sign that said "Hot Dogs." The vendor was selling thin sausages in rolls with yellow sauce on top. It looked and smelled delicious, but I had only a subway token and a dime for emergency phone calls in my pocket. On the subway, I felt as if everyone was staring at me: that kid didn't go to school today. I saw other kids with backpacks going into the train station and I hoped I wouldn't see anyone who recognized me. A policeman stood by the token booth, a gun slung from his belt, and he stared at me as I put my token in the slot.

"Hey!" he said.

I froze, ready to be arrested. But he was looking at another kid who had thrown a crumpled paper bag on the floor.

"You pick that up!" he said.

I passed through and ran down to the train platform.

THREE

Ma and I soon learned that our apartment didn't have any heat. Hopefully, we scrubbed the radiator in the room we slept in, rubbing until we'd taken off most of the flaking paint with the dust, but it remained dead no matter how we twisted the knobs. We explored the third floor of the building and found all of the other apartments to be empty. Trash was piled up everywhere—by the doorways, in the crevices of the steps. There was a stack of half-empty boxes by one doorway, as if someone had disappeared or died in the middle of moving out. The boarded-up storefront below had a faded sign that said "Dollar Store." We found the entrance to the backyard, which was one enormous heap of garbage, probably tossed down by residents and neighbors over the years, and the door to the basement was locked.

When Ma politely asked Aunt Paula about how the heat worked, Aunt Paula understood her real question and replied that she had already asked Mr. N. for permission to fix it. She said we wouldn't be staying at that apartment for much longer anyway.

It was freezing during those days I played hooky in that apartment. After skipping school for almost a week, I saw my first snowfall. Flakes came slanting down from the sky and at first, the concrete sidewalk absorbed them like a sponge. I touched the window with my hands, amazed it was cold when it seemed to me that the falling rice should be warm, as if it were a soup. With time, the ground became a blanket of white and gusts of wind blew snow from the rooftops, flurries swirling in the air.

Even now, my predominant memory of that phase of my life is of the cold. Cold like the way your skin feels after you've been slapped, such painful tingling that you can hardly tell if it's hot or cold. It simply registers as suffering. Cold that crept down your throat, under your toes and between your fingers, wrapped itself around your lungs and your heart. Our thin cotton blanket from Hong Kong was completely inadequate, since Hong Kong shops didn't sell anything substantial enough for New York winters. We slept under a pile of jackets and clothes to try to stay warm. I woke up with parts of my body numb and frozen: unexpected places like my hip, where a sweater had slipped off the mound.

Slowly, a sheet of ice grew over the inside of the windows, a layer of distortion spread thick across the panes. As I stared outside, I used my blueing fingers to melt circles in it, trying to reach the clear glass underneath.

One afternoon, I pulled off a corner of the taped-on garbage bags in the kitchen so I could see what the back of our building looked like. It was a clear day. When I peered out of that opening, I looked down at the roof of a large extension built on our ground floor. That must have been where the dollar store had kept its extra merchandise. People had thrown so much trash onto that rooftop that you could hardly see its surface, but I could discern a large hole in the roof that no one had bothered to fix. A sheet of old newspaper clung to the ragged edge of the hole, flapping in the wind. When it snowed or rained, the inside of that extension must have gotten soaked.

From our kitchen window, I could also see into the apartment immediately next to ours in Mr. Al's building, where it extended deeper than ours. That apartment was strangely close for something so separate, contained within a completely different building yet only a few feet away. I could have stuck a broom out and tapped on its window.

Behind the glass, I made out the form of a sleeping black woman. I could tell her apartment had heat because she was wearing only a thin housedress. She had a few curlers in her hair. Her arm was tenderly cradled around a small blanketed form and I realized it was a baby. The rest of the mattress was strewn with tangled clothes, and above their bodies, a triangular section of plaster was missing from their wall. But I could see how much they loved each other, despite their poverty, and I longed for the simpler times Ma and I had shared.

When it became too cold for me to look any longer, I put the garbage bags back into place.

The next day, I'd just shut the factory door behind me when I saw Matt dragging a massive canvas cart piled high with mauve skirts in the direction of the hemming station. The mountain of clothing loomed over him and he had to walk backward using both skinny arms to drag the cart along. I slung my book bag over my shoulder and started heading for Ma's and my work area in the back, but to my surprise, he called out to me in Chinese.

"Hey, help a hand?"

I went over and grabbed the back part of the cart. Even with him in the front, the floor was so slick with dust that I had to dig my feet into the ground to keep the back wheels from veering off to the side.

He cocked his head to one side to see me around the skirts. "So, had fun at school?"

"Yes," I said.

"Funny school you got. 'Cause no other school in New York's open today."

My eyes stretched wide.

"C'mon, lighten up. Any idiot could tell you were playing hooky," he said.

"Shhhhh!" I looked around to see if anyone was listening.

He went on as if I hadn't said anything. "I didn't see you doing any homework."

"You never have homework either."

"I don't ever do any. You, you're a real homework-doer."

I voiced my real fear. "Do you think my mother knows?"

"Nah, I only know because I did it myself."

"Really?" I warmed to him.

"But I just heard a lady complaining to your ma about having to work today because it's Turkey Day. That's a big holiday here. Anyway, you better think of something fast."

My mind whirled upon itself, panting and empty. "What? What?"

He thought for a moment. "Say you only found out after you got to school, then you went home and did your homework first because you got a big project due next week."

By then, we'd reached the hemming area, which

was at the front end of the factory, near the manager's office. We released the cart and it rolled forward a foot more on its own before stuttering to a stop.

"I really owe you." Ma had taught me that all debts had to be repaid. I turned my pockets inside out to see if there was anything I could give him, but I found only scraps of leftover toilet paper that I had used as tissues stuck to the inner lining.

"Gross," he said. "Forget it." He turned and went back to the seamstresses' area.

I caught a glimpse of Aunt Paula's tall figure in the manager's office and hurried away. I walked down the length of the factory to the finishing station.

Ma's hair was hidden under a kerchief and there was a mauve smudge on her right temple, where she had probably tried to wipe away the sweat beading along her hairline.

I said immediately, "Hi, there was no school today."

Ma folded her arms. "So why didn't you come earlier?"

"I had a big project to work on for next week."

"What's this project on?"

I thought fast. "Current events. I needed to watch the news."

Ma nodded but she still seemed thoughtful. "So you happened to come to the factory at just the same time as you usually do after school?"

I paused a second too long. "I never took the trains at any other time."

Ma started looping a belt through a skirt she had in her hands. Then she said, "What were you and the Wu boy talking about just now?"

"N-nothing," I stammered.

"You seemed surprised at something."

"No, he just wanted me to play with him later." I tried to laugh. "He's always goofing off."

"I think you should be careful with that one."

"Yes, Ma."

Ma put aside the skirt and sat down on a stool. She looked at me. "Don't get too close to the other children here. *Ah*-Kim, you must always remember this: If you play with them, learn to talk like them, study like them, act like them—what will make you different? Nothing. And in ten or twenty years, you'll be doing precisely what the older girls are doing, working on the sewing machines in this factory until you're worn, and when you're too old for that, you'll cut thread like Mrs. Wu."

She paused a moment, as if she were unsure if she should continue or not. "Most people never leave this life. It's probably too late for me. My days of being a refined music teacher are over." At my stricken look, she hastened to reassure me. "That's all right. That's what a parent is for, to do whatever is necessary to give her child a good life. But you, don't forget you were the smartest student our primary school in Hong Kong had ever seen. Nothing can change how bright you are, whether your current teacher knows it or not. Most important, nobody can change who you are, except for you." She drew me close to her for a moment. "I'm sorry I brought you to this place," she whispered.

It was the closest Ma would ever come to expressing regret at her choice to come to America. I understood what my task was now and I laid my cheek against her shoulder. "I'm going to get us both out of here, Ma, I promise."

I had to go back to school on Monday. Pa was dead and no one else could save Ma from this life. The image of Ma cutting thread as an old lady in the factory was unbearable. I thought back to what Aunt Paula had said in passing about my cousin Nelson, that his teacher thought he could become a good lawyer. I wasn't sure what lawyers did exactly, but I knew they made a great deal of money; if even Nelson could become something so powerful, then so could I.

In a way, I was relieved at my decision. The hours in the apartment had been guilt-ridden and fearful. Cold, hungry and lonely. In the back of my mind, I had known that I couldn't get away with it forever. The gods were giving me a second chance. With the turkey holiday, I had a few more days before I had to go back to school and could make up an excuse for the five days I'd missed.

I had hardly any appetite that weekend, anticipating my return to Mr. Bogart's class. Even as I helped Ma finish the factory work, I kept seeing his face before me, the light round head that seemed so malevolent in its hairlessness. Only much later did I realize that he did have very thin hair: it was hair I hadn't recognized as such because it was blond. I imagined not being able to understand anything, getting a zero again. I thought about my teachers in Hong Kong, how they'd always showered me with praise and prizes. I'd felt sorry for the dumb kids who fumbled with their thumbs and stuttered when they gave the wrong answers, but now I was the stupid one with a weight on my heart.

The first thing Mr. Bogart said to me after we filed into the classroom was, "Where's your *accent* note?"

Luckily, I understood the word "note" and I'd known I would have to hand in something to explain my absence from school. I gave him a note I'd forged as best I could, based on my old English schoolbooks:

Dear Sirs,
   Kimberly was sick. Sorry with the trouble.
                    Your obedient servant,
                         Mrs. Chang

Mr. Bogart glanced at it and then filed it away without further comment. I slid into the seat I'd had the first day.

We had a test. Since I hadn't been to class, I had no idea what it was about. Then I saw that we'd been given tables with figures and there was text above each one. *There are three different basketball teams and each has played five games. . . .* It took me a few minutes to try to understand what the word problems were asking, but then I figured out they were simply mean, median and mode problems mixed in with a few decimal problems. It was like unexpectedly running into old friends. They were doing subjects we'd covered in Hong Kong more than a year before.

However, I was still scared under Mr. Bogart's eye. I misunderstood a sentence, then realized too late that I'd made a mistake and I had nothing to erase it with. Would he be angry if I crossed out my work? Probably. And then I wouldn't have enough room for the new answer. I didn't dare ask any of the other kids in case he would think I was cheating again.

My only choice was to ask Mr. Bogart himself. I stood and walked to his desk. At least I knew what I had to say because this exact situation had been covered in one of my old English lessons.

"Excuse me, sir." I tried to enunciate clearly. "May I borrow a rubber?"

He stared at me for a moment and a low titter swept through the classroom.

One of the boys called, "Don't your boyfriend have one?"

At this, the entire class burst into laughter. Why? I wished my hair were long enough to cover my face.

Mr. Bogart's face was flushed. He studied me as if trying to decide whether I'd disrupted his class on purpose. "That's enough. Silence! Kimberly, return to your seat."

Filled with shame for something I didn't at all understand, I hurried back to my seat. I would leave school that day and never come back.

Then the frizzy-haired girl leaned over.

"It's called an eraser here," she whispered. She tucked a strand of her feathery hair behind her ear and pushed a pink eraser across the gap between our desks.

In the end, that day turned out to be a good one. I knew I'd gotten all the answers right on that test, even if I wasn't sure I'd done the equations the way they'd been taught. Later, it turned out that the way I'd carried over numbers from the tens to the hundreds column, writing them down at the bottom of the equation instead of at the top, was not the American way to do it. Mr. Bogart took off some credit for this, so I didn't get a hundred on that test, but I'd seen enough to know that a few minor adjustments were all I required for the next time. This was a fight where I actually had a chance.

Even more important, I'd met Annette, the frizzy-haired girl. After the rubber incident, she subtly elbowed me. I glanced at her, then down at her notebook, where she'd written "Mr. Boogie" with a stick figure of Mr. Bogart, complete with a hole for a yelling mouth. I didn't even know what a boogie was then, but I understood the intention and was delighted. Annette normally didn't raise her hand in class—I think because she didn't like Mr. Bogart—but she often knew the answer. Whenever he asked a question, she wrote the answer down on her notebook paper and showed it to me. Since I could read far better than I could speak, this way of communicating was ideal.

And so Annette made school bearable for me again.

With the freezing cold of December, Ma and I started keeping the oven on day and night, leaving the door open to give us some heat. A few steps away from the small circle of warmth created by the open oven, it was hard to say which felt icier, the kitchen or the room we slept in. The kitchen contained the oven but its windows were only covered by the garbage bags and the other room didn't have any heat at all.

In Hong Kong, I'd had a light blue and white uniform for school, and as soon as school was over, I'd revert to sandals and bare skin in the sun. I was used to seeing the tips of my toes, my bare calves and shoulders; now that they had to be constantly covered, I missed myself. I was embalmed in clothes, layer after layer, and sometimes it was days before I saw my own body. The brief moments when my skin had to be exposed were to be avoided as much as possible. The touch of the air was a bitter hand laid against the flesh, and getting dressed in the morning was an ordeal, shedding the garments my body had warmed in the night and replacing them with clothing that stung my skin.

I didn't have panties like other girls did. Rather I wore two layers of thick pajamas under my corduroy pants. I had several undershirts on under the one red cotton sweater we'd brought from Hong Kong. The sweater had once been pretty, a red cardigan with two pandas on the pockets, but it had shrunk and the white of the pandas had been dyed a light rose through repeated washings. It became harder and harder to pull the sweater over all the under-layers I wore, but I had no choice. Then I put my jacket on over everything. Even stuffed into my clothes, like a lump of sticky rice tied in bamboo leaves, I was still freezing. The only positive of the cold was that it seemed to lessen the number of live roaches and mice.

We did everything we could next to the oven: my homework, folding laundry, getting dressed, working on the sacks of clothing we brought home from the factory. It was practically impossible for Ma and me to keep up with the demands of the factory, and many evenings, she sent me home alone while she stayed to finish as much of the work as possible. When she could, she brought the clothing home in plastic bags. No matter how late I stayed up to do my homework, I almost never remember Ma going to bed before I did. She was always a thin figure bent over those clothes, nodding off and then waking herself up again to go on. If a shipment was going out, we had to stay at the factory until our work was finished, even if that meant staying all night.

The heat from the oven never reached the walls, the floor or the furniture. Everything radiated cold back to our bodies, which were the only other sources of warmth in that dead building aside from the mice. Even in front of the oven, extremities like the tips of my fingers were constantly numb and it was hard to keep them flexible. This was particularly problematic because we often had to finish small tasks on the garments, such as turning sashes the right way around or buttoning jackets. Ma tried to play her violin for me as often as she could, even if it was only on Sundays, but it soon became impossible due to the cold. Her music would have to wait for spring.

· · ·

Despite Mr. Bogart, I looked forward to school: for the joy of seeing Annette, and for the heat. Whenever I got to the delicious warmth of school, the outer ring of my ears, my palms, the bottoms of my feet tingled with needles of regained feeling.

Annette told me she was a serious braces case. When I looked blank, she wrote it down for me and then opened her mouth like a horse to show me. Her teeth looked uneven and bruised because of them. I'd never known anyone with braces. Back home, we just grew up with bad teeth.

She had a blue backpack with little bears and squirrels clipped onto the zippers. I never brought anything for snack time because this concept was still unknown to Ma, but Annette pulled fascinating things from her backpack: crackers with peanut butter and jelly, small blocks of orange cheddar, eggs or tuna fish mashed with mayonnaise, celery sticks filled with cream cheese. She seemed to enjoy my surprise and delight when she shared with me.

I was also secretly fascinated by Annette's coloring. Her skin wasn't the opaque white of a sheet of paper that I'd thought white skin would be; it was actually transparent, and the red you saw was the color of the blood underneath. She was like an albino frog I'd seen at a market in Hong Kong when I was very small. Once, she lifted up her sweater to show me her round stomach and I jumped back in surprise. It wasn't smooth and tan like mine. The skin was blotched and reddened by the waistband of her pants, and fine blue veins ran under the surface. I thought that her skin had to be very thin and easily torn. She had blue eyes, which I had only seen in Hong Kong in blind people with cataracts. It was as if I could look into her brains, and I found it strange that she could see out of such light eyes as well as I could from mine.

She told me my hair was pretty even though it was so short, she said it was so black that it sometimes looked blue, she told me I should grow it into a pageboy. For years, I had the ambition of growing my hair into a pageboy without even knowing what that meant because I was so sure that Annette wouldn't steer me wrong. She thought it was neat that I came from somewhere that wasn't America. She wanted to learn Chinese words, especially insults.

"Crazy melon," I taught her in Chinese.

"She's a *guw guah*," she said, giggling, her tones for *crazy* and *melon* so off that I barely knew what she was saying. No other Chinese would be able to understand her, which was a good thing. Annette was referring to a girl in our class she didn't like because she said the girl was a know-it-all, which she also wrote down for me. It confused me because wasn't it a good thing to know so much?

Like me, Annette didn't have any other friends. It was mainly because she was one of three white kids in the class and the other two were boys, who stuck together. All of the other kids were black. There was clearly a division between the white kids and the black ones. There may have been a few Hispanic kids too but at that time, I mostly thought they were black kids with straighter hair.

I found out that the school was close to a rich white neighborhood. Parents in the rich area who wanted their kids to go to public school had no choice but to send them there. The other kids came from the neighborhood immediately surrounding the school itself, which was a fairly middle-to-lower-class black area. It was only later that I understood it in these terms, but what was immediately clear to me was that Aunt Paula had been right: the neighborhood of my school wasn't nearly as bad as the projects neighborhood, which I'd learned was the name of where I lived.

In many ways, I thought of myself as one of the black kids. The white kids brought sandwiches in brown paper bags. The two white boys sat together at a separate table and kept to themselves. I ate free hot lunch with the black kids, with Annette as the only white person at our table. I also lived in a black neighborhood. However, the black kids were friends with one another and I wasn't. They spoke English rapidly and easily, they sang the same songs in the courtyard, they knew the same jump rope games. One popular song went: *You look like a monkey, you smell like one too. We hate you, Mr. Bogart, we really really do.*

The other kids thought I was strange, of course. I didn't fit in, with my homemade, ill-fitting clothes and boyish hair. Ma cut it as soon as it reached the nape of my neck. She said it was more practical that way, since it took less time to dry in our icy apartment. Although the black kids in my class were mostly poor as well, they had store-bought clothes. On my way to school, I looked more closely at the tall apartment block close to school, where several of them lived. A bit of broken glass littered the ground and some of the walls were covered in graffiti (I had learned what the English writing was called). But the buildings were surrounded by a border of shrubbery, and most of the windows didn't have bars on them. Those people definitely had central heating.

There were some kids who were less well-off, though. One boy suddenly disappeared from school and no one knew where he'd gone. Another girl was picked up by her mother in the middle of the day once and her mother looked like she had been beaten up. Mr. Bogart didn't blink an eye at this. He seemed used to it. Fights often broke out after school, and I'd seen a boy walking away with a cut above his eye that dripped blood. Mostly boys fought boys but sometimes it was girls and girls, or mixed.

The other boys and girls had just emerged from

hating each other into a state of awkward interest, teasing and rude remarks. They were busy with cooties: catching them, getting rid of them and inoculating themselves against them. The transmission of cooties was an excuse for the boys to hit one another as hard as they could and to touch the girls. I had no idea what cooties were and often ended up as the recipient of all the cooties in the class. I'd been taught not to touch another person without permission, so it was hard for me to get rid of the cooties in my possession. Cooties were the one thing that transcended racial lines.

I'd never been a sickly child, but that winter, I had one flu or cold after another. My nose was rubbed so raw that a constant layer of peeling skin and small chapped cuts formed under my nostrils. We didn't have a doctor because we couldn't afford one. When I was trembling with fever, I lay in bed. Ma made rice with large slices of ginger in it. She wrapped the hot rice in a handkerchief and I had to hold it to my head until the rice cooled, so that it could soak up the germs. She boiled Coca-Cola with lemons and I had to drink it warm.

She went to the medicine shop in Chinatown and at great expense brought home many things I had to eat, all of which tasted terrible: deer antlers, crushed crickets, octopus tentacles, human-shaped roots. She stewed them in an earthen crock and cooked an entire pot down to a concentrated cupful. Even though I protested that these things only made me sicker, I still had to drink every drop.

I usually had to go to school even when I was ill, because the apartment was so bitterly cold that Ma was afraid to leave me there. Sometimes, the classroom swam before me, my face burning with fever, my nose dripping.

I'd hoped Mr. Bogart would start praising me once he saw that science and math were my best subjects, but he didn't. He seemed to assume that girls couldn't do these subjects, and often had a half-smile that suggested a girl would be incompetent whenever she went to the board to write down an answer. Then he would make a comment about "the fairer sex," which I thought had something to do with being more honest. I enjoyed proving him wrong. Even though he cut down my grades for any deviation from the path he'd taught, I understood everything perfectly once I could see it written down, and I could learn those subjects faster than anyone else in the class.

But I was failing other subjects even with Annette's help: Physical Sciences, Social Studies, Language Arts, everything that had too much to do with words. I relied on my ability to read and I had Ma scoop out my ears with an earwax spoon so that I could listen better. Ma also gave me $2.99 to buy a paperback *Webster's* dictionary. This cost us almost two hundred finished skirts, since we were paid 1.5 cents per skirt. For years, I calculated whether or not something was expensive by how many skirts it cost. In those days, the subway was 100 skirts just to get to the factory and back, a package of gum cost 7 skirts, a hot dog was 50 skirts, a new toy could range from 300 to 2,000 skirts. I even measured friendship in skirts. I learned you had to buy Christmas and birthday presents for friends, which cost at least a few hundred skirts each. It was a good thing I only had Annette as a friend.

I used that dictionary for years. The cover fell apart, was taped together again and again until it became irreparable, then the top pages started rolling up and falling off as well. I kept using that dictionary even when I'd lost the entire pronunciation guide and most of the A's.

I told Ma we weren't allowed to keep our tests or homework here, which was why I couldn't show anything to her, but promised her I was doing just fine. I said the teacher had recognized what a good student I was. These were lies that hurt me every time I said them. It seemed that Mr. Bogart went out of his way to choose assignments that were practically impossible for me, although now I think that he was simply thoughtless: write a page describing your bedroom and the emotional significance of objects in it (as if I had my own room filled with treasured toys); make a poster about a book you've read (with what materials?); make a collage about the Reagan administration using pictures from old magazines (Ma bought a Chinese newspaper only once in a while). I did my best but he didn't understand. *Halfhearted attempt,* he wrote. *Incomplete. Careless. A pictorial collage should not by definition include Chinese text.*

I wasn't the only child in the class who had trouble with Mr. Bogart's assignments. He seemed unable to understand the abilities or interests of the sixth-graders he actually taught. Many of the other kids just shrugged when he criticized them or gave them failing grades. They had already given up. But I had just come from being the star at my old school, where I'd won prizes in Chinese and math in interschool competitions. I would have given anything to do well in school again because I didn't know how else I would be able to help Ma and me escape from the factory. Mr. Bogart must have realized I was smart, but he seemed to dislike me anyway. Perhaps he thought I was arrogant or mocking him with my formal "sirs" and standing when spoken to. It was so much a part of my upbringing, I found it hard to stop. Or perhaps it was the opposite; perhaps I seemed uncultured in my cheap, ill-fitting clothes, low class. Either way, there didn't seem to be much I could do.

Mr. Bogart didn't mind the white kids as much, and I might have thought he was simply a racist, had it not been for Tyrone Marshall, who was black. Tall and soft-spoken, Tyrone was incredibly smart. He had the highest test scores in every subject except math, where I beat him. He didn't show off, but when he got called on, he was never wrong. One of his book reports, on which he'd gotten an A+, was hung on the wall. I memorized a line from it because it had impressed me, even though I couldn't understand all of the words: "This book takes us into an arena of fierce controversy." His skin was a matte dark brown, like chocolate dusted in cocoa, and he had thick lashes that curled violently away from his eyes. Mr. Bogart loved him and so did I.

When Mr. Bogart lectured about how wonderful Tyrone was, and by implication, what a sorry bunch of underachievers the rest of us were, Tyrone would sink ever lower in his seat.

"You were born in the *get dough*, were you not, Tyrone?" Mr. Bogart asked, pacing back and forth before the blackboard.

Tyrone nodded.

"Were your parents college graduates?"

Tyrone shook his head.

"What does your father do?"

His voice barely audible, Tyrone responded, "He's in jail."

"And your mother?"

"She's a saleslady." A dull red burning was visible through Tyrone's skin, lighting it up from the inside. He was miserable. Much as I understood that feeling of embarrassment, I wanted to be in his place too.

"And YET . . ." Mr. Bogart addressed the rest of us dramatically. "And YET this boy has the highest national test scores this school has ever seen."

Tyrone looked down.

"Tyrone, I know you are *modern* by nature but you must set an example." Then Mr. Bogart continued his speech. "And YET Tyrone reads *Langson* Hughes and William *Golden*. I ask you— what is the difference between a Tyrone Marshall and the rest of you? DETERMINATION. DRIVE." And so he went on.

All of this made Tyrone a complete outcast with the other kids. I wanted to tell him that I had been like him in Hong Kong, that I knew what it was to be admired and hated at the same time, that I knew it simply amounted to being alone. I wanted to tell him I thought he had beautiful eyes. Like so many things I wanted to say, I never did. What I did do was this: when Annette gave me candy, which happened often, I sometimes hid some in Tyrone's desk. I knew he wouldn't tell anyone. A slow, shy smile spread over his face whenever he found it; then he'd look around surreptitiously. I'd quickly look down and I think he never caught me, but I don't know for sure.

Miss Kumar, the black teacher who taught the other sixth-grade class, had colorful posters and guinea pigs in her room, and when her door was closed, I would pause on the way to the girls' room and hear her class laughing. She was tall and elegant, with her long hair always neatly coiled at the top of her head. Mr. Bogart's classroom was barren. We didn't have pets and there were only a few decorations in our room, mainly consisting of signs with block letters: REQUIREMENTS OF GOOD CITIZENSHIP. CHRISTMAS IS FOR CHARITY.

Mei Mei had been my friend in Hong Kong. She'd been both smart and very pretty, with black curly hair and pink cheeks. I was always ranked number one in all of our classes and she was number two. In Hong Kong, the students were seated in the order of their ranking, so Mei Mei sat right behind me every year. She lived in our apartment building as well and we played together often. I gave her little presents like stickers, and I thought she was my best friend. When I told her we were leaving for the U.S., however, I saw envy in her eyes but no sadness. In fact, she started spending time with another girl right away. I think she was happy that she would finally be number one.

My friendship with Annette felt very different. She was always giving me whatever she had: candy, drawings, information. Annette told me her little brother was a pain and I should be grateful I was an only child. When kids chanted, "XYZ

PDQ," and I tried to figure out what the following letters should be—RST? MNO?—Annette informed me that it meant, inexplicably, that your fly was open.

Annette was shocked that no one had ever told me about "the birds and the bees." And then, rather than help to enlighten me as usual, she giggled like mad, which made it especially intriguing. Clearly the phrase had a meaning beyond the obvious. I tried the school library, but the encyclopedia there only offered information on each species alone, nothing about them in tandem. When I asked Ma, she was genuinely mystified but she told me that it must not be something I needed to know if the teacher hadn't taught it in class.

I learned that Annette used Clairol All-Natural Wheat Shampoo to wash her hair and when I told her I used soap, she let me know that that was gross. The fact that we drank hot boiled water at home was weird. She asked me what I did after school, and when I answered that I was usually working at the factory, she went home and asked her father about it. The next day, she told me that that had been a silly thing to say since kids didn't work in factories in America. Annette's friendship was the best thing that had happened to me in America and I was grateful to her for teaching me many things, but that day, I began to understand that there was a part of my life that should remain hidden.

FOUR

We were assigned to work in pairs to build a diorama depicting "some of the basic skills of conflict resolution." Of course, Annette and I decided to work together, and this meant I had to go to her house one day. Ma didn't want me to socialize too much, but any sort of school assignment was sacrosanct, and so I was given permission to go.

After school, Annette's mother was waiting for us in a car. Her gaze was direct and kind, and her wavy hair was streaked with gray. There was a small boy with straggly blond hair already strapped into the seat next to hers. He was absorbed in a comic book. Annette climbed into the backseat and I followed. I'd thought a great deal about getting through this meeting correctly, and as soon as Annette was done leaning forward to kiss her mom, I held out my hand for her mother to shake.

"How do you do, Mrs. Avery?" I asked.

She twisted around and looked momentarily surprised, but then grasped my hand firmly. Her hands were extremely large for a woman's, almost as big as a man's, and they engulfed mine in warmth. She smiled, so I could see the wrinkles around her eyes deepen. "How do you do, Kimberly? It's a pleasure to meet you."

As I sat back in my seat, feeling satisfied that I

had managed to get through at least one occasion according to the rules of etiquette we'd been taught back home, Annette was already tugging on the boy's jacket.

"Let me see that," she said.

"Get your own," he said, not looking up.

"Mom!" she said. "He's not sharing!" She tried to pull the comic book from his hands, but her little brother wrenched it back and then scrunched his wiry body next to the window where Annette couldn't reach him.

"Stop fighting and let me drive," said Mrs. Avery.

It went on like that until we turned onto a beautiful, tree-lined street. The ride hadn't taken long and I'd never imagined that Brooklyn could look like this, especially such a short distance from the school. There was no graffiti anywhere, no housing projects or construction pits. The cobblestone street was lined with low, elegant houses and gardens. Mrs. Avery parked by a three-story house with some kind of stone structure in the front garden. It looked like a well. When I peered in, however, I saw that it was actually a fountain with water spouting from the center, filled with live goldfish and carp. Not long after that, I dreamed of Mrs. Avery giving me an extra goldfish from her fountain in a plastic bag, perhaps a baby that had just been born. I would take it home and keep it alive in one of our rice bowls. Surely, a goldfish couldn't be too expensive to keep, since it didn't eat much.

Annette and her brother had already run to the top of the stone staircase that led to the main door. Annette grabbed the comic book. Mrs. Avery and I caught up to them and Annette's brother wailed, "Mom!"

Mrs. Avery said, "Just give me a minute, okay, honey?" and she managed to get her keys in the lock.

As the front door swung open, I saw a chandelier hanging from the ceiling, sparkling with light like leaves caught in the rain. When we went in, we stood in an entryway with a polished table and a crystal bowl filled with fresh fruit. I wondered how they kept the roaches away from such an uncovered bowl. The smell of lemon cleanser and cookies mingled into a clean and delicious scent, and a thick carpet formed a walkway of flowers into the house.

"We're home," Mrs. Avery called. I looked down the hallway but instead of seeing a person, I saw a dog racing toward us. The white chow chow hurled itself upon Annette. A large gray tiger cat with a white-tipped tail had climbed down the staircase and was rubbing itself against her brother's leg.

"Don't be afraid," Mrs. Avery said. "I know they can be *over woman* if you're not used to animals but they *won't hot* you."

Annette's brother had the cat in his arms and was rubbing his cheek against its thick fur. Annette was giggling like a maniac because the dog was licking her entire face. I couldn't believe that Mrs. Avery allowed this. Weren't animals filled with both germs and a great desire to bite you?

Mrs. Avery bent down to my eye level. "What you have to do," she said, "is *ex-T* your hand like this." She stretched her hand out to the cat. "Come, Tommy. They like to come up to you and smell you, and then you'll be great friends."

I dared to ask a question. I glanced at Annette, who was now sitting on the floor still in her coat and galoshes, bumping her head into the dog's chest. "They have . . . ?" I didn't know what to call them and then pretended I was scratching myself.

"Oh!" Mrs. Avery said. "No, they don't have any *feet*. See this?" The cat named Tommy had approached and was sniffing her hand. She put her finger under the thin collar he was wearing. "This keeps all the *feet* away."

I must have looked confused because then she pretended she was scratching herself under her arms like a monkey. I'd never seen an adult, let alone a lady, do anything so undignified before.

"No scratch," she said. She took her hands away. "All okay."

The little brother had already disappeared into the kitchen and we followed him. I was introduced to the housekeeper, an angular white woman wrinkled like a piece of beef jerky.

I said, "How do you do," and shook her hand.

She cocked her head to one side and said, "Aren't you something."

She made us a snack. It was Ritz crackers, which I'd tasted in Hong Kong, but then she took a block of pale yellow cheese from the refrigerator. She used a metal slicer, which I'd never seen before, and carved thin bits of cheese to put on the crackers. I remembered that taste for a long time: the strange, alien sharpness of the cheese against the buttery crispness of the crackers.

The little brother piled a few crackers in his hands, grabbed the comic book out from under Annette's arm, and raced toward the staircase in the entryway.

"No crumbs on the carpet!" Mrs. Avery yelled after him.

Annette's face started to turn blotchy. "Mom! He took—"

"Stop it, Annette. You'll have time to read it later, and now you have company." Mrs. Avery turned to me. "Kimberly, you'll soon see, it's just a disaster around here."

Annette turned her concentration to her snack and when we were finished, we headed upstairs to her room. As we passed the living room, I saw a black grand piano and next to it, the dog stretched itself out on the large sectional sofa, which shimmered with gold and red stripes. Even from a distance, I could tell the plump cushions were fuzzy with a matted layer of animal hair.

Annette's room was almost as big as our classroom at school. There was a wall jammed full with toys: stuffed animals, board games, building blocks. She had a bunk bed with a ladder for going up and a slide for coming down. No one slept on the bottom bunk, she said, but she had a bunk bed because she liked sleeping high. I climbed up after her and at first I was afraid of getting too close to the edge of the mattress, despite the wooden rail. Once I got used to it, though, it was glorious, heady, to be so close to the ceiling, with my shoes off, a friend at my side, and the anticipation of a slide to return to floor level. It was so warm in their house, I could take off several layers and I lay on her bed in just my undershirt. I felt weightless and happy, as if I were in Hong Kong again.

"Ooooooh . . . the girls are playing in their tree house! Better watch out for bugs!" Her brother's little head stuck out like a dandelion from behind the door.

"I'm going to kill you!" Annette yelled, and she started down the slide but he disappeared before she got to the bottom. She ran to her bedroom door and poked her head out. "You come in here one more time and I'm telling!"

She slammed the door. "I wish I could keep him out, but we don't believe in locked doors in the house." From the way she said it, I could tell it was a phrase she was quoting from her parents. I wished Ma had the luxury of worrying about my behavior; she could barely do more than keep the both of us alive.

I glanced at the clock by her bed. Snoopy's hands showed the time and it wasn't long before I had to leave. "Maybe we start work now?"

Mrs. Avery had set up all our materials on Annette's desk. Everything was new and clean: a large shoe box, sheets of colored cardboard, green and gold glitter paint, watercolors and two types of markers, glue and scissors. Alone at home, I would have needed to do things differently: taking boxes out of other people's garbage, cutting figures out of old newspaper to stick to the box with packing tape, drawing everything with a ballpoint pen. With our pretty materials, Annette and I quickly finished our diorama, which showed some people sitting in a circle on the ground, holding hands and smiling. We used glitter paint to draw the letters of the word "Communication" behind the figures on the ground. It had been Annette's idea and I was glad she knew what we were supposed to do.

When Mrs. Avery drove me home, I asked her to drop me off at the school.

"No, I'll drive you home, dear," she said. "Just tell me where you live. I work part-time as a *really state* agent, I can find anyplace *something*."

"School is okay," I lied. "Ma wait for me at school."

"But the school is cl—" She broke off in the middle of her sentence. She took a breath, then said, "The school? You're sure?"

I nodded.

"The school it is, then. Here we go!" She sounded very bright.

When we got there, all of the windows were dark and there was no one on the pavement. I was afraid Mrs. Avery would protest because, like Ma, she didn't seem to be the sort of mother to let a kid out alone at an empty building.

She pulled up to the curb. "Are you sure you'll be all right?"

"Yes," I said. "I wait for Ma, she come soon. Bye-bye." I slid out of the car and closed the door behind me. I turned back toward her. This was another moment I'd rehearsed. "Thank you for your hospitality."

"You're very welcome." She leaned toward me and hooked a ringed hand around the edge of the open window. "You know, Kim, we'd love to have you over for dinner sometime. You let Annette know when you can come, all right? Just about *somethings* okay with us!"

I thanked her again, and then, to my surprise, she didn't offer to wait. I watched her disappear down the street and suddenly felt lonely. But when I got to the end of the long walk from school and finally opened the door to our building, a car the same style as hers passed behind me. Could she have followed me all this way?

I headed up the stairs.

I thought about the Averys' warm, animal-hair-covered house often. I dreamed of staying in Annette's room. She already had an extra bed and she could smuggle food to me. Sometimes, when I felt the most alone and overwhelmed, I had the fantasy of going to Mrs. Avery for help. Even just the possibility of it gave me real comfort.

But when Annette invited me to her house again, Ma said I couldn't go. I pleaded until finally Ma held me by the shoulders, looking into my eyes, and said, "*Ah*-Kim, if you go too many times to her house, we will have to invite her back to ours one day and then what? Little heart's stem, we already have too many debts we can't repay."

It was always easy to see who had a green card and who was illegal on payday. The illegals all got paid in cash, in Uncle Bob's office. The others had their piecework converted to an hourly wage and that amount was given in check form. We received a check but we also had to go to the office. Each payday, Uncle Bob would limp heavily into our workstation and escort us into the manager's office, where he would cash our check and divide up the money in front of our eyes.

"I want to make sure everything is absolutely clear," Uncle Bob said, sounding resigned. He wrote the different amounts on a pad of paper and put the green bills into separate piles. "So, this is for your medicine, when you were sick in Hong Kong. This is for the plane tickets, this is for the visas, this is the interest over the full amount, this is for the rent—no interest on that, of course—this is for the water, gas and electricity, and this is for you." And then he handed us the smallest pile with a sigh.

The first time this happened, I had been shocked by how little money was left for us. Luckily, we didn't have a phone, or we would have had to pay for that as well. I hadn't known that we were repaying anything else and I hadn't realized how much Ma's tuberculosis treatment and the immigration expenses had been. So this was a part of the reason we couldn't afford a better apartment, although I wished Aunt Paula had given us more time to repay our debts to her. Uncle Bob took their share every week, and we paid our rent and everything else in installments.

One day, Ma tried to talk to Uncle Bob about the apartment too. "*Ah*-Kim is always sick. The apartment is too cold. When will another one be available?"

He looked at me and my perpetually red nose. His face was not unkind. "That's hard to say. Aunt Paula takes care of all that stuff. But come on, let me buy you an iced tea. Have you ever had one?"

Uncle Bob took us to the soda machine and bought me my first American iced tea while a few kids looked on with awe. It was so cold and lemony, better than any drink I'd ever tasted.

"Thank you, Big Brother Bob," Ma said. "Will you keep watch for a new place for us?"

"Hmm? Oh, sure, sure," he said.

In preparation for Christmas, the school was hung with lights and cut-out snowflakes and we all sang songs in assembly. I knew Annette was planning to give me a present, because she spent weeks asking me to guess what it was. I thought only of things like pencil cases or schoolbooks, and so I was continually wrong, to her delight.

If Annette was going to give me something, I had to get her a gift too. Ma and I went to Woolworth's to look for a present. She skipped the toy department because everything was either too expensive or too small. Ma didn't know what we should buy for a white person either. She didn't have much money but she wanted the present to be big enough to look like we'd spent a decent amount on it. She finally decided on a big plastic plant for $1.99, which was 133 skirts. The store wrapped it for us for free and I couldn't wait to give it to Annette.

The last day of school before Christmas vacation, I saw Annette getting out of their car in the morning. I ran up to her, lugging my package.

"Kimberly!" she shrieked. "What's that?!"

I thrust it into her hands. "For you."

"Hi, Kim," Mrs. Avery called from inside the car.

Annette had already torn off the paper. As the green and red mottled leaves were revealed, she held the plastic plant at arm's length, puzzled. "Does it make music?"

I was just getting over another cold and I wiped my nose with a bit of toilet paper while I tried to figure out what she meant. Why would a plant make music? Only much later did I realize that Annette had thought it was a toy, that she couldn't figure out why I'd given her such a thing.

Mrs. Avery's voice interrupted us. "What a lovely plant, Annette. We'll put it right on the *winnie seal* in your room. Thank you, Kimberly."

"Yeah, thanks," Annette mumbled, and then she brightened as she drew a tiny package from her pocket. "This is for you."

When I opened it, I saw it was a little panda clip-on bear, similar to the other stuffed animals she had clipped to her book bag. It had soft brown eyes and neat black ears that were politely folded down; its paws had tiny claws on them that held on to your finger. I had longed for such a bear without even knowing it, although I think Ma felt a bit disappointed that we'd gotten such a tiny present in return.

On that last day of school before Christmas vacation, Ma surprised me. Instead of leaving for the factory in the morning as she always did, she walked to school with me.

"You'll be late," I said.

"Aunt Paula is usually collecting rent today," Ma answered. "And I have a bit of time before the shipment goes out."

"You can't be sure she'll be gone." I had seen Aunt Paula correcting the other workers for small faults like being late. Sometimes, she fired them on the spot.

"I know." Although I was trying to catch her eye, Ma looked only at my school, now appearing in the distance.

"Ma." I pulled on her thin coat. Ma was risking her job and our survival. I was sure that Aunt Paula would fire us too if she got angry enough. In the freezing morning air, puffs of white rose from my mouth. "What are you doing?"

She didn't answer me, but I saw she had looped through her arm a small plastic bag with a take-out container in it. Could this have something to do with my problems with Mr. Bogart? Was she going to throw food at him? With each step, the sidewalk pounded against the rubber of my boots in time with the frightened thud of my heart.

When we arrived at school, I tried to say good-bye to her at the door, but she walked right past the guard and followed me into the school basement, where I had to line up. Mr. Bogart was standing against the wall, talking to the other sixth-grade teacher, Miss Kumar. Ma marched up to them and I trailed behind her, wishing I had the power to make us both disappear.

"Yes?" Mr. Bogart said, drawing the sides of his mouth down into a frown.

"Merry X-y-masy," Ma said in English. Her voice shook. She placed the take-out container in Mr. Bogart's hands.

He raised his eyebrows and then slowly flipped open the cover of the container to reveal a large soy sauce drumstick inside. It was worse than I had expected. For Ma, this was a luxury that we could rarely afford ourselves, but to give Mr. Bogart something as common as a drumstick . . .

His expression was caught between disdain and something else I couldn't identify—could it have been surprise, or even gratitude? I waited for some sarcastic comment, but because of the unusual nature of the gift or Miss Kumar's presence, Mr. Bogart seemed stunned into silence.

Miss Kumar, on the other hand, was smiling openly. "And Nick, you always say you never get any appreciation," she said. She turned to Ma. "Kimberly seems to be settling in just fine, Mrs. Chang."

Ma didn't understand a word Miss Kumar had said, of course, but Ma knew enough to answer, "Dank you."

Mr. Bogart nodded abruptly at Ma and then gathered together our class, most of whom were gaping in surprise at the hated Mr. Bogart's getting any kind of present from a parent.

Ma left quickly and Aunt Paula was indeed away that morning, so we didn't get fired. That incident made Mr. Bogart neither kinder nor crueler to me, for which I was grateful, but I understood Ma was doing what she could to help me with him.

One day close to Christmas at the factory, I saw Matt working with his mother, and I rubbed the panda's forehead in my pocket with my finger.

I walked over and said, "Joyful Christmas." Then I swiftly pulled out the panda and offered it to him. I had thought about this. Much as I liked Tyrone at school, I had never really spoken to him. I was grateful to Matt and he was my only friend who knew what my life was really like; he shared it. I wanted to give him a present even more than I wanted to keep the panda for myself, because it was the only thing I had.

Matt tossed it up in the air and caught it with a quick flick of his wrist. "What's this for?" he asked.

"You helped me before," I said. I wanted to add, "And I really like you," but I didn't.

He smiled at me then, and I saw that he had a bruise smudged across his cheekbone. "Seems to me that this panda wants to be with you," he said, and gently, he put it back in my hand.

I was torn between relief and disappointment

that he'd refused my present. I stared at my fingers, then looked up and asked, "What happened to you?" I nodded at the bruise.

"Oh, that. Some jerks were trying to pick on my brother." He gave a shrug, trying to appear nonchalant, and he looked so small and skinny that I hurt for him.

I already knew the answer but I couldn't stop myself from asking. "Do you get into fights a lot?"

"Nah," he said, grinning at me again. I knew he was lying. "You're a sweet kid."

"I'm not a kid, I'm just as tall as you are."

"Just wait a couple of years," he said, as he walked away with a swagger.

I'd heard about the myth of Santa Claus in Hong Kong, although we'd assumed that he chose not to visit the warmer countries. Since he wasn't an active presence there and no one talked about him much, I hadn't learned that he wasn't real, unlike most other kids my age. Now that I was in the U.S., I assumed he would be appearing like all the other strange things I had heard of but had not seen until now, like red hair and mittens.

We gave Mr. Al a small wooden elephant from Chinatown, to bring him money and a long life. Ma wasn't afraid to give him things she actually liked, because she knew he was crazy about everything Chinese. His wife had died long before and he said that he was going to settle down with a nice

Chinese woman someday. He always made me ask Ma if she had any pretty friends and how to say things like "I love you" in Chinese.

"I'm going to keep this next to my cash register, bring me good luck," Mr. Al said. And he'd given us a small red desk lamp from his store. I put it on the table I did my homework on.

We didn't have a Christmas tree or lights in the apartment, but Ma did her best. She bought a used paperback book of Christmas carols and we sang them together. I'd heard some of them at school, and Ma could read the music if not the English words. She provided the melody wordlessly while I sang in English loudly and off-key. She tried accompanying us with her violin, but it was much too cold and she couldn't play with her gloves on.

I didn't have a stocking, though on Christmas Eve, I laid one of Ma's socks, which was bigger than mine, on the low table I did my homework on. When I woke up, there was an orange and a Chinese red envelope with two dollars in it, a fortune. I saw immediately there was no Santa Claus, only Ma, but that was enough.

A few days after the Western New Year, we found a true gift. Our regular route to the subway took us past a big building and one morning we saw some men working near its dumpster. Soon, they left and we saw what they'd thrown away: several rolls of the plush cloth used to make stuffed animals. The building must have been a toy factory.

We both stopped short, riveted by the sight of the warm material.

"Maybe if we are very fast—" Ma began.

"No, Ma. We can't risk being late with Aunt Paula again," I said. "We have to come back later."

Throughout the long day at the factory, Ma kept asking me questions. "Do you think other people would take something like that? Is there trash collection today?"

The only answer I had for her was, "I don't know." It would be my fault if the material was gone by the time we could leave the factory that evening.

When we finally hurried out of the subway station and rushed to the toy factory, we saw that everything was still there. Ma laughed with joy at the glorious find. Yards and yards of material that could keep us warmer. Even though the cloth was fake fur, lime green and prickly, it was better than anything we had. The streets were deserted in the bitter cold but Ma and I made several trips to pull as many rolls out of the trash as we could and dragged them home.

Ma made us robes, sweaters, pants and blankets out of the toy factory cloth. She used it to cover parts of the floor and windows. She even made tablecloths out of it. We must have been a funny sight, dressed up at home as two large stuffed animals, but we didn't have the luxury of minding. Since then, I have wondered if we would have survived the winter without that gift from the gods. The material was heavy and carpetlike, not having been intended as clothing, and when I slept under our new blankets, I woke with my limbs aching from the weight. However, at least they covered our entire bodies at once, unlike the piles of clothes we'd used in the past, and they were warm.

All of the gods leave at midnight on the night before Chinese New Year, which came at the end of January then. Every year, they return to us at a different time and from a different direction. Ma consulted the *Tong Sing* to find out when and where we had to go to welcome them as they returned. She rubbed a sewing needle against a magnet and then floated the needle in a bowl of water to figure out where the directions were. At four in the morning, Ma and I ventured into the deserted streets, the white clouds of our breaths drifting upward in the frosty gleam of the street-lamps. We headed southeast to greet the returning gods, our gloved hands filled with offerings of mandarin oranges and peanuts.

For the Chinese New Year, the factory was closed because no Chinese would work on this day. I was even allowed to stay home from school. Ma made us the traditional yellow steamed pastries and a vegetarian monk's meal for lunch, and for the night she'd bought us a roasted chicken from Chinatown. Anything that happened on this day was symbolic of the entire year to come, and so we were extremely careful, making sure we didn't break or drop anything.

The next day was the opening of the year, and Ma and I prepared the religious ceremonies to honor the dead. We always celebrated the important holidays first at home and then later at temple. Ma had found one in Chinatown. How many times had my hands laid the small squares of sacred paper into the required patterns over the years: first silver, then gold, then the two rectangular pieces laid horizontally.

Then we set food and wine in front of all five altars in the kitchen, lit incense and bowed to them with stacks of the sacred papers in our hands. We included a set to bring good luck for Ma and me: a promise to the gods that if we made it through this coming year safely, we would offer them roast pork next year. The kitchen was hazy with incense and the smoke crept into our clothes and hair. Ma invoked each of the gods by name, our most vital ancestors, and then our own dead, which meant all of the grandparents on both sides of my family, and Pa. When Ma chanted the prayers for her parents and Pa, she said, "Drink another cup, loved ones," and she poured an extra cup of wine on the floor in front of the ancestor altar.

When she was finally finished, Ma and I took the

sacred papers and rice wine downstairs. The back-yard of the building was overgrown with weeds and trees that stuck up through the two-foot-high layer of garbage covering the ground. A few days earlier, Ma and I had made a clearing in the trash in preparation. A thin layer of ice covered the ground now. We would burn the papers here.

Ma lit the first papers and dropped them in a metal bucket she'd bought in Chinatown. Then she took the flask and swung a chain of glistening rice wine three times counterclockwise around the bucket. The fire leaped under the alcohol. The wine ensured that the petty spirits hidden in the heavens would not be able to steal these gifts from their intended recipients. As she stirred the papers with a long metal stick, the heat radiating outward from the bottom of the bucket first melted the ice underneath it and then dried the concrete in a widening circle. I pictured the sacred gold and silver paper transforming into heavy gold and silver bars in the heavens, the colored papers into the finest silks. The more we burned, the more money our gods and loved ones would have to spend in the heavens, and the more material they would have to clothe themselves. The burning released the essence of the paper from its ashes and created it anew in the spirit world.

The trees were veiled by a haze of gray smoke and a funnel of ash, and partly burned wisps of gold and silver swirled upward into the skies, carrying our offerings to the heavens. Tiny flakes of ash clung to my face and hair.

Ma, her head bowed in prayer, was standing alone at the border of where the earth met concrete in our backyard, and I caught a trace of her words. *Merciful Kuan Yin, beloved relatives, please let good people come to us and allow the bad ones to walk away.* I went over and linked my arm through hers. I thought, *Pa, I wish you were here to help us. Please help me perfect my English so I can take care of us.* Ma pressed my hand gently and we prayed together for our future.

The following Sunday, Ma and I had just returned from buying our weekly groceries in Chinatown when I noticed that the lights were on inside Mr. Al's shop. He also had a large sign in his window that said "Clearance—Everything Must Go." I looked through the door and saw Mr. Al moving some of his things around inside.

Ma shifted her shopping bags to one hand so she could find her keys. "We shouldn't bother him. He looks busy."

At that moment, Mr. Al caught sight of us. He came and unlocked his door. "Come in."

"No, thank you," I said. "We have to put food in refrigerator. But why you here on Sunday?"

"I have a lot of things I have to do. Need to sort out which things I want to get rid of, which ones I want to take with me."

I was aghast. "You are going somewhere?" Mr. Al waved to us whenever he saw us. He was our friend and looked out for us. After we'd gotten to know him better, I told him about the ice-cream-buying incident at the grocery store when the owner had made us pay more than we should have paid.

Mr. Al said, "That guy don't have any right to rip off decent people like that." He must have said something to the owner because the next time we came in, the owner gave me a candy necklace for free.

"What's wrong?" Ma asked me now. She hadn't understood any of this.

Mr. Al looked concerned. "Don't you know? Sweetheart, everybody's gradually moving out of here. This whole area's *boomed*."

"What?" I sounded as confused as I felt.

"Ended. No hope left. The government's going to build some huge *compicks* here. All the buildings on this block and across the street are going to be broken down."

"When?"

"What is happening?" Ma asked again. She was worried.

"I'll tell you later," I said in Chinese. I waited for Mr. Al to speak.

He said, "Was supposed to happen next year, but it keeps getting put off. Lots of people are complaining and trying to stop it. Will probably be another ten years before it actually happens, but could be next year too. *Ant* no one's going to hang around waiting to get thrown out. This is a sinking ship." He patted me on the shoulder with his long brown hand. "You ladies are good people. You should get out while you can. Those landlords aren't going to do nothing for us while we're waiting. No one wants to put any more money in here. My window's been broken in the back for months now. Business is bad, everybody's leaving."

"When you going?"

"My lease is up March first. I'm going to move near my brother back in Virginia."

FIVE

In our apartment upstairs, I explained to Ma what Mr. Al had told me.

"This proves Aunt Paula will let us move when a good apartment opens up," Ma said, smiling. "We can't stay here forever."

"But that can take a long time, Ma. And she knew the area would be broken down. Why didn't she tell us?"

"Maybe she didn't want to alarm us."

I was thinking hard. "What this really means is that Mr. N. will never fix the heat or anything else. Ma, we need to find a new place to live."

She breathed in sharply. "We can't afford it."

"Other people from the factory live in apartments too."

"Don't forget, the rent is only a part of what we pay to Aunt Paula every month. Our debt is so great. And this apartment isn't as expensive."

"Even in Chinatown? They can't cost too much there."

"The really cheap apartments go from family member to family member. Nothing opens up. I've asked around at the factory."

My mind was still turning everything over. "I think it's not even law-following for us to be living here, the building is in such bad shape. That's probably the real reason Aunt Paula had me use a fake address for school." I was getting reckless. "Ma, let's run away. We can find a new job at another factory. Aunt Paula doesn't have to know." Back in Hong Kong, I would never have dared to talk to Ma like this, to openly argue with her about such grown-up topics, but I had never had the responsibilities there that I now did. I had never been so desperate to change our living situation.

Ma's eyes were intense. "And our debt to her, then? She brought us here, *ah*-Kim. She spent the money to cure me, for our green cards and tickets. It's not a question of what we can get away with, it's a question of honor."

"To her?" I tugged at a lock of my hair, frustrated by Ma and her integrity.

"She's given us housing and a job. She's my

sister and your aunt. And no matter how flawed someone else may be, that doesn't give us the right to be less than we are, does it? We are decent people and we repay our debts."

Some of my anger ebbed away. I hated being tied to Aunt Paula but I could see that Ma would have to be a different person before she could renege on something she owed. "Was Aunt Paula always like this, even when you were younger?"

Ma hesitated. I knew she disliked speaking ill of anyone, especially family. "When we were teenagers alone in Hong Kong, Aunt Paula took care of everything. She was smart and resourceful. She trained as a gold-beater so I could finish high school." A jeweler who works with gold. "I was supposed to be the one to marry an American Chinese, since I wasn't good at much except for music, and some people thought I was pretty. But then I started giving music lessons and your pa gave me a job at the school. Soon after that, we were married."

"Was Aunt Paula angry?"

"Well, yes she was. But she's always been very practical, and when Uncle Bob arrived, she just married him herself."

"You were supposed to marry Uncle Bob?" I wasn't sure I could take all these surprises today.

"He went to Hong Kong to meet a number of people," Ma said. I knew that meant he could choose from several different girls. "But an

110

acquaintance of ours had given him my picture. In any case, Aunt Paula has been through some hard times herself."

The next day at the factory, Ma and I spoke to Aunt Paula in the office again.

"Why didn't you tell us that our entire block will be torn down?" Ma asked gently.

Aunt Paula raised her thin eyebrows, surprised that we knew. "Because it wasn't important. I told you it was only temporary that you would be living there. You see that you didn't have to worry? You can't stay there too long even if you wanted to."

"How much longer will it be?" Ma asked.

"Not much," Aunt Paula said. She scratched her cheek absentmindedly. "I'll let you know as soon as I have any news. Now, we'd all better get back to work." She tightened her lips. "You came close to missing the deadline on that last ship-ment."

"I know," Ma said. "I'll work harder."

"We are family, but I can't have people saying I'm being unfair."

Her threat was clear and we left quickly.

As we went past the thread-cutters' station on the way to our workplace, I was surprised to see Matt there working alone, without either Park or his mother.

"Where is your ma?" I asked.

"She doesn't feel too well sometimes," Matt said, not slowing down. He had to cover his mother's workload. "She kept Park home with her today so I could really get some work done." He seemed proud. "Park isn't a big helping hand sometimes."

"Can I get anything for your mother?" Ma asked. "If it's her lungs, crushed bumblebees in salt are very effective."

"It's her heart," Matt said. His eyes were warm as he glanced up at the both of us. "And she has her own medicine, but thank you very much, Mrs. Chang."

Ma smiled at me as we walked on. "He's a nicer boy than I thought."

I had to perfect my English. Not only did I write down and look up the words I didn't know in my textbooks, I started with the A' s in my dictionary and tried to memorize all the words. I made a copy of the list and stuck it to the inside of the bathroom door. I had learned the phonetic alphabet in Hong Kong and that made it easier for me to figure out how the words were pronounced, even though I still often made mistakes. Our class went to the public library once a week and I always took out a stack of books, starting with the embarrassingly thin ones for little kids. I slowly worked my way up in age. I took these books with me to the factory and read them on the subway. Almost all of my homework was done either on the subway or at the factory. For the bigger projects, I caught up on Sundays.

By the time report cards were given out at the beginning of February, I wasn't doing well but I was passing most subjects. I'd taken the national reading and math tests with the other kids but I didn't know what the results were yet. On my report card, I got a few Satisfactories for Science and Math, a few Unsatisfactories, and the rest were all Fairs. In the comments section, Mr. Bogart wrote, "Kimberly must learn to apply herself with more effort. Please come see me at the PTA meeting. Submit dental note!" How were we supposed to pay for a dentist? I didn't know what a PTA meeting was, but I wasn't about to let Ma see any of this. I let her believe that we got report cards only once a year, at the end. I forged her signature, which was easy since I'd been signing her name since the beginning.

The ice across the inside of the windowpanes in our apartment slowly dissolved and I could see through to the outside world again.

At the end of February, the class bully started staring at me in class. His name was Luke and he'd been left back a few times so he was a head taller than the rest of us. He had a barrel of a chest covered loosely by the same stained gray top that he wore every day. His nostrils were flared like a bull's, and even Mr. Bogart seemed to have given up on him, leaving him alone most of the time. I saw Luke shove the other kids around. If a kid dared to fight back, Luke became doubly vicious. His main weapon was his legs and he liked knocking people to the ground and kicking them. There was a rumor that once a kid had rammed him in the stomach with his head and Luke had pulled a knife and cut him. He also used a lot of words I didn't know, like *cock* and *mother finger*.

I asked Annette if she knew what *cock* meant.

"Everyone knows that." Her smile was confident. "It means poop."

Annette had recently told me that she was going to a private school called Harrison Prep next year. I would go to a public junior high school, of course. How would I manage without her?

We said good-bye to Mr. Al. A large moving van had taken away most of his inventory, although he'd saved a few folding chairs and a single mattress for us.

"Thank you, Mr. Al," I said. I was thrilled to have my own place to sleep again.

"*Mmm sai*," he said, trying to say "You're welcome" in Cantonese.

"Your Chinese is very good," I lied. Luckily, I knew exactly what I'd taught him, so I could usually guess what he was trying to say.

"You beautiful ladies take care of yourselves,"

he said, and he gave us each in turn a big hug. He smelled like tobacco.

"May you have the strength and health of a dragon," Ma said softly in Chinese. She looked in her shopping bag and pulled out a short wooden sword she'd bought from the kung fu store in Chinatown. She gave it to him.

His broad face shone with pleasure as he ran his finger over the carvings on the handle.

"She say, 'Good health,'" I said, not knowing how to translate it further. "You supposed to lay that under pillow."

"What? And waste a good weapon?"

"It takes away worry and bad dream."

"All right, then. If you say so." He grinned at us as he walked away to the subway, waving his sword like a ninja.

I felt sad when I saw Mr. Al's empty store downstairs. Up in our apartment, I took a look at his building, pulling up the garbage bags over the kitchen window.

I wanted to see the sleeping black woman and baby in the apartment above his store. The mother wasn't there but I could make out the baby, bigger now, alone in an old mesh playpen. He was hanging on to the sides. He had his mouth wide open, crying, but no one came.

I had always liked toy cars more than dolls and I had no interest in real babies at all, but I wished I could pick him up and comfort him.

115

• • •

Through all of March and into April, I continued to feel the bully Luke's eyes on me but I pretended I didn't notice anything. He had started grabbing girls by their hair and kissing them whenever Mr. Bogart wasn't looking. Finally, one lunch period I was crossing the cafeteria, holding my tray, and passed the table where he was sitting with some other boys. He stuck out his foot. I stepped over it and kept going. The rubber legs of his chair screeched against the floor as he pushed himself away from the table and stood up.

"Hey, Chinese girl."

I didn't look around. I had just set my tray down at my usual spot across the table from Annette when I felt his hand on my shoulder. On reflex, I lowered my shoulder and turned at the same time, so that his hand fell off.

"Wow, that's kung fu," one of Luke's friends said.

"You know karate?" Luke asked, with real interest.

"No," I said. That was the truth.

"She does," his skinny friend said.

"I want to try out your moves. Let's fight after school." Luke said this as if he were inviting me to play at his house. Then he and his friends went back to their own table.

Annette was staring at me from across the table. I sat down, trembling.

"Are you crazy?" she asked, her voice pitched higher than normal. "He'll kill you!"

"What must I do?"

"You gotta tell somebody. Tell Mr. Bogart."

I just looked at her.

"Okay, forget that." Annette wrinkled her forehead in thought. "My mom's got to work today, so my housekeeper's picking me up from school. We could tell her."

I thought about her housekeeper, who had looked so dry and serious. She didn't seem like someone I could trust. If only Mrs. Avery were going to pick Annette up that day instead. "No, I don't want you tell her."

"Why not?"

"She don't help." I knew it was true. "And I'm not a telly-tale."

Annette lowered her voice to a hiss. "Look, Kimberly, I think Luke carries a *knife*. It's okay to tell someone!"

I shook my head. I was afraid of Luke but I was more afraid of grown-ups. Maybe Annette's housekeeper would try to talk to Ma or Mr. Bogart. Everything I had hidden from Ma could come out: the forged signatures, the failed tests, the dental note, the report cards, the PTA meeting.

Annette grabbed my wrist. "Okay, you just come home with me, then. We'll get in the car and drive away. We can drop you off at your place."

I wanted to agree. But how could I show them

where I lived? And Ma was expecting me at the factory. Besides, Luke would just wait for me tomorrow, or the day after that. It would only get worse. He'd been staring at me for a while now.

"No," I said. "I fight him."

After school, I could taste the sour from my stomach in my mouth. I'd never been struck before. Even though I'd often seen fights in the school yard, I'd never been punched or kicked or spit upon. I had never hit anyone either. I'd done some tai chi in the park with Ma back home, but since most of the other students had been in their seventies, what we'd learned had hardly trained me for a street fight in Brooklyn.

Everyone had heard about the brawl, and a tight circle of kids reined us in. The words *fight fight fight* pulsed in the air like drumbeats. Annette disappeared into the ring of faces and I stood in the center alone, facing Luke. He was waiting: large, gray, a battleship. I came up to his chin and he weighed twice as much as I did. He came from one of the toughest neighborhoods in Brooklyn, where the mailman wouldn't even go to deliver parcels, and had only recently moved to this area. I was so scared, I would have given anything never to have come here.

I did not run. There was no place to run to. I felt a great stubbornness rising from my core, even though my fingers were numb and cold. The calm of terror swept over me. I am born from a great line of fighters; my ancestor was one of the greatest warriors during the Tang dynasty, and I wouldn't flee. Methodically, barely audible, I began to curse him in Chinese: *You have a wolf's heart and a dog's lungs, your heart has been eaten by a dog.*

"What the *fuh* you saying?" Luke said.

I didn't answer. I continued under my breath as if I were praying. We circled each other, his shadow looming over me.

"You're so weird," he said. Suddenly, he took off his book bag and swung it, thwacking me in the side. The blow twisted me around, so that my back was to him, and I felt a thud on my book bag, from where he'd kicked me. I took off my bag and connected with his arm. Left, right, I beat him on either side of his fleshy body, the material of his jacket catching against my bag. To my surprise, he didn't try to hit me back. Then I swung my right leg and connected with his calf.

"Shit!" he cried. For a second, something wild flared in his eyes but he still didn't strike me again. Instead, he took my shoulder in one hand and gave a casual push, so that I stumbled back a few steps. Then he swung his bag over his shoulder and sauntered away.

Annette was hugging me. "I didn't know you could fight!" she said. "You can do kung fu!"

I didn't tell her otherwise, but I knew that I

couldn't fight, that I hadn't fought. I walked home in a daze. He could have killed me. What had happened?

The next day, Mrs. LaGuardia, the principal, opened our classroom door in the middle of Social Studies and said, "Mr. Bogart, I need to see Kimberly Chang."

A number of kids whispered "Ooooooh" and clasped their hands against their mouths. Even though quite a number of jokes about La Guardia Airport were made behind her back, Mrs. LaGuardia was well respected and universally feared. I felt my chest freeze. I glanced over at Luke, who didn't meet my eyes. Who had told on us?

Mr. Bogart nodded. "Do try to be good, Kimberly."

I had to hurry to keep up with Mrs. LaGuardia's smooth strides. When we reached her office, she shut the door behind us and took off her spectacles, letting them hang over her bosom on a silvery chain. I sat on the chair facing her desk and my feet barely brushed the floor. I knew what happened to students in the principal's office: they were annihilated.

"The results of the national test scores have just arrived. Miss Kumar *noty* yours and asked me to take a look. Especially your math scores are very *something*. Of course, your reading scores are low."

I stared at my fingernails and my blood thudded harder. I understood this meant that my English scores were not good enough, an embarrassment to the school. I was going to be suspended on the grounds of grades and fighting. Or perhaps they'd found out about my forgeries of Ma's signature too.

"Tell me, what are you planning to do next year?"

So that was it. I was going to be kept back. Everyone else would graduate from the sixth grade except for me. How could I hide this from Ma? I was really going to be in trouble when I got home. I slunk down lower and tried to think of an answer that would appease her.

"Honey, look at me."

I was so startled by the word "honey" that I obeyed. I had heard Mrs. Avery using it for Annette. This was not a word principals used back home. Mrs. LaGuardia's face looked strangely naked without her glasses. Her lashes were short but her eyes were kind.

"You're not in trouble," she said.

I straightened a bit in my chair even though I knew better than to believe her.

"Unfortunately, there aren't many good choices when it comes to public junior high schools in this area. I've been *lobbing* to change this fact because all of our children deserve to go someplace first-rate after graduation, but this is still the way it is.

The closest public junior high school is still quite far from here and it's not in the safest neighborhood. A child of your *cola brr* usually gets into one of the specialized public schools for bright children, but your English scores aren't high enough yet. I also know you haven't had the easiest time here so far."

I was looking at the seat of my chair again: the upholstery was violently green. I felt vaguely sick.

She went on. "The truth is, Kimberly, I'm worried about what might happen to you if you get thrown into a school without the *faciltees* to help you *nur chore* your abilities. Off the record, I think you should consider a private school. Most of our students wouldn't have a *really stick* chance of getting in or of being able to pay for it, but you might."

Now I was alarmed for a different reason. Somehow, Mrs. LaGuardia had mistaken me for one of the white kids, the ones who had housekeepers waiting at home, ready with an afternoon snack. I had to play it cool until I could get out of that office, throw her off the scent and then bolt.

"Thank you, Mrs. LaGuardia," I said.

"I know of several good schools, if you should need some names," she said.

I stared at her blankly.

"Do you want some *recordy shunts*?" she repeated.

"No, thank you." I was too quick to answer.

She looked at me. No one ever said Mrs. LaGuardia was dumb. "Don't you want to go to private school, Kimberly?" She was beginning to sound annoyed. "Or if you can tell me how to reach your mother?"

I shook my head and stared at the floor.

She sighed. "It's your decision."

I could hear she'd given up and instead of feeling relieved, the unhappiness in me grew heavier.

"I want go," I mumbled. I could feel her leaning forward across her polished desk to hear me better but she didn't interrupt. "But we should pay."

"I should have been clearer." Her tone was brisk now. "No one would expect you and your mother to pay for it all yourselves. I meant that the private school would naturally have to offer you a scholarship. I can't promise anything, but I believe there is a chance they would."

"Really?" I had never imagined that I might get to go to a fancy school like Annette.

"But don't get your hopes up too much, because this is very late to apply. The normal application process is already closed. Any school who accepts you, if they do, would have to squeeze you in and their budget may already be *ex-sausaged*."

"Maybe Harrison?" I asked. That was where Annette was going.

Mrs. LaGuardia laughed. "Well, you do set your sights high. Why don't you let me make some phone calls? I'll get back to you, Kimberly. You may go now, but again, don't hope for too much. It's a long shot."

After I came back from Mrs. LaGuardia's office without being expelled, Luke wanted to fight me every day. We had our exchange of backpack blows a few more times when another girl caught on to what was going on before I did. She was beginning to develop a woman's body and she was much prettier than I, with her soft brown curls and creamy skin. She started challenging Luke as if she were defending me.

"You better not pick on my friend," she said, pushing her face close to his. She had never spoken a word to me before this, but I was still grateful.

It wasn't long before Luke transferred his attention to her.

"You wanna fight?" he asked.

They had to fight only once before they started necking in the school yard. Finally, I understood. I hadn't been involved in fights: it had been a courtship, the rules of which I'd violated by kicking him so hard the first time. I felt ashamed. In any case, the whole episode earned me a kind of respect from the rest of the class and I began to feel more at home.

There were several other notable events that spring: Easter, a holiday about rabbits and eggs, and the school photo. Ma and I couldn't afford to buy the pictures, so I kept the print they gave me, which had the word PROOF stamped across my chest. The new PTA meeting came and went without Ma's knowledge.

After Easter, I heard from Mrs. LaGuardia that Harrison Prep was indeed interested in me as a scholarship student, which I understood to mean they might be willing to pay for me as long as I got into a good college in the end. That seemed to be a reasonable bargain to me. What else could I offer?

Mrs. LaGuardia made an appointment for me and Ma at the school, which was in a part of Brooklyn I had never seen.

Ma was breathless with excitement when I told her. "What a chance! I am so proud of you!" But her brow furrowed when she heard the date. "So soon? The shipment is going out that night."

"It's all right. I can go by myself."

"Can we reschedule the appointment for another day?"

"Ma, I'd like it if you came with me but I don't want you to get into trouble at the factory. You can't miss any day there."

Ma looked sad. "I wish you didn't have to do it alone but I'll light incense for you."

I was allowed to miss my own classes that day and I had to take three subways to get to Harrison Prep. Then I walked for a while, following the map

125

they'd given me, until I came to a huge wooded area. This was a part of Brooklyn I hadn't dreamed existed. It didn't look like anything else I'd seen, not even Annette's neighborhood. It was so beautiful and peaceful it seemed like I was in the country.

I thought I was walking along a park but it later turned out that this was already a part of Harrison's campus. The school was so old that it owned a great deal of property. The trees and shrubbery turned into a high wire fence and through it, in the distance, I could see high school kids playing a game on an enormous and immaculate lawn. They were wearing shorts that were so wide, they seemed to be square. These kids and their game were completely alien to me. At my current elementary school, at least I wasn't the only nonwhite child and I certainly wasn't the only poor one. No one I'd ever known had done things like what these students were doing, and if I stayed here, I would also have to run with a netted pole, be expected to catch balls and toss them to some figure waving in the distance. I would also have to run in square shorts. We could never afford square shorts.

I stopped walking for a moment and thought about turning back, going back to who I was. If they knew that Ma made even my underwear for me, that we slept under pieces of fabric we'd found in the trash, they would surely throw me out. I was a fraud, pretending to be one of the rich kids. What I didn't know then was that I shouldn't have worried about pulling any of this off; they weren't fooled at all.

I finally reached a large brick building set in the same smooth lawn. The door was made of carved wood inset with pieces of colored glass. It was so heavy, I could hardly get it open. Through the lighter parts of the glass, I could already see a young woman at a desk in front of an enormous curving staircase. She was in a crisp white blouse and high heels, her light brown hair neatly pulled back in a bun.

I felt very small in that hall. A portrait of a bearded man holding a Bible watched me as I walked up to her. I looked at the crumpled slip of paper in my hand, even though I already knew it by heart. I'd thought a lot about how to get through this appointment.

"Do you know Dr. Weston?" I asked in a squeaky voice.

She looked faintly surprised, then took a breath and said, "Do you have an appointment with her?"

"Yes," I said, relieved she'd understood me. She would take over from here.

"You must be Kimberly Chang."

I nodded and handed her the stack of forms I'd had to fill out for my application.

She glanced behind me. "Is your mother parking the car?"

I looked down. "No," I said. "She is ill today."

"Someone else must have brought you, then?"

I should have thought of this and been ready with an answer. Lies flashed through my mind—someone brought me but they were waiting in the car, someone brought me and left.

She interrupted my thoughts. "Did you come alone?"

The engine of my mind stuttered to a halt. "Yes."

She paused, then smiled at me. "You must be tired from all the traveling, then. Why don't you take a seat and I'll tell Dr. Weston you're here."

She led me to one of the wooden chairs set against the wall and left with my pile of paperwork. She hadn't been unkind but I wasn't reassured. Her heels echoed in the hall.

When she returned a few minutes later, she was accompanied by a compact older woman in a beige suit with a face like a bulldog, the jowls hanging below a pointy nose, and close-set bright eyes.

The older woman stopped before me. "Hi, I'm Dr. Weston," she said.

"How do you do?" I said, glad that I had practiced this with Mrs. Avery. I extended my hand to her and she shook it without hesitation. Her hand was pale and soft except for the hardness of several square glittering rings.

When I was seated in her office, Dr. Weston leaned back. A silver stopwatch rested on the yellow legal pad on her table. My forms also lay on her desk. She gave me a smile that only moved the bottom half of her face. I knew this was supposed to put me at ease but it only made me more nervous.

"We normally do this in written form but because I've been told you're a special case, I'm going to ask you a few questions myself, all right? Just answer them as best you can, and if you don't know the answer, tell me."

I braced myself: Where is your mother? Why didn't she bring you here today? What do people wear for Easter? Which hand should you hold your knife in when you eat? I gripped the armrests of my chair.

"Would you please count from one to forty in threes? I'm going to time you. It begins one, four, seven . . . ?"

I blinked. This, I could handle. "Ten, thirteen, sixteen . . ."

"Good. Now, a boy is sixteen years old and his sister is twice as old. When the boy is twenty-four years old, what will be his sister's age?"

She went on like this for about an hour. It was the strangest conversation I'd ever had with anyone but I liked it. I understood it was a test, of course, but all such conversations are tests and this, at least, was one for which I understood the rules. In a world of uncertainties, I was on concrete ground. When I didn't know a word, she explained it to me. I had to skip a question only a few times and then she asked me something else. Finally, she stopped and looked up at me.

"Excellent," she said. "Now, there is one last thing."

She handed me a sheet of paper and a pencil. "Draw a picture for me. Anything you like. A house, a girl, whatever."

I didn't want to draw a picture of our house. For a girl, I imagined she meant a non-Chinese girl, and I drew the only kind of girl I knew about, the sort I'd read about in books: a princess. She had long blond hair with a crown on her head and a Cinderella ball gown with puff sleeves and an impossibly narrow waist.

When Dr. Weston took the sheet of paper and saw the drawing, she gave a short bark of laughter. She contained herself immediately and riffled through her papers, but I didn't know why she had laughed. I must have looked hurt as I wondered if it was because of the incongruity between my clothes and the beautiful ones I'd drawn.

She glanced at my face. "Your results on the test were so *impersee*, I'd forgotten how young you were. Listen, why don't you take a tour of the school and we'll talk again afterwards, all right?"

I nodded. The first lady came in and took me around. First, she showed me their trophy show-case, which was in the main hall where I'd entered. I heard her talking about the awards the school had received, but I was looking at the pictures of the kids who had won them. They were all wearing blazers. No one wore blazers at my school. We made them sometimes at the factory, but these were different. I could tell they weren't made of polyester. These blazers looked stiff, reining in the students' shoulders, making sure that they didn't take up any more space than they were allowed.

The students who were smiling showed even, white teeth to match their even, white skin. Was I going to be the only Chinese person in the whole school? Was that why they were interested in me? The framed pictures were arranged one above the other, with the older classes at the bottom. The older classes contained only boys, and then there were both boys and girls, but as the photos moved forward in time, one thing hardly seemed to change: a few darker faces appeared here and there, but those were rare exceptions.

Then, to my surprise, I was taken to several other buildings, all large and spacious, the walls paneled with wood. I had thought the first building was the entire school. Inside the other buildings, I tried not to stare at the statues of women with bare breasts, their whiteness glowing in the alcoves; they even had nipples. This too was something Western. As we passed some classrooms, I saw they were filled with students who looked just like the kids in the pictures.

We took a walk around the campus, and I gasped. I was completely dumbfounded. I had never imagined there could be such a place in New York. The woman pointed out the tennis courts and the football field, as if it were completely natural to have access to such things. Leaves were sprouting everywhere. I'd never seen so many trees, but what struck me the most was how open it was. Not the vacant lots where Ma and I lived, or the fenced-in patch of asphalt we had at school, or even Annette's pretty little backyard had been like this. I didn't know much, but I knew this place was special.

SIX

When we arrived back at Dr. Weston's office, she was on the phone. She excused herself, hung up and gestured for me to sit down again.

"What do you think of the school?" she asked.

I had to think a second. "It is quiet."

"Of course it's quiet." She looked a bit irritated and I knew I had said something wrong. "That's how our students can *achiff* such *spectacles* academic results. Did you hear about the prizes we've won?"

I said yes even though I didn't remember, because I didn't want the younger woman to get into trouble.

"Harrison is one of the best college *prepator* schools in the country, comparable in terms of the *facilies* we offer to schools like *Exit* and *Sand*

Paul, only with the advantage that you don't need to *bord* here. We are actually a *boring* school without the *boring*."

She'd used more words I didn't understand in one breath than she had in the entire time I'd been there. I had absolutely no idea what she was talking about, only that she was repeating a memorized speech like a person in a play and I should acknowledge that by smiling and nodding, which I did.

Then there was a silence while Dr. Weston flipped through her legal pad, scanning her notes from our interview. Her eyes lingered a moment on my homemade pants: red corduroy, well-washed and visibly pilling around the elastic waistband.

"All right, then. For the final scholarship decision, I am going to need to *consle* with the financial aid committee but I can tell you now that no school in their right mind would *denee* you *admissee*."

I was trying to understand if this was a good or a bad thing when she switched tactics.

She smiled at me and this time, her smile was truly kind. "We like you, Kimberly. We want you to join our school. Is that something you want too?"

I could breathe more freely now. I even smiled back. "I like school."

"But . . ." She waited for me to finish her sentence.

I hesitated a moment. "The kids look different from my school."

"You mean our dress code? Everyone has to wear a dark blue blazer but you can choose your own. It's not really a uniform."

I started to nod again just to be agreeable but then felt compelled to add, "Maybe I am too different."

"Ah." Her small eyes were sad. "We truly try to recruit children from different backgrounds, but it isn't easy. Harrison *is* quite expensive, and due to financial *limiteetees*, we cannot . . ."

She kept talking, but I had stopped listening after I heard what she said about the school. Now that I'd actually seen it, I knew it had to cost a lot of money. I'd expected a simple concrete building like the one I went to now. How naive I'd been, to think that such a school would let me in for free.

"Kimberly?"

I looked up and she was waving her right hand, trying to get my attention.

She spoke again. "Don't worry. We do have a financial aid program. You are applying after the normal process has closed, but I'm sure we can make an *excession* for you. Sometimes we even offer up to fifty percent of the *twosheen* costs."

I swallowed something in my throat. "Thank you."

I didn't know what the fifty percent that we would have to pay would mean, but I knew we could never afford it. Now that it was impossible,

134

I wished I could stay. This was a chance to get both Ma and me out of the factory, out of that apartment, and I realized I wanted it desperately.

"What are you thinking? Please tell me, Kimberly. I need to know so I can help you."

I felt myself grow hot. "I'm sorry," was all I said.

"We may even be able to go up to seventy-five percent, although I can't make any promises."

"Yes, thank you. I am sorry, you are busy." I stood up so hastily I almost knocked my chair over. I'd wasted her time and gotten us all into an embarrassing situation.

She raised a hand to stop me. "No, wait a moment. Please don't make any decisions in your head until I've had a chance to talk to your mother, okay? I'm sure we can work something—"

"We not have phone." By now, I could feel the tips of my ears burning.

Dr. Weston dropped her hand. "All right, maybe we could schedule an appointment."

"My mother work. And she don't speak English."

There was a moment of silence, very awkward for me, then she said, "I see."

She set her papers aside and escorted me to the door. "Thank you for taking the time to come and see our school."

While we were working on a science experiment in class, I mentioned the test I'd taken at Harrison to Annette, who had already gotten her acceptance letter weeks before. Her father had gone there too.

"Did you do okay?" she asked, worried for me. "That is a really hard test. And they look at all kinds of other things too. Lots of kids get rejected from Harrison."

Her voice had risen and I saw Mr. Bogart, who was standing at the next table, glance over at us. I tried to shrug and looked away.

"So?" she said. "Do you think you passed?"

I wanted to tell her the truth, that I'd been accepted but we couldn't afford to go, but I was too ashamed to say it out loud. I made myself shake my head.

Annette's face fell. "Oh no," she said. "They have to let you in! I want you to come with me!"

"It is okay," I said, although my disappointment grew hotter behind my eyelids until I was afraid it would spill over into tears. It was much too late to apply to another private school. "I will go to public school, like I should before."

"I don't care how you did on that test, you are so smart. You have to talk to someone and get a second chance."

"No, I do not want this."

She thought about it for a moment. "Okay, then I'll stay in public school too."

I blinked. Generous, loyal Annette. Of course, her parents wouldn't allow her to do that, but

136

would I have, could I have, offered to do the same for her? I laid a hand on her shoulder. "You are good friend."

The end of the school year approached.

A craze of autograph books swept through the sixth grade. A few kids had them and started asking their friends to sign and within a few weeks, many children were circulating their auto-graph books around the room. I begged Ma to buy me one and she did, for 59 skirts from the Dime Shop. It had a red fake-leather cover. I learned from watching everyone else that after someone signed a page, I was supposed to fold the edges down or up to make alternating patterns of folded triangles in my book.

Annette wrote in my book: "2 Friends 4-ever!" The other kids wrote things like "Wish I had known you better" and "Too bad we didn't know each other." I wrote "Good luck for the future" in everyone's book except for Annette's and Tyrone's. In Annette's I wrote: "You are my best friend." When Tyrone shyly handed his to me, I saw that on the page before mine someone had written: "You are the King of the Brains." I thought a moment and wrote in Chinese: *You are a very special person and may the gods protect you.* Then I signed my name in English.

"Wow," he said. "What does it say?"

"Good luck," I said.

He stared at the page. "That's a lot of words for 'good luck.'"

"It take long time to say something in Chinese."

In my book, he wrote, "Wish I had known you better."

The sixth-graders had a graduation ceremony, and our class spent weeks practicing parading on and off the auditorium stage.

Ma had been deeply disappointed we couldn't afford Harrison. At first, she'd said we would somehow find a way to pay, and wanted to take on an extra job, although she was already working as hard as she could. I explained what the campus looked like, however, and how much the tuition actually was, and finally, she'd reluctantly given up. Then she hugged me and said, "I am still so proud of you. You have been here less than a year and you already found this opportunity. You just need a little more time."

I was now worried about how she would react to my report card. I would be forced to show it to her this time because she hadn't seen anything yet this whole year, and even though I was now passing everything, I knew it would be far from the perfect grades she'd seen from me back home. I slept badly in the weeks leading up to the graduation ceremony.

Ma bought a pretty brown flowered dress on sale for me. There was lace trim at the neck and sleeves and the hem flared when I turned. It cost a fortune for us, 1,500 skirts, but Ma bought it a size larger so I could wear it for longer. It was loose but it still looked all right, and I had a pair of new brown Chinese slippers to go with it.

On the day of my graduation, I got dressed.

"Ma," I said, "do I look pretty?" I knew it was not what a decent girl did, asking for compliments, but I wanted so much to look nice.

Ma tilted her head to the side. I think that because Ma had been known as something of a beauty herself in Hong Kong, she never commented on how I looked. She'd always taught me that other qualities were more important. "You look fine."

"But am I pretty?"

Ma hugged me. "You are my wonderful, beautiful girl."

All of the kids looked different in their formal clothes. The girls were wearing dresses and some of the boys had ties. Even Luke was wearing a new white shirt, although he had the same gray pants on. Now that I'd seen Harrison and how different things could be, I realized how much more at home I felt here, where many of the other students were poor too. When we went into the auditorium, I searched the faces for Ma's and I found her sitting near the back in the center. Aunt Paula had made a "very unusual, one-time exception" to allow Ma to be here this morning and we'd have to catch up on all the work tonight. I wished with sudden intensity that I could make Ma proud of me as I once had. Back home, I'd always gone up to the stage to receive awards and I'd won Best Student every year. Ma had been so delighted at those ceremonies.

When the sixth grade sang onstage, I looked for Ma and tried to sing extra loudly. Then, after all of the singing and speeches, the awards were given out and my name was not called once, not even for Science or Math. Tyrone went up many times and Annette won a few too. I was so ashamed, I wished Aunt Paula had not let Ma come after all. I wondered what she was thinking. Had it been only a year before that I'd been such a different person?

Mrs. LaGuardia was now saying something about laying foundations, good citizenship and bright futures. She seemed to be finishing up. "Sometimes, here at P.S. 44, we have students who go on to achieve *spectacuur* results despite what may seem to be *overwoman* odds. In particular, I would like to congratulate Tyrone Marshall on getting into Hunter College High School, a public school for gifted children."

Tyrone stood up to a round of applause. Although he sat down again quickly, he looked happy, and a black woman in the audience was cheering so enthusiastically that she knocked her feathered hat askew.

"And Kimberly Chang for being granted a full scholarship to Harrison Prep, an *un-president-ed* honor for a student from our school."

Everyone clapped again but I thought that I couldn't have heard her correctly. I didn't move.

Mrs. LaGuardia was looking at me and continued to talk. "Kimberly came to our school barely speaking English and we are very proud of what she has *ah-cheed* here."

The girl sitting next to me hissed. "Get up, you gotta get up."

I finally stood up for a second and the applause became louder. The blood pounded in my eyes so that I couldn't see anything. As I sat down and my head cleared, I looked around for Annette. She was craning her neck to find me too, and when our eyes met, she clasped her hands together in excitement. Over her shoulder, I saw Mr. Bogart, blinking rapidly with his mouth open. I tried to see Ma's face too but she was too far in the back, with too many heads in between. I hoped that she had seen me too, that she knew the applause had been about me. I couldn't wait to tell her the good news.

Ma was beaming when I found her in the crowd of students and parents after the ceremony.

"What was that about?" she asked.

"Ma, the principal said I won a full scholarship to that private school!"

We hugged each other tight.

141

Ma's eyes glowed. "What an opportunity! This is the beginning of a new direction for us, *ah*-Kim, and it's all due to you."

I looked up to see Mrs. LaGuardia standing in front of us. She said, "You must be Mrs. Chang. It's a real pleasure to meet you at last."

Ma shook her extended hand. "Hello," she said in English. "You very good teacher."

I said in rapid Chinese, "Ma, she's not a teacher, she's the principal!" Then, in English, "Prin-ci-pal."

Ma flushed, then said in English, "Sorry, so sorry. Mis-sus Prin-ci-pal."

Mrs. LaGuardia smiled. "No matter at all. You have a very special child and she has really done her best here."

Even though I knew Ma hadn't understood a word of what she said, Ma realized it was a compliment and said in a nervous rush, "Thank you. You so good. You good teacher."

I couldn't believe Ma had said it again, but Mrs. LaGuardia didn't seem to notice and she said to me, "I'm sorry about announcing the scholarship in front of everyone. I could tell you were surprised. I just got the news yesterday and I thought you must already have heard. Didn't you get a letter?"

As she spoke, I understood what must have happened. There must have been a letter informing me of the scholarship, but it would have gone to the fake address we always used, the one my school had on file. This meant it was likely that Aunt Paula would be the one to receive it, and bring it to us at the factory later. "I think letter will come. Thank you, Mrs. LaGuardia. You help me so much."

She bent down and, as a cloud of perfume enveloped me, gave me a kiss on my cheek. "You're very welcome."

I saw Tyrone leaving arm in arm with the woman in the feathered hat, who must have been his mother. He waved to me as they went outside.

Annette hugged me from behind. "I can't believe you're going to Harrison too! We'll have so much fun!"

As I disentangled myself, she cocked her head and asked, "How come you told me you didn't pass the test?"

"I was not sure," I said. Annette seemed satisfied and turned to her parents, who were standing behind us.

"Hi, Kimberly," Mrs. Avery said. "A very big congratulations to you." She extended her hand to Ma. "It's so nice to meet you at last, Mrs. Chang."

"Hello," Ma said. Ma shook her hand and then Mr. Avery's. He was quite a bit shorter than Mrs. Avery, and seemed to have to crane his neck to allow his head to emerge from the top of the tidy suit he was wearing.

"We're all going out for a celebratory lunch," Mr. Avery said. "Would you both care to join us?"

Ma looked at me in confusion. I translated for her, hoping that just this once, she would say yes.

"No, dank you," Ma said. "We go . . ." Her voice trailed off as she couldn't think of the words for a polite excuse in English.

"Home," I said. "We must do something."

"Oh," Mr. Avery said, "that's a pity. Maybe next time."

"Dank you," Ma said. "You very good."

After the Averys left for their lunch, Ma and I also withdrew from the celebrating crowds at the school and went into the subway station to go to the factory. I was still basking in the excitement of the ceremony. Ma was so happy about Harrison Prep that she barely glanced at my report card on the train.

Once we were at the factory, Ma and I were working as fast as we could to catch up when I saw Aunt Paula standing in front of us. She didn't usually come to our area unless it was time for her to check the pieces before a shipment went out.

"How was the graduation?" she asked.

"Very fine," Ma said. "Thank you for letting me take the morning off."

"Would the two of you come with me?" Her tone was polite but Ma and I exchanged a worried look. I wondered if something had gone wrong because

144

Ma had been absent from the factory that morning.

We trailed behind Aunt Paula and went past Matt, who was just leaving the men's room. Behind Aunt Paula's back, he caught my eye and pretended to scratch himself, in an imitation of her. I stifled a laugh.

When we entered the office, Aunt Paula invited us to sit down. Uncle Bob must have been out.

"I have some mail for Kimberly." She held out a thick manila envelope with the crest of Harrison Prep stamped on it.

I took it. Despite Aunt Paula's casual manner, I felt nervous. Why hadn't she just given it to us at our workstation? Bringing us here meant she wanted to talk or to find out something.

"Are you applying to that school?" she asked.

I nodded. Ma took a breath, probably to tell Aunt Paula the news but Aunt Paula spoke first. "Why didn't you ask me for advice?"

Ma must have changed her mind about what she was going to say. "We meant no disrespect."

"Of course not. It's just that this is a very competitive school and I could have helped you choose a school possibly more suited to Kimberly."

"Do you know Harrison Prep?" I asked.

"Of course. I had to do a lot of research before figuring out where Nelson should go. Harrison Prep is a famous, beautiful school. But it is also very difficult to gain admission, and it is extremely expensive."

"Yes," Ma said. Like me, she didn't say more. I think we were both waiting to see Aunt Paula's true face. We wanted to know what she would say to help or discourage us, before she knew the truth.

Aunt Paula laughed. "Little sister, I am surprised you let Kimberly hold on to her hope when you must suspect how much this school costs! You should throw that application form away! Even Nelson couldn't get accepted there. And it is much too late anyway."

I finally spoke. "It's not an application form. It's a letter of acceptance with a full scholarship. My principal told us today."

Aunt Paula stared. A flush crept up her neck and the dark mole on her lip trembled. "*You're* going to Harrison Prep? The two of you did this behind my back?" Her voice was furious.

I heard Ma gasp as I clutched the envelope to my chest. Aunt Paula's sudden open anger caught both of us by surprise.

"Older sister," Ma said quietly, "what strangeness are you speaking?"

Aunt Paula put her hand to her hair to calm herself. Her fingers were shaking with emotion. "I am just surprised that something so important was done without asking me."

"It happened quickly and we didn't think it would be successful." Ma tried to placate her. "We are grateful to you, for everything you've done."

Aunt Paula had recovered herself. "Of course, I

am glad for this opportunity for Kimberly. And to think, I worried that the two of you would be a burden to me here."

"We can take care of ourselves," I said, meeting her eyes.

Aunt Paula studied me as if she'd never really looked at me before. "I can see that."

Later, when we were back at our finishing station, Ma and I didn't speak openly about what had happened. I knew Ma didn't want to admit Aunt Paula's weaknesses to me. But I had understood what happened anyway. For just a moment, Aunt Paula had flipped her polite face over and we had seen the black face underneath. We would be allowed to work and not cause any trouble for her, but she didn't want us to be any more successful than she was. And I wasn't supposed to do better than Nelson. In other words, Aunt Paula wouldn't mind if we stayed at the factory and that apartment all our lives.

That summer, Annette sent me postcards. She always addressed them to "Miss Kimberly Chang" and she signed off with "Yours Truly, Miss Annette Avery." I'd given her my real address because I didn't want these letters to have to go through Aunt Paula and I figured that even if Annette looked it up on a map, she was too innocent to know what sort of neighborhood I lived in anyway. From camp, she wrote:

I am so bored here! There is no one fun and all of the activities are dumb. The only thing I like is swimming. When it gets hot, the water is cool in the lake. They make us sing stupid songs and play stupid games. I wish I was back in NY with you!

I'd never seen a lake and I'd never been swimming. Like many people in Hong Kong in those days, Ma and I hadn't had the money to do such things. Often, when I was working, I pictured being at that cool lake with Annette. Summer in the factory was one long rush of heat amid the deafening roar of the fans. It was impossible to hear one another over the noise and so the summer became a wordless time for us. The windows remained hermetically sealed, probably to deter any inspectors who might look in, and the huge industrial fans were the only relief we had.

Each fan was tall and black like a sarcophagus, swathed in dust. Thick strands of filth hung off each part of the wire hood, swaying in the wind until they broke off to splatter against my face or worse, the piece of clothing I was working on. The air they blew was a sweltering wind, merely redistributing heat from the steamers and scorching motors of the machines to our own wet bodies and back again, yet we were glad of them because there was nothing else. During our breaks, we were too hot to play, and Matt and I stood with arms outstretched in front of the fans, our hair streaming out behind us, pretending we could fly.

The factory dust became worse than usual because we were bathed in sweat and the fabric fibers clung to us. My bare shoulders and neck were streaked where I'd wiped the dust off with my fingers.

Despite the expense, Ma bought me a few stamps so I could write back to Annette, because Ma thought it was educational for me to write in English. I wrote this:

> *Sorry it is boring there! New York City is relaxing. I enjoy it to rest and read books. Songs and games are greatly stupid. I hope you come back soon. Maybe my mother and me will go trip soon.*

From Florida, Annette wrote:

> *Your so lucky you get to relax in NY! Well, my grandmother's house is pretty neat. Yesterday, we had a barbeque and I got to eat my hot dog while I was sitting in the pool! Where are you going? I hope you have a great time! Don't forget about your best friend when your gone!!!*

She also sent me a postcard with a picture of a castle and the words "The Magic Kingdom" printed on it.

I answered:

I had a hot dog one time and I liked it very greatly. Only I not like the yellow sauce. Ma and me maybe not go trip now because it is too nice in New York City. When I go trip in future, I will buy you a present. What you like? Thank you for a beautiful post-card. I like it very much. Your grandmother belong to your mother's side or your father's side? I hope she has good health.

Every night, when I got home from the factory, I reread Annette's letters. I longed for a story of my own to tell, about a trip to New Jersey perhaps or Atlantic City, where some of the sewing ladies went. If I were rich, I would buy Annette and Ma many presents, from places all over America.

In our apartment, the roaches and mice had returned with a vengeance and we couldn't leave anything unsealed even for a moment, not even the toothpaste, or we would return to find a roach licking it, with its long waving antennae. We took off all the garbage bags from the windows in the kitchen. The sunlight streamed in from the back for the first time. I looked for the woman and baby in the apartment next door but their room was empty. Even the bed was gone. As soon as the weather became warm enough, Ma took out her violin almost every Sunday evening. I would clean up after dinner while she played, sometimes only for a few minutes, because we usually had so much work from the factory to finish at home.

I said to her once, "Ma, you don't have to play for me every week. You have so many other things to do."

"I play for myself too," she'd answered. "Without my violin, I'd forget who I was."

Finally, the heat got so bad that Ma bought us a small fan and we set it in front of our mattresses. After work, we both caught our breath in front of that fan, sitting on the mattresses on the floor, our backs resting against the wall. Slowly, two yellowish human-shaped stains developed against the cracked paint: a small one for me and a larger one for Ma. Those stains are probably still there in that apartment, and I've dreamed about them, about our skin cells, our droplets of oil and sweat, sunk into that porous wall, bits of us that will never escape.

One Sunday afternoon near the end of the summer, Annette appeared at my apartment. Ma and I were buttoning up some jackets we had brought home from the factory. I jumped at a loud noise. It was so unfamiliar, it took me a moment before I recognized it as the doorbell.

"Who can that be?" Ma said.

I ran to the front window as Ma said behind me, "Kimberly, stop! They'll see you!"

I was already peering down and saw Annette's round face framed by her halo of hair, turned up toward us. My knees buckled. I ducked down and hid myself below the window. I hoped she hadn't seen me. I'd caught a glimpse of their car on the street with a short man inside, probably Mr. Avery.

The doorbell rang again, then again. Ma and I stared at each other, not daring to whisper, as if the factory inspectors were at our door. Finally, the ringing stopped and I heard the car drive away.

"I think they're gone," I said.

"Don't look yet," Ma said.

We waited another ten minutes before I dared to check that Annette and her father had left.

A few days later, I got another letter from Annette:

> *You are going to be very disappointed! Because I actually came to your house, just to say hi! But you weren't there. I thought I saw a face in the window but no such luck. Hey, what's your phone number? How come I still don't have it? See you very soon . . . at our new school!!!!*

In preparation for Harrison, Ma bought me some new clothes. I had to get a dark blue blazer to conform to the dress code, but it was hard to find one we could afford. Finally, in a discount store, we bought a navy blue one for $4.99. It was made of scratchy polyester and the sleeves were so long they covered my hands. The shoulders were padded and protruded into the air past my own, but at least it vaguely resembled the ones I thought the other kids had been wearing. We got a white shirt and a dark blue skirt at Woolworth's.

When I had the entire outfit on, I looked in the mirror and I saw a small Chinese girl with short hair, her torso and arms engulfed by a boxy blazer. A cheap shirt peeked out from under the blazer and below that, a stiff skirt jutted out above skinny calves. The skirt had large rhinestones around the waistband because we hadn't been able to find a plain one. I wore my brown Chinese slippers, the only shoes I had that could go with a skirt. The entire outfit was uncomfortable. I felt lost in the contours of someone I didn't recognize.

I was as ready as I ever would be to start Harrison Prep.

Now that I was a student, I could take a private bus to Harrison that stopped close to my old elementary school. I stood there in my ill-fitting clothes, and when the bus pulled up, I didn't recognize it for what it was. It was sleek and gray, with a white board showing the number 8 in the front window.

Inside, the seats were arranged around the perimeter instead of in rows. The bus was half full, with about seven other kids of different ages already on board, all of them white, all in blazers. I slid into the closest seat, next to an older boy who was so tall he stretched his legs out into the middle of the bus.

We made another stop in what looked like Annette's area, and three more white kids got on. Their parents waved as we drove away. Annette was going to school with her mother today, but after this, she would be on my bus too. Although I'd been in the U.S. for almost a year now, I had never seen so many white people in one place before. I didn't want to stare, but their coloring was so interesting. The boy next to me had hair that was the pale yellow-orange of boiled octopus. His skin was as light as Annette's but blotched. A girl who had gotten on the bus at Annette's stop was sitting diagonally across from me. She had dark brown hair and eyes, very much like a Chinese person, only everything was lighter and her hair was flipped back from both sides of her face. Some of the other kids made a lot of noise welcoming one another back from the summer and chatting about their new classes.

We pulled into a large parking lot already filled with other buses like ours, all showing different numbers in the front window. There must have been at least nine buses there, and more kept coming in. Most were empty but a few had just opened their doors and kids were getting out.

I followed the other kids past the parking lot for normal cars. I didn't see Annette or her mother. A father hurried by me, asking his child, "Are you sure you know where your classes are?" I went by a small group of older students laughing together outside the main building. Everyone I saw was white. I had studied the Harrison map carefully and I found Milton Hall, which was covered in vines, with no problems. My homeroom and most of my classes were there. As I walked up the steps, I felt so nervous, I could take only shallow breaths. Two girls who looked like they could be my age went into the building before me.

Just inside the door to my classroom stood a small huddle of boys and girls who seemed to be inspecting everyone who entered. I found out later they'd all gone to Harrison Elementary School together. A few of the girls had bracelets with sparkly shapes hanging from them and several of them were already wearing eye shadow and lip gloss.

When I went past them, one boy with hair as red as sugared ginger whistled and said distinctly, "*Nice* skirt." There was a burst of giggling from the group.

I pretended I hadn't heard and hurriedly sat down in a seat against the wall, but I wanted to keep walking, through the wall and into the distance. I resolved to remove the rhinestones from my skirt that night and I quietly picked at them with my fingernails as I watched the rest of the kids come in.

Although at first glance all of the blazers had looked the same to me, I could now tell that they were quite different from one another. Some of the girls had blazers that were shorter and more fitted than those of the boys. I was glad to see that many of their blazers had padded shoulders too, like mine did, although my blazer was much longer and wider than theirs. I had received a written description of the dress code at home (blazer required, no denim, no short skirts, no sweatshirts). Now I saw that quite a range of clothing was allowed within those rules. One girl, a part of the group of kids who had laughed at me, had on a tan skirt that ended a bit above her knee. Below that, she wore what looked like woolen tubes or footless, slouchy socks over a pair of short boots. A tall boy with a lion's mane of sandy hair was playing around, arm wrestling with the ginger-haired one, and when the tawny boy's blazer fell open, I saw that the T-shirt he had on underneath was spattered with paint.

I spotted the girl with the long brown hair from my bus sitting near the back. Like many of the other girls, she was wearing a headband to keep her fluffy hair in place. At that point, the home-room teacher came in. She would also be our math teacher. She was blond and thin, moving with the quickness of a bird. She took attendance and gave us our schedules, then explained a lot of practical things like where our lockers were. I was thrilled at the idea of having a clean place where I could keep my own belongings.

I'd known Annette wouldn't be in my homeroom but I still missed her. I followed the other kids when we traveled together from room to room, trying to stay away from that group of kids and especially the mean ginger-haired boy. Our Social Studies teacher was Mr. Scoggins, a heavyset man in a suit and tie. He told us in his deep voice that we would need to keep up with the news in his class. We would also be simulating buying stocks on the stock market, following our stocks' ups and downs in the coming weeks to see if we earned or lost money. I bit my lip, wondering where I would get access to a newspaper for the stock prices.

In our classes, I didn't volunteer to give any answers yet. By now, I could understand most of what the teachers said, although the effort of listening so hard in English was tiring. I was exhausted by the time I met Annette at the cafeteria at lunchtime.

Annette hugged me and the metal of her braces gleamed. "I'm so glad to see you!" she said. "Everyone here is so weird."

She hadn't gotten much browner over the summer although the density of her freckles seemed to have increased, making her look darker if you squinted from a distance. She'd become taller and a bit thinner but the buttons on the shirt around her stomach still strained against the fabric. Her hair had grown as well, and instead of balling out around her head, it now jutted out like a pyramid behind her neck. To my surprise, she took a tray and got into line with me for the hot food.

"Do you have free lunch too?" I asked.

She giggled. "Silly. Everyone eats at the cafeteria here, it's a part of the tuition."

There was an extensive salad bar with all kinds of items I'd never had before, like olives and Swiss cheese. The main dish that day was sweet-and-sour pork over steamed rice, but it tasted as foreign as everything else. The rice was hard and tasteless, and the pork had only been painted red on the outside instead of actually being grilled in *cha-siu* sauce. But I felt happy again, sitting there next to Annette.

After lunch, we had Life Science, which I enjoyed because we were being introduced to subjects like scientific notation and cell structure, which I hadn't studied in Hong Kong. At the end of the class, the teacher wrote a challenge question on the board:

> The E. coli genome is 4.8 million base pairs compared to a human genome of 6 billion base pairs. How many times larger is the human genome than that of E. coli?

"At home, think about how you would approach this," the teacher said. "Anyone already have an idea?"

No one stirred.

Slowly, I raised my hand and at the teacher's nod, said, "It is 1.25×10^3, sir." I almost bit my tongue for allowing the "sir" to slip out again.

Without looking at his attendance list, he smiled and said, "Ah, you must be Kimberly Chang."

Scanning the faces I passed throughout the day, I saw that I wasn't the only minority in the school, but I was one of only a handful. Everyone else in my homeroom was white but I had seen an Indian girl and an older black boy in the hallways.

The last subject of the day was gym, and I was glad I'd remembered to bring my sneakers from home. At my elementary school, gym had been a time for the kids to fool around, to hide behind other people when the ball came your way. At Harrison Prep, gym was a serious business. We would have it several times a week, we were told, and I could already see it was going to pose a problem for me. Ma had taught me never to do anything that could be considered either unladylike or dangerous: a lesson passed down from her own formal upbringing. "Unladylike" meant anything that allowed your knees to be parted from each other or that could cause a skirt to flip up. Whether you were even wearing one or not was irrelevant, it was the idea that counted.

"Dangerous" covered most other categories of motion. I had often been in trouble with Ma because of my carelessness with the skirt issue and my penchant for running too fast. Standing in that gym, I felt guilty toward Ma before we even began to move.

But it was after we lined up to be given our gym uniforms (green T-shirts and the wide shorts I had seen earlier) and crowded into the locker room that I knew I was really in trouble.

SEVEN

All of the other girls began stripping down. We'd never had to change for gym at my old school. We'd only had to switch to sneakers if we weren't wearing them already. I clutched my new clothes as I saw everyone else was wearing store-bought panties. Some even had on cotton bras or sleeveless camisoles. All of their underwear was colorful and expensive.

Some of the girls were completely flat-chested and I envied them. I had begun to develop small breasts that summer and I did everything I could to hide them. It was inevitable that a solution would have to be found for them, and I would have to be the one to find it. Everything under my clothes had been made by Ma and thus was badly sewn: a pair of thick cotton shorts unevenly trimmed in red for good luck, a stained and pilling long-sleeved undershirt. All the girls were checking one another out from under lowered eyelids. Then I spotted the toilet stalls against the wall. I silently thanked the gods and ducked into one to change.

This first gym class was to be our individual evaluation. We were timed in our running, measured in our jumping, counted for our push-ups, and then the gym teacher put a racket in our hands, fired balls at us and counted the number we hit. Working in the factory had made me strong. I was far from the best but I was also not the worst. It was such a relief that I stopped feeling guilty for acting unladylike.

I was beginning to see the importance Americans put on a kind of general athleticism, which was new to me. Back home, a student was praised if she did well in her classes at school, but for these kids, good grades were not enough. They were also expected to play sports and an instrument, and have straight teeth as well. I too would be expected to become attractive and well-rounded.

By the end of the day, I'd learned some of the kids' names: Greg was the mean one, Curt the one with hair like a lion's, Sheryl was the girl in the leg warmers (I'd heard the term when another girl admired them) and Tammy was the brown-haired girl on my bus.

After gym, school was over for the other kids but I was scheduled to work in the library three days a week and to get special tutoring in English on the fourth—though I had yet to figure out how I was going to fit all of this in with helping Ma at the factory too. The library work was a requirement of the scholarship I'd been given.

I knew that the library I would be working in, the one in Milton Hall, wasn't the main research library but rather a minor one mainly used for studying. I expected a modern sterile space, similar to the public library in Brooklyn. I opened the door to the library and caught my breath. It was small, intimate and lovely. Long streams of sunlight drifted through the high stained-glass windows. A few students were curled up in large leather armchairs, reading.

A man in a striped maroon silk tunic was watering a gardenia on one of the tables. Aside from the gym teacher, he was the only man I'd seen the whole day who wasn't wearing a suit and tie. He looked up and saw me, then approached. I saw his tunic had an embroidered stand-up collar and he was wearing white cotton trousers.

His hair would have been as dark as mine, only his was shot through with silver. "Are you the new scholarship student? I'm Mr. Jamali." He spoke English with a slight lilt.

We shook hands and then I couldn't help asking, "Where are you from?"

"Pakistan," he said. He saw me looking at the intricate thread work on his tunic.

"Ah. You noticed. The headmaster has tried to

162

get me in a suit for many years but I have resisted. I am also the theater director and that justifies a bit of flair, don't you think?"

Mr. Jamali showed me the mechanics of my work, which were very simple. He told me that since this library had a limited selection of books, most students came just to read or study. I understood this meant I would have some free time when working there, maybe even enough to do my own homework. There was even a typewriter in the back office I was allowed to use. I wanted to clap my hands for joy.

"Mr. Jamali, can I change the hours I have? I like to be here more early in the day."

"Why?"

"Because . . ." My voice trailed off. "My mother work and I must help her after school."

"I see." He looked at me with his intelligent eyes. "Well, in that case, we shall see what we can do."

At the factory, Matt noticed my new clothes right away. "Well, if it isn't the landlady's daughter," he said.

I must have looked hurt, because he immediately added, "I didn't mean it like that. I meant, you look pretty."

I knew he was only being kind, and also that I'd never forget it: the time Matt said I was pretty.

But it made me realize that coming to the factory

in my school clothes could cause trouble for me with the other factory kids or even with Aunt Paula, who clearly didn't need to be reminded of my new private school. From now on, I would make sure I changed into my work clothes as soon as I arrived and never mention my new school.

"How did it go today?" Ma asked. Seeing her warm, familiar brown eyes, I relaxed for the first time in hours, and I realized how much stress I'd been under the whole day, how foreign the entire world of Harrison was.

I stood close to Ma and, without answering, leaned my forehead against her shoulder. I wanted so much to be her little girl again. Her shirt was made of polyester and was damp with sweat.

"You crazy girl," she said affectionately. She ruffled my hair.

I lifted my head. "Ma, I think I need some new underwear."

"Why? What's wrong with what you have?"

"We all change together for gym and the other girls will be able to see it. They're going to laugh at me."

"No decent girl would look at someone else's underwear. Did they make fun of you today?" In Ma's world, underwear was something that was invisible. With money so scarce, she believed it should be spent on things people could see, like my uniform.

"No, but—"

Her tone was indulgent. "*Ah*-Kim, you should not be so sensitive. I'm sure all of the nice girls are changing where they cannot be seen. The whole world is not looking at you." She gave me a quick squeeze and turned back to her work.

I stared at Ma's back, the bony ridges of her spine visible through her thin shirt, and I was suddenly so angry that I wanted to push her into the pile of dresses stacked in front of her on the counter. But then, as I breathed in the factory air, perpetually damp and metallic from the steamers, I felt guilt slice into my anger. Ma hadn't bought a single thing for herself in the whole time we'd been in America, not even a new coat, which she desperately needed.

As soon as I had a break, I tried to remove the rhinestones from the skirt, but it was impossible. The colored plastic had been glued to the waistband, and taking it off would mean leaving unsightly stains on the cloth. I searched through the cart filled with rejected fabric remnants and found a strip of dark cloth that could double as a sash. It wasn't exactly elegant but the stones were at least covered. There were also several skirts that hadn't passed Aunt Paula's examination and I wished I were big enough to wear adult sizes.

As usual, Ma and I ate the rice she'd brought from home. For Chinese people, rice is the actual food and everything else—meat, vegetables—is just an accessory to it. We had so little money during these days, though, that Ma put hardly any meat in with the rice anymore.

When we got home, at around nine-thirty that evening, I was finally done with my day. It was the first chance I had to think about everything that had happened. I had spent the entire school day as the only Chinese in a crowd of white people. The ginger-haired boy, Greg, both fascinated and frightened me. It wasn't only that he'd made fun of me. He looked so alien, with his incredible hair, pale green eyes and veins under his skin. And the girls in my class, with their blue eyelids and sunken eyes, their thick upswept lashes. I stared in the paint-flecked bathroom mirror at my face. I didn't look anything at all like those girls. If they were pretty, then what was I?

The next day, I went to meet my English tutor, Kerry, in an empty classroom. When I stepped inside the room, she got up and shook my hand. She was quite short and I could see the gap in between her two front teeth when she smiled. She told me she was a senior.

I sat down and waited for her to tell me what to do, expecting her to pull out a grammar book. She waited as well.

Then she said, "What should we do, Kimberly?"

I stared at her. She was the tutor. In Hong Kong, I'd never heard of any teacher or mentor allowing the students to influence the material.

She leaned back. "What would help you the most?"

I needed help in everything. I thought for a moment. "To speak."

"Good. How about if we talk and I'll correct everything you say that's wrong?"

"Yes! Thank you!" I was so glad to have someone actually help me to improve my English. I wanted to hug her.

In our ensuing conversation, I found out that she was a scholarship student too.

Reacting to my surprise, she said, "Not all the scholarship students are minorities, you know. This place is really expensive."

"How you like Harrison?"

"How DO you like Harrison," she said, correcting me. "It takes some getting used to, especially at first, but it helps a lot if you get involved in some activities. You know, like tennis or lacrosse. Or the school newspaper."

"Yes, that good idea," I said, but I knew I wouldn't do anything extra after school. Ma couldn't get the shipments out on time without my help.

Greg and his friends were feared. He had his targets, and his taunts were cruel and calculated: Elizabeth, so shy she rarely spoke, the whiteness of her skin punctured by freckles ("Miss Chicken Pox"); Ginny with her faint mustache ("Forgot our razor today?"); Duncan and his deep nasal breathing ("Duncan Vader"). He'd also smelled the mothballs in my clothing, which Ma and I used to keep the roaches away. All Greg had to do was pinch his nose when I walked by and a wake of laughter from his friends would follow me down the hall.

My classes were much harder than those at my elementary school. Despite the relief of not having Mr. Bogart as a teacher anymore, I struggled to keep up. One of the biggest hurdles was the daily current-events quiz in Social Studies, which I failed time and time again. Mr. Scoggins did not understand why we couldn't simply watch the six-o'clock news each evening, or take a peek at our parents' *New York Times*.

"If you don't understand something, ask your parents about it," he said. "Discussing the news is one of the most important things we can do with each other."

I imagined Ma and me having long discussions over a polished dining room table like the one at Annette's house, Ma explaining the intricacies of Watergate. I did try to ask Ma about wildlife conservation when we had to read an article on it for class.

"Why would anyone want to save animals like tigers?" she'd asked, baffled. She looked sad. "A baby in our old village in China was taken by one."

I saw her looking through my books sometimes, attempting to sound out a word here or there, but she kept trying to read from right to left. She had a thin book she'd bought in Chinatown to learn English and I tried to teach her on Sundays, but Ma had always been bad at languages. And the two languages were so different, it was as if I were asking her to change her eye color.

At the factory, I kept the radio on while we were working, and tried to grasp the main events, but the boiler was right next to our workstation and made a regular hissing sound, drowning out many of the words. There was so much vocabulary I didn't know. Even when I could understand the sentences, I usually didn't have enough background to understand most of the stories.

I managed in Life Science and Math because those subjects came naturally to me, but in my other classes it took me three times longer to read the textbooks in English than if they'd been in Chinese. I couldn't skim at all. If my concentration sagged for even a moment, the sentence became incomprehensible and I had to reread the whole thing. Every few words, I had to look one up in the dictionary. Often, I could barely understand the questions, let alone the answers I was supposed to be finding.

Trace the theme of violence in the story from inception to its inevitable climax; how is violence unleashed in each of the main characters?

I looked up to see Ma getting ready for bed. Her fragile frame was weighed down by layers of clothing, bound together by a furry vest made out of the stuffed animal fabric we had found. She had pulled on her gloves but she still rubbed her hands together to warm them. That past summer, I had read a passage in a children's book in which the father sat down with his daughter to teach her how to write a check. I thought about that scene often.

"Can I do anything to help you?" Ma asked.

"No, Ma."

She sighed. "You have to work so hard. Don't stay up too late, little one."

I wanted to go to bed. I felt the back of my neck growing heavier, weighing down my head, my eyes. The apartment was dark and empty. A few mice scurried in the kitchen.

I rubbed my temples and studied the question again.

A few weeks later, I had just finished dressing in the toilet stall when I heard a noise from above. There was a large skylight in the ceiling and I saw shadows moving in it.

One of the girls shrieked, "Boys!"

There was the sound of laughter and footsteps above our heads, and then the shadows disappeared.

Instead of being upset, many of the girls seemed pleased by this event and there was a great deal of whispering. The next day, Greg yelled down the hall as I passed by, "Are those *boxing* shorts comfortable?"

The boys and girls around him exploded with laughter. I kept on walking as I burned with embarrassment. Something had to be done.

"The other kids have started teasing me about my underwear," I said to Ma at the factory.

She flinched and I was glad, glad to punish her by having been right. This was Ma's fault.

"How did they see you?" she asked, not meeting my stare.

My pain from all the teasing cracked open like a rice pot from the heat. "I told you, everyone changes together and everyone looks at each other! This isn't China, Ma!"

She was silent. Then she said, "We can go shopping on Sunday."

I had to endure the rest of the week before our shopping trip. When we had gym, Sheryl started peeking into the stall where I dressed. I heard her and the other girls giggling outside, and their laughter had become more merciless, as if the fact that I was still wearing the underwear was my silent consent to their teasing.

On Friday of that week, in desperation, I wore my one swimsuit instead of my homemade underwear under my clothes. A neighbor back home had given it to me as a going-away present. It had become too small and the straps cut into my shoulders. The bright yellow material was faintly visible through the white of my shirt but its tightness was reassuring to me. At least this was new, store-bought; at least this was taut and trim like the others' underwear.

In gym class, Greg made a point of saying to everyone, "Hmm, are we going swimming today?"

I realized I had only made things worse.

We bought a package of panties for me at Woolworth's, but the store didn't have any bras that were small enough, so we had to go to the Macy's across the street. Aunt Paula talked about shopping there and we knew we couldn't really afford it, but there was nowhere else we knew to go.

Under the sparkling lights, saleswomen sprayed passersby with perfume but ignored Ma and me. We were too poorly dressed, too Chinese. The counters were crammed with things we didn't dare look at: leather handbags, fake diamonds, lipsticks. Girls were perched on stools having their makeup done by women in lab coats. The entire store smelled ripe and exotic.

In the lingerie department, multicolored nightgowns, corsets, slips, bras were displayed like candy. Ma picked up a price tag, looked at it and shook her head.

It was clear I could never fit into any of those huge bras on display. They were for women with real breasts, not the little bumps I was growing.

"Ask someone for help," Ma said.

I wanted desperately for her to be able to ask someone for me, to take charge as I was sure Annette's mother would have. But I picked up a bra, hanging voluptuous and full even though no one was wearing it, and brought it to one of the salesladies. Ma stayed behind me.

My entire body felt flushed even before I spoke. "Do you have this? For me?"

To my horror, the black lady burst out laughing. When she saw my face, she tried to stifle her giggles. "I'm sorry, honey, it's just that you so little and this so big." Her voice boomed.

"Come on," she said. "What you need is a training bra. What size are you?"

"I don't know. Seventy?" I made a wild guess based upon Ma's bras, which had come from Hong Kong and were based on the European sizing system.

The woman started laughing again. "You just too much. Someday, I promise, you will grow up to be a real woman. No need to rush things, baby. Now, let me measure you."

I pulled up my sweater as she took out a tape measure. I was embarrassed by my homemade undershirt, but at least this one didn't have any holes in it. If the woman noticed, she didn't say anything. I stared at the ground as she wrapped the tape measure around my chest.

"Thirty triple A," she announced. The whole store could have heard her. She took a cardboard box out of a display and gave it to me. "You wanna try it on?"

"No, thank you."

I grabbed the box, Ma and I paid fast, and we left.

When I tried the bra on at home, I saw it was only a piece of flat cotton, but when I put it on, it looked like what some of the other girls had been wearing.

But the new underwear came too late. The teasing had already begun and borne by its own momentum like a speeding train, it continued.

The complexities of these kids were beyond me, and I thought about telling Annette. She and I talked every day on the bus and at lunch, but she babbled about her classes and the kids who shared them with her, telling me often that none of them were as nice or smart as I was. Most of our talks consisted of my reassuring her that one boy or another didn't hate her. She didn't notice that I rarely said anything about myself, but I didn't blame her for this. The truth was, I enjoyed not talking about myself. It was such a relief to be in her world and, by my silence, pretend I shared it. I didn't want her to know what a hard time I was having.

I brought it up at my tutoring session with Kerry and she'd looked thoughtful.

"That is really not okay," she said. "You should tell the teachers."

I worried that if I complained, the school would see me as a problem and regret letting me come. And in Hong Kong at least, the teachers would ask the parents of the kids involved to talk to each other, and how could Ma possibly stand up against Greg's parents?

I finally decided to ask Matt at the factory.

"I need your help," I said.

"You know I'm the boss," Matt said.

"There are kids at school who pick on me." I was ashamed to have to admit this. "I want them to stop."

His golden eyes were kind. "That's not right. Some idiots tried that on me and Park too." Now, his grin faded.

"What did you do?"

"I fought the leader. But that's not a good solution for a girl."

"I was in a fight once, with the biggest boy in my class."

"You? Miss Skinny Arms?"

"Okay, it wasn't much of a fight. It turned out he actually liked me."

"Maybe that's what's happening now."

"Oh no. Absolutely not." Then I smiled. I was sure Greg did not have a crush on me, but Matt had still given me an idea.

• • •

And so I waited until the next gym class. Up to the last moment, I wasn't sure if I would be brave enough to see my plan through. My heart was pounding so hard I could barely breathe. I paused in the doorway of the huge indoor hall, then walked up to where he was standing in the midst of all his friends. "Greg."

Hardly any of these kids had ever heard me speak at all, and certainly not directly to them. Everyone quieted down.

Greg looked at me.

Despite my trembling legs, I smiled as kindly as I could. "I'm very sorry."

He looked confused and also the tiniest bit ashamed. He probably knew he should have been the one apologizing. "For what?"

"You keep try to get my attention but I just not like you in that way." Then I reached up to give him what I hoped would look like a patronizing kiss on the cheek. I missed in my nervousness, though, and kissed him on the corner of his mouth instead, which must have made my performance more convincing to all of the spectators. Despite his bravado, Greg was also only twelve years old at the time, and he was so shocked by my kiss that he started to sputter violently, as if he'd been stung by a hive of bees, and all of the skin that was visible in between his freckles flushed a dark red.

I was still unaccustomed to the vivid colors that

white people could turn and he scared me so much that I sprang backward, but by this time the entire hall had exploded in laughter.

"Greg's got a crush on Kimberly, Greg's got a crush on Kimberly," the boys chanted.

"Oh, come on," he finally got out, but he was touching his lower lip with his finger—I think out of surprise—and it only made the teasing worse.

"Still feeling the kiss?" Curt asked with a wicked smile.

I don't know how many of the kids actually believed me and how many simply took the opportunity to get back at Greg, who'd been hurtful to almost everyone at one point or another, but this turned the tide. He started avoiding me, and the teasing stopped soon after that.

As much as I tried to avoid her, I crossed paths with Aunt Paula one day as I entered the factory. I was still in my Harrison clothes and she looked me over with speculation. I greeted her, then hurried into the bathroom to change.

Later, she came over to our workstation.

"Big sister," Ma said, worried. It wasn't time for the usual quality inspection yet. "Is there something wrong?"

"Of course not," Aunt Paula said. "I was just thinking that it has been so long since you've eaten rice at our house." Rice meant dinner. "Why don't I have Uncle Bob pick you up on Sunday?"

Ma tried to hide her surprise at this generosity. Since we moved into our own place more than a year before, Aunt Paula had invited us to her house only once. "You give us so much face."

"No, no. And let Kimberly wear something nice, maybe her school outfit."

Now I was surprised as well. After Aunt Paula left, I turned to Ma. "I thought she was so angry that I was going to Harrison Prep."

Ma thought for a moment. "Aunt Paula isn't one to fight against things she cannot change. She's too practical for that."

"So she isn't upset anymore?"

"I didn't say that. You must be very small-hearted when we are at their house." Ma was telling me I should be careful. "You must be humble."

"If Aunt Paula is still calculating-self, why did she invite us over?" Calculating-self means jealous.

Ma sighed. "*Ah*-Kim, you are not supposed to ask such direct questions. That does not befit a well-behaved Chinese girl."

"I just want to understand so I know how to act there."

Ma hesitated, then decided to answer. "If Aunt Paula cannot alter something, then she will see how it can best benefit her and her family."

I finally had it. "Nelson. She wants me to set a good example for him."

Ma nodded. "Be nice to him."

• • •

Aunt Paula's house was deliciously warm. I found myself lingering by the radiator in the living room.

Nelson noticed me there and sauntered over. He was wearing his school uniform too, a dark green blazer and tan pants—and then I knew. We were both in our school clothes because Aunt Paula wanted to show off the fact that Nelson was in private school too. She'd made me wear my outfit so that he could wear his.

Nelson spoke softly so the adults wouldn't hear. "When you see our home, your eyes glow red, don't they?"

Nelson could never out-insult me, and certainly not in Chinese. I patted his arm. "What a pity your mind is like a cowhide lantern. No matter how often you try to light it, it will never be bright."

Aunt Paula's voice from the kitchen interrupted us. "Time to eat rice!"

We were all crowded around their table: Uncle Bob, Godfrey, Nelson, Aunt Paula, Ma and me. The table was loaded with delicacies like stir-fried shrimp with lichee nuts, steamed peppers stuffed with meat, and a whole sea bass poached with ginger and scallions.

"You're serving us a golden dragon on a platter," Ma said. My aunt had gone to elaborate lengths.

She had never made such an effort for us before, and I could see that our status in her mind had been raised. It wasn't just that she was impressed by my achievements, though. I understood her well enough to know it couldn't be that simple. Perhaps she realized I could become more of a threat to her now, and that she ought to treat Ma and me a bit better, just in case.

Over dinner, Aunt Paula wanted to know all of my standardized test scores and how exactly I had managed to get into Harrison Prep. I gave her a general impression of what had happened, leaving out most of the details.

"And what are your grades like, now that you're at such an exclusive school?" she asked.

I stared at my bowl of rice. "The classes aren't so easy."

"Really? For such a smart girl?"

"I got a hundred on my last English test," Nelson interjected. "What did you get?"

I had just put a lichee nut in my mouth, and I bit down so hard on my chopsticks I could feel my teeth imprint on the wood. "Nelson, we don't even go to the same school."

"I know. So what did you get?" he said.

I was ashamed but I had to be honest. "A sixty-seven."

Nelson beamed. Uncle Bob paused in the middle of feeding Godfrey a spoonful of rice.

"Aaah." Aunt Paula breathed out. There was relief and satisfaction in her sigh. Obviously, her wish for me to be unsuccessful was greater than her desire to use me to inspire Nelson.

Ma's forehead was furrowed. She had never heard of me receiving such a score before. "You didn't tell me that, *ah*-Kim."

"It's all right, Ma," I said. "I'm working as hard as I can."

"You must be careful with your scholarship, Kimberly," Aunt Paula said, though I knew she would be glad if I actually lost the money. "You wouldn't want to be disqualified."

"I know," I said. This was a secret worry of mine and I hadn't wanted to share it with Ma. Of course Nelson and Aunt Paula had exposed me. I looked Aunt Paula in the eye. "I'm at the factory until so late, I don't have much time to study."

Ma interrupted us. "You can release your heart, older sister." This meant that Aunt Paula didn't need to worry. "*Ah*-Kim always tries her best in everything. Do take another piece of stuffed pepper." She speared a piece with her chopsticks and put it in Aunt Paula's bowl, while staring at me to be quiet.

I obeyed and Ma changed the subject.

Annette was having a hard time fitting in at Harrison too, although not in the same way I was. She came from an affluent family like most of the other kids, but she was too funny-looking and out-spoken to fit in easily. Every morning on the bus I saved the seat next to me, and as soon as she boarded, we would spend the rest of the ride talking about our classes and the boys Annette thought were cute. I didn't care for any boys. I was too busy struggling to keep up in my classes, and the boys in my class only seemed to be interested in playing around and teasing the girls.

The brown-haired girl, Tammy, glanced over at us sometimes on the bus, and in class she sat next to me once in a while.

"I tried to call you for the homework yesterday," she whispered to me once in Math. "But I couldn't find your number in the school directory."

"Our phone number changed," I said. These were the same lies that I had used with Annette until she stopped asking.

"What's your new number? I'll write it down."

"Now we have a problem with the line. They are working on the road outside."

"Oh." Tammy looked at me strangely. After that, she sat more often with Sheryl, Greg and their group of friends.

I paid attention to everything my English tutor Kerry taught me, and she told me that she'd never seen anyone improve so fast. I knew there was still a long way for me to go, though, and I studied English in all of my spare time.

By the second semester of seventh grade, I had more trouble understanding my fellow students than I did my teachers. The combination of the kids' use of slang and my lack of cultural context made their discussions bewildering. One day, I thought I'd found an opportunity to learn something about religion when I heard Curt, sitting at the end of the cafeteria table, talking about the afterlife.

I wasn't really listening at the beginning because Annette had been chattering to me but I caught a few of Curt's words like, ". . . Pearly Gates . . . nun meets Saint Peter . . . he says . . . Sister, life you led . . . go back to earth."

I paid more attention then because I was interested in their faith. I hadn't expected Curt to be so thoughtful.

Curt continued speaking. " 'I'd like to be Sara Pipeline in another life,' the nun said. She pulled out a newspaper article and gave it to Saint Peter.

"He read it, then said, 'No, dear, it was the Sahara Pipeline that got laid by fourteen hundred men in six months.' "

From the way the other boys laughed especially loudly, as if showing off their comprehension, I saw that what I'd thought was a spiritual discussion had actually been a dirty joke. I had no idea what in the world the Sahara Pipeline had to do with a nun, or how a pipeline could be dirty in a sexual sense. Annette had kept on talking the entire time so I couldn't ask her about it without exposing the fact that I'd been distracted away from her.

Despite all of this, however, I was thrilled to go to Harrison Prep every day. When I left our graffiti-covered area in Brooklyn and arrived at school, with its green lawns and birds circling overhead, I felt like I had gone to paradise.

It was also a relief not to have "fun" assignments like dioramas and posters anymore. Instead, my assignments were tests and papers, which were easier and didn't require any extra materials. I sometimes still missed the teachers' sentences in class, but it mattered less because much schoolwork was based on reading I'd done at home, so I already had some background knowledge. When I made mistakes in my writing, the teachers were kind.

My teachers graded my English skills only by my improvement and not by how I compared with my classmates, who were all native speakers. Some teachers actually corrected the mistakes in my writing, which helped me enormously.

Mr. Jamali was rarely in the library itself when I was working, although I always knew I could find him in his office upstairs or at the theater if I needed him. Sometimes, though, he would suddenly appear behind my shoulder. When he found me studying books like *How to Improve Your Vocabulary in 90 Days*, Mr. Jamali started giving me old books and magazines the library threw away. They were a random assortment: *Philosophy Through the Ages*, *Moll Flanders*, *The Wonders of Your Own Window Garden*. I read them all and kept them in a pile by our nonworking radiator in the apartment.

By the end of the year, I had managed to do decently in most of my classes except for Social Studies, and Mr. Scoggins allowed me to write an extra paper to make up for the current events quizzes I'd failed. I hadn't lost my scholarship and slowly, my talent for school was beginning to reassert itself. However, Ma and I were careful not to tell Aunt Paula.

When eighth grade began, the school told me I didn't need an English tutor anymore. I would miss having someone like Kerry to advise me, but I took it for what it was: a compliment. My English had improved. In other ways, though, I still lived in a different world. Most of the kids in my homeroom were the same as from the previous year, but I didn't really know them. As they participated in whole new activities and developed social lives after school, I could only observe. They were in plays, did lacrosse, basketball, tennis; there were football games and a whole group solely devoted to cheering. I overheard them enough to know that they also started going out places in groups at night. But what struck me most was how relaxed and happy the other kids all seemed together. I often saw Tammy laughing along with her friends, although she continued to be nice to me as well. Curt and Sheryl, the two coolest kids in the grade, flirted with each other like crazy, for the rest of us to see.

The other girls (with the exception of Annette, who thought Sheryl was shallow) regarded Sheryl with admiration and envy. When she pushed the limits of the dress code and came in with her skirt rolled up to mid-thigh, many of the other girls did the same within a week, flashing their pale legs. And as for Curt, he just seemed to glow with promise. It wasn't that he was so handsome, but the way he wore the knowledge that he was someone special.

In a way, I gave myself the excuse of not even trying to get close to the others because I knew I couldn't be a part of their lives. I still had my responsibilities at the factory, but even without that, Ma wouldn't have allowed me to go out anyway. That wasn't what nice Chinese girls from her background did.

At the beginning of one lunch period, I happened to be walking down the hallway a bit behind Greg and a group of his friends, including Tammy.

"You going to *Rocky Horror* tonight?" Greg asked Tammy.

"Sure," she said. "You guys could meet at my place beforehand, if you want." To my surprise, she turned and smiled at me over her shoulder. "Do you want to come too, Kimberly?"

"Oh, I don't know," I said, stalling for time. I knew I couldn't go, but I wanted to pretend it was a possibility. "What time you are meeting?"

She glanced at Greg, who looked as shocked by

her inclusion of me as I felt. "Around eleven, I guess?"

I blinked. Didn't we have school at eleven o'clock in the morning? Luckily, I didn't say anything to reveal my ignorance, because then Tammy continued, "It'll take us less than half an hour to get to the city, so we'll have plenty of time to make it to the Village by midnight."

"No, let's meet earlier. I can get some *bears*," Greg said.

While they discussed the logistics of their evening, my mind whirled. A show that started at midnight. And some bears? Then I realized he had to mean the alcoholic drink, beer.

When I finally looked up, Tammy was saying something to me again. "So, can you make it?"

"It is not a problem for your parents?" I blurted out the question in my thoughts. "Beer?"

She shrugged, looking a bit sheepish. "My parents are divorced. I live with my dad. He's out a lot, and almost anything goes, anyway."

"Oh." I hesitated. "I am busy. Maybe another time, okay?"

She gave me her warm smile. "Next time, then."

I knew there would be no next time, but felt pleased by her invitation. It allowed me to imagine that I could have been one of the other kids, for a moment.

• • •

We had a big Physical Science test in two weeks, covering topics like mass, force and acceleration, and everyone else seemed scared. I was actually relieved to have a subject that involved so much math, but I saw some of the other kids huddled around the lockers after school one day, trying to do their homework and complaining that they didn't understand a thing.

"I flunked the last test," I heard Sheryl saying to her friends. "I'm going to get grounded if it happens again."

"This one's going to be even harder," Curt said. "Everyone will fail and then they'll have to throw away the results."

At that moment, Sheryl caught sight of me. Her tone was dry. "Not everyone."

I ducked my head and kept on walking, but I could feel them watching me.

On the day of the test, our desks were arranged in rows. This time, I was sitting behind Tammy, and Curt was in the next row, directly across from me. Our teacher, Mrs. Reynolds, was walking around the room, passing out the tests.

Tammy turned around and spoke to me. "Do you have an extra pencil? My point just broke."

I nodded and gestured at the one I'd placed on my desk.

As she reached out to take it, a small piece of folded yellow paper fluttered from her sleeve to the floor. I automatically bent down and picked it up, but by the time I straightened up, Tammy had already turned back around in her seat. Could this be a note for me? I didn't pass notes in class but I'd seen others do it with friends, shaking with suppressed laughter. Feeling flattered and curious, I was beginning to open the note when Mrs. Reynolds came up from behind and took it from my hand.

She finished unfolding it and I watched with horror, sure it said something private. Mrs. Reynolds studied it through her round brown glasses. "I hadn't expected this of you, Kimberly."

Tammy was staring straight ahead, as if she hadn't done anything at all. Mrs. Reynolds's lips were compressed in a thin line of disapproval and she held the note up for me to read. I could barely make it out but realized it was filled with what looked like scribbled definitions for Newton's Laws, plus formulas for things like velocity and speed.

I figured out what had happened. My face flamed. I would never cheat, even in subjects where I had trouble. That wasn't the way Ma had brought me up. How little everyone here knew me, to even think I could do such a thing. Tammy turned her head now, behind Mrs. Reynolds's back, pleading with her eyes for me not to tell on her.

"That is not mine," I said.

"Please come with me." Mrs. Reynolds gestured for the assistant teacher to take over the class. She left the room and I followed her, feeling the eyes of the entire class upon me. I felt nauseated as we went down the hallway to the office of the director of the science and math department, Dr. Copeland.

Dr. Copeland looked up as Mrs. Reynolds knocked on her open door. The director was so thin as to be gaunt, with old scars etched into both sides of her face, as if she'd once been in an accident of some kind. Mrs. Reynolds shut the door behind us, then explained what had happened. She handed over the incriminating piece of paper. I clasped my shaking hands together.

"We take cheating very seriously here," Dr. Copeland said in a deceptively mild voice, but her eyes blazed into mine. "Students have been expelled for it."

"I wasn't," I said, my fear making my voice tremble.

"Mrs. Reynolds found this in your hand."

"I just pick it up."

Her face was white with tension. "I'd like to believe you, Kimberly, especially since you're such a good student, but if it's not yours, then why would you do that? It's hard to argue with the fact that you had a cheat sheet for the test in your possession."

I thought about the desperate look in Tammy's eyes and couldn't say anything. My face and neck were flushed with embarrassment and anger, mostly at myself. I couldn't believe I had gotten myself into so much trouble. What was going to happen to me?

At my silence, Dr. Copeland continued. "Whether you created the note or someone else did that for you is not the point."

My panic was so great by now I could only take shallow breaths. I knew I could be expelled when I was completely innocent. Why couldn't I open my mouth to tell them the truth? My emotions were all jumbled up inside and I felt paralyzed. I was still in a state of shock at the cheating accusation itself. And in part, I was so stunned Tammy would cheat that I couldn't bring myself to accuse her. How could I have thought that it had been a personal note for me? I burned with shame at wanting so much to be liked, to belong to a circle of friends, that I had picked up something during a test. What would Ma say if I not only got kicked out, but for cheating!

Both women were staring at me, waiting for my answer.

There was a knock on the door. Mrs. Reynolds cracked it open. "Yes?"

To my surprise, I heard Curt's voice. "The assistant teacher gave me permission to come here. I have something to say."

After he entered the office, Curt spoke in a clear voice. "I saw Kimberly pick up that piece of paper."

191

Dr. Copeland tapped her cheek with one finger. "And it was just lying there?"

Curt swallowed. He didn't know what I'd already told them. "I didn't see anything else. Only her picking it up."

"So, Kimberly, either you were very foolish or you were picking up something you had dropped yourself. Or your friend is covering up for you."

My eyes shot to Curt's. "He is not my friend," I said, before I could censor myself.

Curt had a wry smile on his face. "She's right. We've hardly ever spoken to each other before."

I saw Dr. Copeland glance at Mrs. Reynolds, who gave a slight nod. Mrs. Reynolds was agreeing that Curt and I weren't friends.

"So the question is, were you picking up something dropped by someone else or by yourself?" Dr. Copeland said.

"It is not my penmanship," I said.

"The writing is so small, it's hard to tell."

The time had come for honesty. "I am too smart to cheat," I said, feeling my face grow warm at my own arrogance. No good Chinese girl would say such a thing about herself. "It is under me."

Dr. Copeland pulled one corner of her mouth back in a half-smile. "You mean it's beneath you. All right, the two of you may return to the class and take the test. Mrs. Reynolds and I are going to discuss this further."

EIGHT

As soon as Curt and I were out of their hearing range, I turned to him and asked, "Why did you do that for me?"

He shrugged. "Because I did see you. And I heard Sheryl give Tammy the idea."

"You mean, to put the note in her sleeve?"

"Yeah."

I looked at him for a long moment. "Thank you."

He grinned. "I'd hate to see you get kicked out since I always cheat off of your tests."

I stopped short. "What?"

He gave me a playful punch. "Just kidding."

When we entered the classroom, all the kids looked up from their tests in progress, their curiosity plain across their faces. Tammy's eyes were swimming in tears. I angrily wondered if the tears were from guilt or having to work through the test without her cheat sheet. I was sure everyone else thought I was a cheater, and felt grateful that Curt had come and walked back with me, as indirect proof of my innocence. I took the test with even more care than normal because I knew the school's final judgment of the situation would depend partly on how I performed without any notes. The assistant teacher kept a keen eye on me. After a short while, Mrs. Reynolds came back and resumed her seat at the front of the room as if nothing had happened.

When the bell rang, everyone got up and handed in their papers. Mrs. Reynolds said, "Kim and Curt, you have ten more minutes since you started late, but no more than that." Her tone was hard to read, but I was afraid I had lost the respect of a teacher I liked a great deal.

When our time was up, she took our papers and silently handed us late passes for our next class, which had already begun. So it wasn't until lunch that Tammy was able to catch up with me.

She slipped in next to me on the lunch line and squeezed my arm. Since she hadn't been called to the office, she knew I hadn't told on her. I stared at her hand on my blazer sleeve, torn between fury, confusion and the desire to forget the whole incident. She didn't say a word, and then moved away again.

The next day, I found a card she'd slid into my locker that said, "I'm so sorry! Thank you!!!!" I wondered if she might feel closer to me now. I had hoped we were developing a friendship. Would we really become close now? But after that, she avoided me.

I was hardly able to eat or sleep until our Physical Science class the next day. I didn't dare tell Ma or Annette about this. The whole experience made me feel ill and I was not at all sure I had handled it right. Most of all, I was embarrassed and disgusted at myself for thinking Tammy might pass me a note. Would I be summoned to the office again, or simply get a letter at home telling me I'd been expelled?

The class came at last and Mrs. Reynolds solemnly handed back everyone's tests. She'd graded them faster than usual. I saw Mrs. Reynolds give Tammy a hard look when she returned her test. She knew as well as I did who had been sitting in front of me. By craning my neck, I could see Tammy had failed. I felt sorry for her, but vindicated as well.

Mrs. Reynolds laid my test on my desk. I'd gotten a 96. She bent down and whispered, "We're going to give you the benefit of the doubt."

She put her hand on my shoulder with a smile, and I saw that she, at least, was convinced of my innocence. I glanced at the other students surreptitiously and saw most of the class watching us. The knot in my stomach began to loosen.

I only hoped that Dr. Copeland didn't have any remaining doubts either.

It was also in the eighth grade that we finally got a phone at home. I knew the monthly payments pained Ma, but I was too ashamed to be the one omission in the stapled school telephone directory everyone received. It seemed to be a public declaration of poverty that came too close to showing everyone the truth about the way we really lived.

Ma had finally agreed to the phone, persuaded by the argument that I needed it to discuss homework.

But most things hadn't changed, they'd simply become routine. I grew into the space that Ma's foreignness left vacant. She hadn't learned any more English, so I took over everything that required any kind of interaction with the world outside of Chinatown. I pored over our income tax forms every year, using the documents the factory provided for us. I read the fine print repeatedly, hoping I was doing it right. If Ma needed to buy something at a store or to make a complaint or a return, I had to do it for her. The worst was when Ma wanted to bargain, the way she had in Hong Kong, and I had to translate for her.

"Tell him we'll only pay two dollars," Ma said to me at the American fish store near our apartment.

"Ma, you can't do this here!"

"Just say it!"

I gave the fishmonger an apologetic smile. I was only thirteen. "Two dollars?"

He was not amused. "Two dollars and fifty cents."

Later, Ma scolded me for not having had the right attitude. She was sure that if I'd been firmer, we would have gotten a discount.

At school, I still kept mostly to myself. In the middle of winter, some kids started coming to school with tanned cheeks and white rings around their eyes from their ski goggles, exultant about places like Snowbird in Utah and Vallery in France. There was a rage for a certain brand of ski jacket, tight and short, with a high collar around the neck, and soon most kids in my homeroom class were wearing one. I heard the jackets cost at least 20,000 skirts each.

More of the girls in class also started wearing makeup to school, or applying it in the restrooms or at their lockers. This interested me more than the ski jackets. It seemed to have a magical quality that would somehow make you more normal. Once, in the girls' bathroom, Annette had pulled out what she called a cover-up stick and rubbed it over the surface of a pimple she had on her chin. I couldn't believe it. The pimple hardly showed afterward. I immediately thought about using it to cover my nose, sometimes raw from the colds I got.

"Take it," Annette said. "The color's too dark for me anyway."

Moments like this showed me that despite my constant evasions, Annette understood my situation in a way that no one else at school could even begin to, but I still couldn't bring myself to talk about it. And even as kind-hearted as she was, there was no way she had any idea exactly how poor we really were.

Now that I was older, I wasn't as sick all the time, although a runny nose often plagued me. What worried me more was when sometimes Ma became ill. Whenever she coughed, I worried she would have a relapse of tuberculosis, though fortunately it never happened. Our living conditions didn't change but with time, I stopped allowing myself to be conscious of my own unhappiness.

At home, Ma and I kept hoping for the wrecking ball to appear outside our building, forcing Aunt Paula to move us to a new apartment, but it never did. Ma had asked her one last time about when we'd be able to move, and Aunt Paula allowed her black face to be seen for a moment.

"If you're really so unhappy there, no one is stopping you from making other choices."

After that, Ma didn't dare to ask again. We were still paying Aunt Paula back and it was clear that she simply did not care to move us. As far as she was concerned, it was most convenient and best to leave us where we were. And the truth is, caught up in the vortex of work and school, we had become too exhausted to fight against the roaches and mice, our frozen limbs, the stuffed animal clothing, and life in front of the open oven. We had been forced into acceptance. Sunday was our only free day, but it was packed: we did all our grocery shopping then, but also had to catch up on factory work, my schoolwork, and prepare for any Chinese holidays. Our one bright spot was when we went to the Shaolin temple in Chinatown. It was on the second floor of a building in the Lower East Side and was my sanctuary.

It was run by true Chinese nuns, complete with shaved heads and black robes, and they always served free and delicious vegetarian food: fried noodles with tofu, rice and thin, ruffle-edged black mushrooms called cloud ears. When the nuns handed me my food, I could feel how present they were in every gesture of kindness. After lighting incense and bowing to the enormous triple Buddhas in the main room, we would pay our respects to our dead, and most especially to Pa. I felt at peace in the temple, as if we had never left Hong Kong. As if there were forces of compassion that were watching over Ma and me.

I couldn't get away from the factory much. Once in a long while, when we had a bit of time before the next shipment went out, I lied to Ma and snuck off with Annette for a few hours in the afternoon.

On one of those days, Annette tried to convince me to go with her to a movie. I had never been to one in this country and I hesitated for a moment, wondering if it was even possible.

Misunderstanding my hesitation, Annette tried adding more incentive. "I'll bring my makeup and we can put it on before the movie. Don't worry, we'll wash it off afterwards."

I made up an excuse for Ma, and Annette and I went to see *Indiana Jones and the Temple of Doom* at a theater close to her house. I worried about what it would cost, and if I would have enough, but when we got to the ticket window, Annette insisted on paying. I protested but secretly felt relieved. I didn't have any spending money of my own. The money in my pocket was change I had borrowed from the grocery budget, which I would have had to make up for in skirts.

We were early for the film, and the theater was huge, half empty and cavernous, with lights set into the floor, as there had been on the airplane from Hong Kong. I inhaled the smell of popcorn and butter, and then Annette rushed me into the ladies' room, where, grinning, she pulled out a pink plastic makeup case. It looked new. She sifted through small packages with different colors of powder and explained the set had been a gift from her cousin.

"You have great cheekbones," Annette said, putting more blush on me and giggling.

"You too." I wasn't sure what made a cheekbone "great" but that seemed irrelevant.

When we were done, I peered in the mirror and was amazed at how different I looked. Heavily shadowed eyes, tons of blush and lipstick: hardly an inch of my skin had been left its original color. It would be very American to look like this all the time. I touched my great cheekbones with my fingers.

A woman leaving the bathroom smiled at us as she left. "You look lovely, girls."

We felt beautiful. Then we sat in the dark for a

few hours watching the film, which I didn't follow at all. I kept feeling the velvet of my seat with my hand and imagining the glow of my face. Indiana Jones did seem very heroic. The movie was similar to martial arts films I had seen on television in Hong Kong, only less comprehensible, with too many villains, tribal people, and children needing to be rescued. But it was so exciting. When the film was over, Annette and I went back to the bathroom to scrub our faces. She wasn't allowed to wear any makeup either. I didn't mind. Now we had a secret together, a happy one.

When school let out for the summer, Annette went off to a camp at a college upstate and I returned full-time to the factory. I needed to lighten Ma's burden as much as I could, and any extra work I did meant more income. That was the summer I learned exactly the pattern in which my bra would get soaked by sweat: first the band below the breasts would begin to get wet; then the sweat would slowly move upward. It traveled more quickly under the arms and in the center of the back, then would rise between the breasts to soak the cups and finally the straps. The entire thing was wet within half an hour of work.

My specialty in the finishing process was the bagging. This was the most physically demanding job, but I learned to do it fast. There was a tall black metal rack with an enormous roll of plastic garment bags at the top. You took a garment from the right side, hung it on the hook on the rack, then opened the plastic bag and fit it over the item. Then you had to separate the bag from the previous ones in the roll and, finally, lift the entire garment up over the rack and hook, and hang the garment on the rack to the left. It was important to be careful not to rip the bag or you would have to start all over again.

The finishing process started when we got the garments and ended after they were bagged; it included hanging, sorting, belting, tying sashes, buttoning, tagging and bagging each item. For all of this work, we were paid one and a half cents per skirt, two cents per pair of pants with a belt, and one cent for an upper garment. I was still too short for the rack so I had to stand on a chair. I timed myself with the large factory clock that hung on the opposite wall. It took Ma about thirty seconds to bag a piece, which worked out to bagging about 120 pieces an hour. It was easy to figure out that Ma was making much less than two dollars an hour.

This was no way to survive. At first, when I was doing it the slow way, separating each bag with two hands and carefully fitting it over the garments, it took me twenty seconds to bag a piece. Then I tried different tactics to refine my methods.

I figured out that the fastest way was to grab the next bag in the roll with my hand, which was moist with sweat and thus sticky, give the bag a slight twist so that the bottom dropped open and then, as I pulled it down and over the hanging garment, to strike the serration line with my other hand so that the bag separated from the others in the roll as it fell. Before the plastic had fully dropped to cover the entire garment, I was lifting it up by the hanger to get it off and onto the rack on my left. Then I grabbed another one with my right hand.

Pants took slightly longer because most of them were belted, which made them unbalanced on the hanger, and if you didn't grab them with both hands as you lifted them, they would slip off. I developed hard muscles in my arms from all of the lifting.

By the end of that summer, when I'd hit my rhythm, I could get almost five hundred skirts bagged in an hour, about seven seconds per skirt. Later, when I was older and stronger, I would reach a top speed of a bit less than five seconds per skirt, doing more than seven hundred in an hour.

Despite my dislike of Aunt Paula, I worked harder and faster whenever she passed by to show her that we were industrious people, valuable workers and loyal to the factory. I still hoped that maybe we would be rewarded for our good behavior.

Once, Matt was hanging around the finishing station, helping us tag some skirts in his free time. On the days a shipment went out, we finished in the order we were placed in the garment proce-dure. Since he helped his ma with thread-cutting, a much earlier part of the process, his part of the work for the final shipment had been done earlier in the day. As the finishers, Ma and I were always last. Matt could leave but sometimes he stayed to hang around me.

Ma gave him a smile. She had to speak loudly to be heard over the noise the steamers made. "You're growing up, Matt. I never realized what fine human material you were made of." She was saying that he was handsome.

Matt grinned and flexed his muscles. "It's all that thread-cutting, Mrs. Chang. Makes a guy strong."

I was a few feet away, bagging as usual, but I couldn't help sneaking a glance at his shoulders. He was still skinny but the white undershirt he wore revealed the broad frame of a young man's body. Matt glanced at me, as if to see if I had heard Ma's compliment, and caught me looking at him.

He struck a pose, with one arm raised and the other on his hip. "How do I look?"

I giggled. "Like the Liberty Goddess!"

He pretended to be insulted. "What would you know about that? You probably don't remember what she looks like."

I sobered up, remembering all my old dreams of New York. I'd thought we'd be living in Times Square, known in Cantonese as the Tay Um See

Arena, and what I'd gotten was the slums of Brooklyn. "No, actually, I've never seen it."

"You must be talking the big words." He meant I had to be lying.

"I'm serious."

"You mean, you haven't seen Min-hat-ton?" He pronounced "Manhattan" the Cantonese way.

"Only Chinatown."

"Hey, I'll take you out on Sunday. You can't live in New York and not see the real Liberty Goddess."

I could feel my lips form a small, delighted "O" but I didn't know how Ma would react. She had her back to us, working and pretending not to be listening.

"Mrs. Chang?" Matt said. "How about I act as your tour guide on Sunday?"

I felt a rush of disappointment even as I recognized his cleverness. Ma would be much less likely to say no if she'd been invited too.

Ma turned around with a teasing smile on her face. "Now, I wouldn't want to be a lightbulb."

"Ma!" I was glad I was already flushed from the heat, or I would have turned bright red. Her joke, that she would be there as a chaperone—stopping the lovers from kissing because of her presence, like a lightbulb in a darkened room—made public my private hope: that Matt's invitation might actually be a date.

Matt shook his head like a dog, hiding his embarrassment, but he managed to look flirtatious at the same time. "No, no. You look so young, everyone would think you were only coming along to shell peanuts." It was a good line. He meant the younger brother or sister who is sometimes sent to accompany a couple to the movies, shelling peanuts and preventing them from making out.

Ma laughed. "You have such good mouth skills. All right, I'd like to—"

Suddenly, one of the men at the steamers started to scream. It was Mr. Pak. I didn't know much about him except for his name. I didn't think he had any other family working at the factory. He was surrounded by steam, so it was hard to see what had happened, but the other three men who worked on the steamers raced to his side. They were working to release the metal top of the steamer as Matt, Ma and I rushed up. Finally they got it open and Mr. Pak clutched his hand. He was still howling. I didn't dare look at his hand directly.

I immediately knew what had happened. When the men at the steamers are under pressure, they need to work so quickly that they simply slam the top lid down hard enough that it latches closed by itself. Then they open the lid and switch garments at lightning speed. Matt had told me that if they weren't fast enough when they slammed the lid again, their hands could get caught.

Aunt Paula and Uncle Bob had arrived, and they

pushed their way to the front of the crowd that had formed.

"Why are you so clumsy?" Aunt Paula yelled. She grabbed Mr. Pak, who was sobbing and hunched over his hand, and she pulled him in the direction of the exit. Uncle Bob hurried after her, with his swinging limp. She called over her shoulder, "Nobody call a lifesaving-car! We'll take him to the factory doctor! Everyone, get back to work, tonight the shipment goes out!"

As the crowd dispersed, I turned to Matt. "I didn't know there was a factory doctor."

His voice was low, shaking a bit from what he'd just seen. "He's just a friend of Dog Flea Mama's. Someone who won't report the accident."

I was trembling too. "You probably want to go home, Matt. Don't worry about us."

"No one's at home anyway. My ma is getting the needle-rescue treatment for her pains."

Later, I was working as fast as I could bagging skirts—I still had to finish them all before the shipment could go out—when I saw Aunt Paula had returned to our work area. She moved briskly, and I thought she seemed stressed by what had just happened.

"I was going to talk to the two of you about something anyway when that incident occurred. There's been a change in the factory policy." She didn't bother to use her false smile. "Due to bad economic conditions, after this shipment goes out, the rate for skirts will have to drop to one cent a skirt."

"What?" Ma said.

"Why?" I asked. And then I knew. Aunt Paula had seen me working fast. Too fast. We'd started earning more, and she'd calculated that we could receive less and still survive. And I'd imagined I was impressing her.

"Sorry, but that's the way it is. Company policy. For all the finishers."

We were the only finishers at the factory.

"That's not fair," I blurted. Ma, standing behind me, poked me under my shoulder blade.

Aunt Paula turned her attention to me. Her lipstick was smudged in one corner. "I wouldn't want the two of you to be unhappy. You're free to make your own choices if you feel uncomfortable. There's no slavery in America anymore, is there?" And she started to walk away.

Ma, who never touched anyone casually, shoved past me, ran after Aunt Paula and grabbed her arm. "Older sister, I'm so sorry. She is such an outspoken child."

"No, no," Aunt Paula said. She sighed. "Those bamboo shoots, they're like that. Don't worry about it."

"Bamboo shoot" was a term for a kid who'd been born and raised in America, meaning he or she was too westernized. *I'm a bamboo knot,* I wanted to say: *born in Hong Kong but brought*

208

over here young. A bamboo knot blocks the hollowness of the bamboo shaft, yet the knot gives the bamboo its strength as well.

"Thank you," Ma said. "Thank you."

I suddenly heard Matt's voice. I'd forgotten he was there. "You enjoy having bamboo shoots for your midnight snack, don't you, Mrs. Yue?"

I stopped breathing, even my heart seemed to stop beating. What was he doing, what had I done by starting this whole fight?

Aunt Paula started to laugh and her laughter chilled me. "The older Wu brother is turning into quite a man, isn't he? All right, if you're so grown-up, you can take over the empty steamer spot tomorrow."

"No!" I realized we had played right into what Aunt Paula needed. "You know Matt, he's always joking—"

Matt interrupted me. "It's okay. No problem, Mrs. Yue, I've been wanting to build up my muscles anyway." And with a shrug, he set off slowly for the exit. "Bye, Mrs. Chang, Kimberly."

Aunt Paula stared at his back and then stalked off in the direction of her office.

Once she was gone, Ma whirled on me. "Don't interfere when adults are talking! Who will fill our mouths with food when we don't have any work?"

"It *is* a free country, Ma. Why do we have to work for her?"

"Free country! Who do you think owns the other

clothing factories? They're all family or friends with each other. The whole Chinatown garment industry. And what is going to happen to Matt now?"

I looked down. The ragged edge in her voice had turned into frustration and despair. Like me, Matt was only fourteen, and who knew what would become of him when he worked on the enormous steaming press, which only grown men operated.

Ma's voice became gentler. "*Ah*-Kim, I know you mean well. It's just that everything in you gets spoken right out." She meant I was too honest, and at that moment, I agreed with her.

The next day, I lingered by the steamers. The three men who worked them were constantly appearing and disappearing behind billows of steam. They laid garment after garment across the steamers with military precision and as the massive lids clamped down, scorching clouds were expelled in enormous gusts. When the lids were pulled open again, remnants of steam trailed behind like saliva between jaws. Even an accidental touch of the steamer surface resulted in a rush of blisters.

Matt was a small figure in between the muscled men. I saw he wasn't as fast as the others yet, but he was working hard with his left foot on the vacuum and his right foot on the steam paddle. He lifted a skirt onto the surface of the steamer. He ducked his head away when a cloud of steam poured over him and was lost in the fog. The next thing I knew, he was coming up to me with his fist clenched.

I shrank back. I saw that his undershirt, all that he was wearing, was soaked, and droplets of sweat and steam rolled from his neck down onto his chest.

"Guess I got a big mouth," he said.

"Me too."

"Hey, someone has to find the rice, right?" To earn the money.

I felt so guilty, I couldn't answer. It made it worse that he was being nice to me. "Can I help?"

"Maybe when you're older. Work pays well and you get into shape too. You work here, you'll become a stud like me."

Normally I would have laughed and I tried to, but something in my body stopped me and it came out as a kind of a cough instead.

At that, he looked at me seriously. "I need this anyway. My ma can hardly earn a dime anymore. Her heart hurts, her lungs hurt. And Park can't work. I'll be okay." He didn't wait for an answer but changed the subject. "Hey, can you take this to her for me?"

I held out my hand and he poured something metal from his closed fist into it. It was a necklace made of gold, with a jade Kuan Yin hanging from it. This Kuan Yin was carved with a multitude of arms, each hand holding a different tool. People call her the goddess with an infinite number of arms to help all those in need.

I had noticed Matt wearing the necklace before, but thought nothing of it. It was common for parents to have their children wear gold and jade jewelry underneath their clothing to protect them from evil. They never take it off. Some families with barely enough money for food save until they can afford this kind of protection for their children.

I must have looked puzzled that Matt had just handed it to me, because he said, "Look." He pulled open his T-shirt and I saw the red marks the necklace had burned onto his skin.

"It's too hot for you to wear any metal so close to the machine," I said flatly, the guilt flooding over me again.

"Duh. Hey, we're going to the streets on Sunday, right?"

I couldn't stop the huge smile from breaking across my face. "Really? You still want to?"

"Sure, have to get back to work so I don't fall behind too much." And he went back to his spot by the steamer.

The jade Kuan Yin glowed as green as tender leaves in spring and I could see how valuable that necklace had to be. I brought it immediately to Mrs. Wu, whose back was to me. She was scolding Park for something. He was half turned away from her and there was no way he could have read her lips. To my surprise, he responded by turning to her and clumsily patting her arm.

I looked at her face more closely and I saw that Matt was right, she didn't look healthy. In addition to the large bags she always had under her eyes, both her skin and her lips were sallow, and the whites of her eyes seemed very yellow. That was when she saw me.

"You," she said.

Terrified, I held out Matt's necklace, but she only cast it a scornful look. "You going to be nice to my son?"

I didn't dare speak. She clearly knew I was responsible for Matt's being at the steamers.

"And to think I thought you were a boy," she said. Her disgust made her Toisanese accent in Chinese even more pronounced. "He has a good heart." She took the necklace from my hand. "Course, he would give this to you," she muttered.

Suddenly, I heard Ma's voice behind me. She must have come over when she saw us talking. "Mrs. Wu, I cannot face you. We are responsible."

Mrs. Wu gazed at Ma, then the tension seemed to leave her. "We all have no choice. He's a good boy. He'll be all right."

"Kimberly's not a bad girl either." Ma's glance was warm. "They're both so young and impulsive. We have to give them time."

The two mothers looked at each other.

"Kids," Mrs. Wu said.

I ran back to our workstation but their words flickered on the walls of my mind. Was Mrs. Wu implying that Matt could actually like me, perhaps just a little bit? I thrilled to the thought, but it was also strangely painful, like an ache in my lungs.

Matt didn't just take Ma and me to see the Liberty Goddess, he started by meeting us at Times Square, the Tay Um See Arena. We got out of the enormous subway station, drawn along by the sea of people, and I was relieved to see Matt at the Burger King on the corner, just where he'd said he would meet us. Standing by his side, Ma and I looked around. Finally, this was the New York I'd dreamed of. A long white limousine drove by, surrounded by dozens of yellow taxis. We strolled by movie theaters and restaurants, signs that said "Girls Girls Girls" and massive billboards advertising Broadway shows. I felt strangely at home. The crowded streets and bustling city reminded me of the fancy parts of Hong Kong, although the Tay Um See Arena was bigger and richer. The people on the street were dressed in every imaginable way, but some of the women were especially elegant, with high heels and suits with shoulder pads. Many people were white, but I saw an Indian man with a turban, some black people in traditional African dress, and a group of singing monks in melon-colored robes. Ma put her hands together and bowed to them. One monk paused in his chanting to bow back.

"Oh, look at that!" Ma said to me, pointing to an enormous musical instrument store. I shielded my eyes from the hot sun to see through the window: an expanse of grand pianos, cellos and violins. In the back were what appeared to be cases filled with musical scores.

"Let's go in," Matt said.

"Oh no, we can't buy anything," Ma said.

"No harm in looking," I said because I knew how much she wanted to enter, and Matt and I ushered her in through the double doors.

A burst of air-conditioning met us. It felt like heaven. There were enough customers wandering around, examining instruments and looking at musical scores, that Ma started to relax. Some were seated at the pianos, testing them out. I longed for this clean and carpeted life. Ma was as wide-eyed as a young girl. She started leafing through a stack of scores by Mozart, completely absorbed.

Matt and I walked around by ourselves.

"I didn't know your ma liked music so much," Matt said.

"She was a music teacher." I paused. "Back home. What about your parents? What do they care about?"

"My ma's so busy, just taking care of Park. And my pa's gone. So I have to look after everybody."

I smiled. Matt always took his responsibilities so seriously. But this was the first I'd ever heard about his father.

"You mean he's passed away?"

Matt nodded without meeting my eyes, then said, "Where's your ma?"

I turned around to look for Ma and found her lingering by a grand piano. I cocked my head in her direction, and Matt and I crossed over to her.

"This is a handsome instrument, isn't it?" Ma said, flipping through the sheet music that some-one had left on the piano. "It must sound lovely."

"Try it out," Matt said. "You're allowed to push a few keys."

"Oh no," Ma said.

"Please." I caught her eye. I desperately wanted her to play for Matt, to show him that we were more than what we seemed to be at the factory.

Slowly, Ma sat down. "Your pa used to love this piece," she said, and ran her fingers up and down the keyboard in a series of runs before she started playing Chopin's Nocturne in A-flat.

Matt's mouth was slack.

I closed my eyes, listening and remembering how it had been when we had our own piano in our apartment, how Ma's delicate fingers had moved so gracefully over the keyboard. She played the beginning and then stopped. By then, we had attracted the attention of a salesman, despite our simple clothes.

"Madam plays beautifully," he said. "The piano has a wonderful tone, doesn't it?"

I wondered how I could turn him away politely, but Matt spoke first.

"Yeah," Matt said in English. "Thanks, but we're just looking."

For once, someone had taken the burden off me.

We wandered around the Tay Um See Arena, looking at the skyscrapers.

"Oh my, I have to look up three times before I can see the top," Ma said, laughing as she peered up at one particularly high building.

"I can span it with my hands," Matt said, stepping back and pretending to measure it.

That reminded me of something I didn't want to bring up, but I needed to know.

"What's going to happen to Mr. Pak?" I asked Matt. Since he lived in Chinatown and knew a lot of people from the factory, he heard most of the gossip.

"He won't be coming back to the factory. His skin was badly burned and his wife thinks the work is too dangerous."

"What will happen to him, then?"

"She works for that jewelry factory on Centre and Canal, so I bet he'll do that with her when he heals."

"What is that?"

"Making bead bracelets and other costume jewelry. You can bring all your work home, but it pays even worse than our factory. And you need to have very fast hands."

I looked at Ma. Could this be a way to get out of the clothing factory?

She shook her head. "Remember how cold it gets at home, *ah*-Kim?"

I nodded. In our unheated apartment, we would never be able to string beads with a needle and thread.

Finally, we went to see the Liberty Goddess. Ma had tried to pay for Matt's subway tokens but he'd been too quick for her.

"Now, we're not going to actually get off at the Liberty Goddess," Matt said. "That boat costs too much. What we'll do is to take the Staten Island Ferry, which is only twenty-five cents, and you get an even better view."

"Perfect," Ma said.

We climbed aboard the large yellow ferry, which reminded me of the ferries in Kowloon Harbor, and Matt led us up to the top deck. Ma said it was so windy there that she had to go back downstairs to sit down.

It was wonderful, standing against the railing with Matt by my side, the cool wind blowing the heat away. The ocean stretched out before us.

"We're going to get a first-rate look soon," Matt said, and he left to go downstairs to get Ma. I marveled at how he could be tough yet considerate.

I held my breath when we finally got a good view of the Liberty Goddess. She was so close and so magnificent. Ma and Matt were right next to me. Ma squeezed my hand.

"How long we've dreamed of this," she said.

"We're here," I said. "We're really in America."

Matt was looking thoughtful. "Doesn't she remind you of Kuan Yin?"

We nodded.

Later, when Ma and I were finally back in our apartment, she said to me, "I was wrong about that Wu boy. He's more than handsome, he's got a human heart too." She meant he had compassion and depth.

I didn't answer but I hid my face in my pillow, thinking about Matt.

Ninth grade marked the transition to high school. Most of us had been there for seventh and eighth grade but some new students entered in ninth, and the school year began with placement tests in math and science to determine which level classes we should be in. The other students, especially the better and more competitive ones, were nervous about the tests because spots in the accelerated science and math program were limited and coveted. Although the tests were supposed to be a simple evaluation of our abilities, many kids had tutors to help them do some extra studying on their own. There was a rumor that some colleges accepted only students who had gotten into the accelerated program.

After the dusty, physical work of the factory, the scientific world created a clear and logical paradise where I could feel safe. Just for pleasure, I had started reading library books about subjects we'd touched upon in school: amino acids, mitosis, prokaryotes, DNA forensics, karyotyping, monohybrid crosses, endothermic reactions. And mathematics was the only language I truly understood. It was pure, orderly and predictable. It gave me great satisfaction to work on mathematical puzzles and forget about my real life at the apartment and factory. So I might have been the only student who actually looked forward to the placement tests and enjoyed taking them.

When I received my scores, they seemed impossibly high, even to me. I was overjoyed. However, after a few weeks in the accelerated science and math program, Dr. Copeland, the director of the science and math department, called me into her office. My heart thudded in my throat. I didn't have good memories of that place.

"Kimberly, I am concerned by your performance in your classes," she said.

My breath seemed to lodge in my throat. What could be wrong this time? I'd been getting close to perfect scores on every test so far. As an extra credit assignment in Biology, I'd devised a lab activity my teacher had raved about: using drated juice to identify solutes, solvents, solution, concentration, and to simulate enzyme activity. "Is there a problem with my grades?"

"To tell you the truth, you're doing a bit too well." Dr. Copeland stared at me with narrowed eyes to gauge my reaction.

Now I understood. She hadn't forgotten that incident with Tammy last year. With the fear clogging my throat, it was hard to get the words out. "I'm not a cheat."

"I hope not. All of your teachers seemed to be convinced of your intelligence, and I do want to believe them. However, no student your age has ever gotten the results you got on those placement tests. And you are doing extremely well in your classes, while your middle school grades were less consistent. You may or may not know this, but tests have been stolen in the past." Her face was filled with suspicion. She leaned in closer to me. When she finally spoke, her voice was so low I could barely hear her. "I was a pretty bright student too, as smart as they come, and I couldn't have learned as quickly and as well as you claim to be doing. If you prove me wrong, I'll be glad—glad to have such a brilliant young girl in science—but, well . . . you understand why we need to be sure of this, I think. You will be taking a new combined placement exam, an oral one, conducted by the entire science and math faculty. Each teacher will contribute his or her own questions."

I didn't answer. I was terrified of losing everything Ma and I had worked for. What if I couldn't understand the English well enough, since it would all be spoken? What if I happened to make a few mistakes or just did less well than usual on her test? They could wrongly decide I'd been cheating and I would have to leave the school. I stared at her but her face no longer made sense to me. It had become a blur of shapes and light.

"I'm not out to get you, Kimberly. If you're doing everything honestly, you have nothing to worry about." And she turned back to her desk.

I walked slowly out of her office. Why couldn't I just be like everyone else?

"You okay?" Curt was passing by, arm in arm with Sheryl.

Sheryl turned her head, her forehead furrowed. Perhaps she was as surprised as I was that he'd spoken to me. Maybe he also remembered the last time I'd been in that office.

"Sure," I said. I blinked my eyes a few times. "Thanks."

"See you," he said, moving away.

NINE

I had a few casual friends, but at some point, we always hit an invisible barrier. There was Samantha, who was something of a snob. At the school cafeteria, I once asked the lady behind the counter for a cheese croissant in my careful English and Samantha corrected me with an exaggerated French accent, "*Crois san.* It's so uncultured to pronounce the *t.*" And nowadays, Tammy spent her time pretending I didn't exist.

Finally, there was boy-crazy Lucy, who said things like, "Hey, I know what. Let's dress up in our shortest miniskirts and go shopping in the city! I went out last Friday and these guys were drooling all over me!"

In the end, Annette was my only true friend. In ninth grade, she became political, as she put it. She started wearing buttons and tried to get people to sign petitions. With being political came a new set of friends too. They were mostly the kids who worked on the anti-racism newsletter she set up: a few of the older scholarship students, a Swedish exchange student, some of the kids with punk hair. Now she wanted me to sign petitions fighting apartheid in South Africa, and I did; she wanted me to go to feminist marches with her, and I couldn't. She became more extreme, using her newsletter to comment on the lack of students of color at Harrison. She started calling herself a Communist. With my family's history, how could I believe in Communism? Even more than that, though, with all the time I spent trying to appear normal, I was too conscious of the dangers of sticking your neck out.

The younger Annette I'd known had been easily

distracted, filled with different and contradictory passions that flew from one extreme to the other. That simpler Annette had been easier to handle, only really concerned with herself and her comfortable world. There was a more serious Annette emerging now, one that started asking difficult questions.

"So how come we're so close," she began once, "and I've never been to your house?"

"My apartment is small. You would not be very comfortable," I said.

"But I don't mind."

"My mother care. Just wait, I will ask her if you can come, okay?" I was hoping that this would appease her until she forgot about the whole thing. It was not until several years later that Annette showed me I was wrong; she'd never forgotten.

What Annette didn't understand was that silence could be a great protector. I couldn't afford to cry when there was no escape. Talking about my problems would only illuminate the lines of my unhappiness in the cold light of day, showing me, as well as her, the things I had been able to bear only because they had been half hidden in the shadows. I couldn't expose myself like that, not even for her.

In some ways, getting the phone had only made things worse. Once, when I was working in the library, Annette had come by to hang out and started talking about an assignment for Social Studies, a class we shared this year. She was working on a paper titled "Marx and Aristotle: The Nature of Morality." I hadn't had time to start mine. I didn't even have the topic yet.

"I tried to call you yesterday afternoon." She tucked a lock of hair behind her ear. "Why aren't you ever home after school?"

I tried to look innocent while I thought. "What do you mean?"

"You never answer until so late. Where do you go?"

"Nowhere. Sometimes it takes me a long time to get home."

Annette tightened her full lips. "Kimberly, are we or are we not best friends?"

Miserable, I met her eyes. "Of course."

Her eyes were fierce. "I'm not stupid."

"I know." I hesitated. "The truth is, I help my mother at work."

"In Chinatown? Are the stores open that late?" I'd once told Annette my mother worked there and allowed her to believe that Ma worked in a shop.

I decided to tell her a part of the truth. "Do you remember I told you once we worked in a factory?"

"Maybe, kind of." Annette's voice started to rise. "Do you really? Aren't you too young? Isn't that illegal?"

"Annette. Stop it." I looked around the library. There was only one other student seated at the other end of the room. "This is not some abstract idea in your head. This is my life. If you do something to protest, we could lose our job." I paused and looked down at my calloused hands, then up to her eyes again to say, "We need the work."

"I won't do anything you don't want me to. But are you okay?"

"Yes. Really. It's not so bad," I lied. "There is a soda machine."

"Oh. Great." She sounded sarcastic. "If there's a soda machine, you've got to be in heaven."

I started laughing. "You can even get iced tea in it."

She giggled too. "Now I'm really convinced." Then she sobered up. "Thanks for telling me. You can trust me."

I paused and looked at her. Annette had grown taller and her freckles had faded, but she was still the girl who had been my loyal friend since our days in Mr. Bogart's class. "There's something else." I hadn't told her anything of the school suspecting me of cheating—mostly because I found the whole thing so horrible I couldn't bear to speak of it. Now I told her the whole story, starting with what had happened last year with Tammy and ending with my approaching oral exam.

"Kimberly, I can't believe you didn't tell me any of this! And why didn't you just say it was Tammy who was really cheating?"

"I'm actually not so smart."

"No, you're just not a telly-tale, that's all. You remember you always used to say that?"

We both started to laugh again but I remembered where we were and shushed us.

"You'll be all right," Annette said. "You can take anything they throw at you."

"I hope so." I wasn't so sure. "But they can make the test very hard."

Whenever we got home from the factory, Ma would cook our dinner for the next day so that we could bring it with us to work. Afterward, if it wasn't too cold, she'd play her violin for a little bit. That was always my favorite part of the day. And then, if she didn't have work she needed to finish from the factory, she would fight exhaustion to study as much English as she could. Now she had also started practicing for the naturalization examination. As I did whenever I was doing schoolwork, she kept a roll of toilet paper by her to crush any roaches that tried to run across the pages of her book. While she studied, I finished my own homework and worked on some books I'd borrowed from the library for my upcoming exam.

At fourteen I couldn't take the naturalization test myself, but I would automatically acquire U.S. citizenship if Ma passed. This was essential if I wanted to qualify for the financial aid programs at colleges. Ma had bought a cheap tape player and a study book with a cassette. After listening to the questions repeatedly, she memorized what she needed to answer by the sounds alone. I peeked in her notes and they were full of phonetic symbols like a musical score. I'm sure she had no idea what any of the sentences meant. When I tried to explain their grammar and meaning to her, she listened politely, but I never saw anything like understanding in her eyes.

"Are you Communie?" Ma asked herself in English.

The book made it clear that there was only one correct answer: "No!"

Whatever Annette called herself, I knew that if you said yes to this question, you would have trouble with your U.S. citizenship. We weren't natural-born Americans like her. They could still throw us out.

Having spoken to Annette about my problems at school earlier in the day, I realized that I needed to talk to Ma as well. Before we went to bed, I told her the whole story.

She held her head high on her slender neck and her eyes blazed. "My girl would never cheat."

"They are worried because they think I might have, before."

"If you're as straight as an arrow, you'll have to beg for a living," Ma said with a sigh. She was quoting a Cantonese expression about the dangers of being too honest. "Do you want me to talk to that teacher?"

"No, Ma." I didn't mention the language barrier. "No one can convince her that I'm innocent except for me. I have to pass her exam."

A week before my big oral examination, Annette decided I needed to relax, and despite my protests that I should study in all of my free time, she insisted she was taking me to Macy's. Since our initial bra-buying expedition two years before, Ma and I had returned there a few times to buy new underwear for me, but we always felt so uncomfortable that we got out as fast as we could. It was hard for me to see how this trip would be relaxing, but as always I let myself trust Annette.

I constantly had to lie to Ma when I did social things with Annette, because Ma found nonschool things to be unimportant and she was afraid that something dangerous would happen to me when I was out. Plus, I knew that if I told her what we did, she would feel the need to return the favors.

This time, I stayed a bit behind Annette. She went up to each of the perfume ladies and stuck out her round wrist with confidence. I followed. The spritzes of perfume were cold against my skin. Then we put our noses up against our own and each other's arms, although we could have smelled each other from the other room.

After we'd been to all of the perfume ladies, we circled the glossy white counters, picking up the test bottles and spraying each one on a new spot. It became hard to find an exposed piece of our bodies that hadn't been sprayed: we started with our wrists, moved up our arms, then did our necks and collarbones and chests as well. Annette and I giggled like mad, and I felt as glamorous as the ladies in the posters by the time we said good-bye.

When I showed up at the factory a few hours later, though, Matt looked up from the steamers. Then he started convulsing with laughter while he waved his hand in front of his nose.

I was aghast. Despite the enormous clouds of steam, he could still smell me.

I doubled back to the bathroom and scrubbed off as much as I could but it was impossible to remove it all. When I approached Ma at our workstation, she said, "*Ay yah, ah*-Kim! What have you done?"

"Annette had a bottle of new perfume with her. She let me try some."

"Some! You must have taken a bath in it!" Luckily, Ma didn't pursue it any further.

But that night, as I bent over my books, I could still smell the lingering perfume on my clothes and wrists, and I felt surrounded by the warmth of Annette's friendship, by her confidence in me. I wondered if that had been her plan all along.

I'd gotten my working papers and Mr. Jamali gave me extra hours at the library. I was actually paid for this time since my work was beyond what I was required to do for my scholarship. I made sure I only filled up some of my free time slots during the day so I could help Ma at the factory as much as possible after school. I had opened a bank account in Ma's name and we put everything extra there for college.

I had mostly lost my interest in makeup. It wasn't that my looks didn't concern me, because they did, but I just couldn't fathom ever being popular or beautiful. I didn't understand how that all worked. No matter what colors Annette put on my face, I realized I was still the same underneath. I was also so busy, working at the library and the factory, trying to keep up in my classes, doing papers and homework and tests. Even aside from the upcoming oral exam, I was always worried I would come across something I couldn't handle. If I didn't understand an assignment or a topic in class, Ma couldn't help me. She had never been good at school, only in music, and with the added confusion of the different methods and language here, it became impossible for her to be useful. Ma had told me that Pa had been a brilliant student, with a talent for both languages and science, and that I'd gotten my intelligence from him. I used to take comfort from that, but now I just wished he were here to help me.

All I wanted was to have a break from the exhausting cycle of my life, to flee from the constant anxiety that haunted me: fear of my teachers, fear at every assignment, fear of Aunt Paula, fear that we'd never escape. In the library one day, I picked up *Car and Driver* instead. Paging through the photos of glossy convertibles, I felt something open up in my head. Car and motorcycle magazines became my escape. I wanted just to ride a Corvette into the wild night and not have to fill out the income taxes for Ma, not have to be responsible for everything that was in English. I was always afraid I had done something wrong and an inspector would appear at our door, demanding answers to questions I didn't even understand.

One day at the library, I was leafing through an old copy of *Cycle* that Mr. Jamali had given me. An article about a particular motorcycle caught my eye. I didn't understand at first why this model seemed so familiar but then I recognized the Indian head on the gas tank. It matched the toy replica Park always kept with him.

Later that afternoon at the factory, I looked for Park. He'd wandered away from his mother again, as he often did, but as long as he didn't cause anyone else any trouble, people tended to ignore him. He was standing next to one of the sewing machine ladies, staring at the spinning wheel at the end of her machine. He seemed hypnotized by its whirring. As usual, he was holding his Indian motorcycle.

"Scares me to death," the sewing lady said to the one sitting next to her, never pausing in her work. Each piece of clothing was a blur as it raced through her machine. "Wish he'd find someone else to watch."

"As long as it's not me." The other lady laughed.

"Glad I don't have a boy like that. He has the white disease." She was calling Park retarded. I felt annoyed at her remark, but then wondered if Park could actually have a deeper problem than simply not being able to hear.

It was more to startle them than anything else that I called, "Park, I have an article on your motorcycle."

To my surprise, he turned around with an eager look on his face. Both sewing ladies froze.

"Here," I said.

He grabbed the magazine, brought it inches away from his face and turned it around and around, rotating it around the picture of the bike.

I gently pried the article out of his hands and read him the beginning:

"The 1934 Indian Chief is a true classic, featuring Indian's famous headdress logo on the gas tank. The company's enormous factory in Springfield was called the Wigwam. . . ."

When I finished reading, both Park and the ladies were staring at me. Whispering to each other, the ladies turned back to their sewing. I handed the magazine to Park.

"Matt can read you the rest later." I waited to see if he would respond.

A slow smile started in the corner of his mouth.

It took time to cross his face, as if he wasn't used to smiling much. He looked almost handsome, and very much like Matt.

I went back to work but over the last few months, I'd become constantly alert to where Matt was. When he was on his way to the bathroom this time, I saw Park intercept him and show him the magazine. They flipped through some of the pages together.

An hour or so later, Matt came up to me, dripping with sweat. "Thanks. Where'd you get it? Can I pay you for it?"

"From school. Don't worry, they gave it to me for free."

"Wow. They must like you a lot."

"Mmm." I stared at the floor, then up at him. "I'm not so sure."

"Oh?"

"They think I'm sending out the cat." Cheating.

He raised his thick eyebrows. "You? What's wrong with them?"

I smiled at his faith in me. "How do you know I'm without crime?"

"No bad-hearted person could be as nice to Park as you are." Matt looked at me through his lashes.

I flushed. To change the subject, I asked him the question that had been on my mind all day. "Why do you pretend he's deaf?"

He coughed. "I don't know what you're talking about, Kimberly."

I persisted. "Are you just covering up?"

"What?"

"That he doesn't talk. Or that he can't talk."

There was a pause. "Never heard him talk. Not even when he was little. Only sounds." His golden eyes were sad. "Should've been me. I could have handled it better."

"Being born like that?"

He nodded. We weren't just talking about being deaf or dumb. Park's problems were clearly much bigger. I was touched that Matt let me know this. I also understood why they tried to disguise Park's limitations. In Chinese culture then, having a disability in the family tainted the entire group, as if it were contagious.

"You could take it better? You don't seem so tough to me," I said, ribbing him. I knew this kind of talk would snap Matt out of his melancholy.

He grinned. "And what about you, then?"

From then on, Matt still signed to Park in front of other people but not me. I slowly learned some of Park's signs, so that I could understand most of what he wanted to say to me. There was something restful about him. Now that I'd made contact with him, he didn't completely ignore me the way he did most people, and the truth was, I was glad to have someone who liked the same things I did. I could babble away at him about motor sizes and cylinders and he always nodded, as if my talking pleased him, even though he often didn't meet my eyes. I often brought my car and motorcycle magazines to the factory after that and I showed them to Park, pointing out the ones I wanted the most.

A shipment needed to go out at the factory the night before my big oral exam, so we didn't get home until past two a.m. I stayed up the rest of the night studying and didn't sleep at all. Wrapped over many layers of clothing, I wore a robe made of the stuffed animal material, which Ma continued to recycle as I grew. There was only Ma's sleeping body to give me comfort and the night was damp, filled with the taste of my own fear. Beyond the circle of my lamp was only darkness. I found myself close to despair that night but far from slumber.

"You shouldn't have come to the factory with me," Ma's voice, clogged with sleep, came from the depths of the mattress. Then a pause. "I shouldn't have let you come. Your exam tomorrow is too important."

"You couldn't have finished without me."

"Let me make you some tea."

"Ma, I really need to study. Go back to sleep."

The next morning, my entire body was trembling as I stood in front of the blackboard on a stage. Dr. Copeland and the rest of the science and math faculty sat in the first two rows. The rest of the room was empty. The rounded backs of the vacant chairs formed a field of doubt before me. I felt as if I were a scarecrow in a high wind. At any moment, I could be blown out of balance, all of the pieces that composed me would scatter and I would wake to find nothing left of myself, nothing left of the person I wanted to be. I knew my lack of sleep would affect my concentration. What if I floundered now and led them to think that I'd actually been cheating all along?

A man in a blue shirt stood up. He wasn't one of my teachers but I recognized him as an upper-grade chemistry teacher. He approached me and silently handed me a copy of the periodic table. He stared intently over his glasses.

Finally, he spoke. "Good morning, Kimberly. Could you please tell us how you would write the formulas of the ionic compounds formed by the following elements: nickel and sulfur, lithium and oxygen, and bismuth and fluorine?"

I took a deep breath. Although I had read about how to predict formulas of ionic compounds, I had never actually done it before. "May I have some paper?"

"The blackboard would be fine." He gestured toward the chalk.

I picked up a piece in my shaking hand and started writing on the board.

At the end of the long session, there was a silence, and then slowly, the teachers started to clap. Startled, I stood frozen in front of the blackboard, the front of my blazer covered in white chalk dust, until the chairperson of the program stood up and strode over to me. She was flushed with excitement.

"I'm afraid I've misjudged you, Kimberly," she said, extending her hand. We shook and then, smiling broadly, she said, "Thank you for the lesson. I'm delighted we have such a brilliant student at our school."

Instead of skipping me one year ahead in the accelerated science and math program, they decided to let me skip two.

"I have to give my pa something today. You want to see where he works?" Matt asked. His face had suddenly appeared in front of me at the factory, floating above a maze of cream-colored shirts.

"Sure," I answered, surprised. Hadn't Matt told me that his father was dead?

I made an excuse to Ma that I had homework and left early. This wasn't something I normally would do, but the temptation of being with Matt for a few hours was too much.

"What about you?" I asked.

Leaving early was easier for Matt. Now that he worked the steamers, he was treated as a grown-up. He could come and go as he pleased as long as he fulfilled the tremendous daily quota. That often meant working late, like Ma and me.

"Don't worry about me, I have it covered," he said.

I took that to mean he'd have to come back to work late into the evening but I simply shrugged. The fabric dust had accumulated on my jacket and book bag, which I kept inside a plastic bag on the work counter. At the end of every work shift, I had to shake long strands of filth off the bag before I could get my things out.

Matt met me downstairs wearing a light jacket and holding a cargo bike. The large wooden box attached to the back of the bike was painted green. "Antonio's Pizza," it said in curly letters that grew out of the glossy mustache of a beaming Italian man.

"Where did you get this?" I asked.

"My other job. Bet you didn't know I had so many talents."

"How do you have time to work as a delivery boy? I mean, with school and all."

"Aw, school doesn't take up much time," he said, staring at his steering wheel. I realized he was cutting school for his other job. I was sure his ma didn't know.

He swung his leg over the bike and waited for me. "Get on."

I wasn't sure exactly where I could do such a thing, but the only choice seemed to be to climb onto the box behind him, which is what I did. Then I scooted around so that my legs dangled from either side of him, almost kicking him in the process, and carefully wrapped my hands around the underside of the bicycle seat. He started ped-aling and we were off with a lurch.

The bike swung as he gained momentum. Then he really started to race.

"You sure you don't want to hold on to me instead?" he asked. "It'd be safer."

"I'm okay," I breathed. I did desperately want to put my arms around him but I was already so aware of his body that shyness overwhelmed me at just the thought of it.

Gaps opened up for us in the solid wall of people on the street as they sprang back with fear when they saw us coming.

"You flying boy!" one woman yelled. A gang-ster, one of those kids that hung out on the streets, definitely not a compliment.

"You have the nose of a pig and slits for eyes too!" Matt called over his shoulder.

I was looking back at the woman apologetically when he swerved to avoid a delivery truck and we bumped onto the curb, pedestrians leaping out of our way; then we were in the street again. He seemed to slow down by the Chinese American Bank, and I wondered if his father worked there. Then I saw he was just looking at a pretty girl in tight jeans. I hated her at that moment, and him too. But seconds later we were past and out of Chinatown, and the traffic was less congested.

As we zoomed up the Bowery, I tossed my hair back and started to relax. After all of my dreams of traveling at high speed, this was the closest I'd come. Everything passed behind us, the wind streamed through our clothes and I wasn't even cold, thrilled as I was at being close to Matt. The late-afternoon sun shone on my upturned face. Ahead of us, a pigeon spiraled upward between the concrete buildings, its wings extended as it headed for the sky.

He turned back to look at me. "You scared?"

"You trying to scare me?" I felt I was glowing, all of my happiness emanating for the world to see.

He grinned and turned back around. "Nah, you're not going to hold on to me anyway. You have one big gall bladder." He meant I was brave.

Finally, he slowed down by an alleyway. I knew we were still in Manhattan because we hadn't crossed a bridge, but where we were exactly, I didn't know. We stopped by one of the abandoned buildings, then Matt held the bike still while I climbed off. A homeless man and his shopping cart sat sprawled a few doorways away. Everything was boarded up, but from the upper floors, I could hear a baby wailing. Laundry fluttered from the fire escapes and the chatter of Spanish drifted in the wind. I was breathing shallowly, trying to avoid the stink of urine and car exhaust, but I wound up with their taste in my mouth instead. It looked like my neighborhood.

Then he went down a few steps to the doorway of an abandoned storefront. That sunken area served as a collection point for trash, and he had to kick away an empty can and a pile of what looked like toilet paper before he could get to the door. The glass window was completely covered by yellowing newspapers. I followed him down the stairs and stood next to him. When I peered more closely at the writing, I saw it was made up of Chinese characters.

He rapped out a drumbeat on the door, obviously some kind of code. The whole building looked so forsaken that I was still surprised when a tiny corner of newspaper was peeled back and a pair of eyes gleamed in the darkness.

"Wu, it's your kid," a man's voice said.

The door was unlatched and we went in. I felt curiosity and anticipation but no fear, maybe because I was with Matt. The back of a man was disappearing down the murky hallway. The hallway was cramped and made even more so by the boxes piled high on either side, and in an alcove, a dark stairway led upward to nowhere. A bicycle tire, twisted and bent, leaned on top of a heap of magazines.

"From your last bike?" I murmured to Matt.

He gave a snort of laughter and we followed the man into a crowded room. It looked like it had once been a bar. The air was thick with smoke, and a group of Chinese men gathered around a card table piled high with cash. The bills were worn but lay on top of one another in neat stacks, except for the large mound in the middle of the table. The men had made sure that the room was entirely invisible to the outside world by boarding up every window, though tiny cracks of sunlight squeezed past the slits and caught the tarnished bronze of the barstools.

And in the yellow glow of the few dangling lightbulbs, Matt was watching me as if to ask if it was okay that he'd brought me there. By showing me his father in such a sordid place, he was letting down his face, which told me I was as close to him as anyone could be. I gave him a little nod. He seemed satisfied and turned away.

By this time, the men had seen me. "This isn't a tourist stop," one man said.

"She's with me." Matt had unfolded a chair in a corner behind the table. He let me sit down and stood next to me, shielding me from the rest of the room.

I had seen so much money on the table in front of me that when I breathed in I thought I could smell its acidic odor underneath the blue cloud of smoke.

"Here, have something to drink, kids," the man behind the bar said, and he slid two open beers toward us.

Matt took them and gave me one. I'd never had alcohol before. I took a swig. The taste was bitter and made my eyes water, but I managed not to show my distaste. After my initial swallow, I sipped only a little from the bottle. Matt drank as if he did it all the time.

The men returned to their game. They had glasses of liquor in their hands and more cards were thrown onto the table. Matt went up to the man sitting in front of us and tapped his shoulder. So this had to be Matt's father. His father turned but seemed annoyed at being interrupted in his game. Then Matt handed him a thin envelope from inside his jacket. To my surprise, his father opened it, gave a satisfied nod and immediately added the contents to his pile of money on the table: it was more cash. Then he dismissed Matt by pushing him away with the back of his hand. There had been no greeting, no thank you.

Matt's shoulders were hunched when he returned to me. He didn't meet my eyes. I stood up and gave his arm a squeeze. Then, to cover up this impulsive gesture, I pulled him down into my recently vacated chair.

I said, "You sit down. I want to see better."

From this vantage point, I could observe the cards they were laying on the table. My head began to whirl from the alcohol and the smoke, but I was fascinated by the Chinese game they were playing, unlike any I had seen in the West. When I stared long enough, it seemed to me I could begin to make out a pattern to the cards.

After some time, the phone rang and the barman said, "*Ah*-Wu, it's for you."

Matt's father stood up and the barman tossed him the phone, attached to the wall with a long black cord. He paced back and forth as he spoke and I could see his face well for the first time. It was clear where Matt had gotten his looks. His father was handsome, the heavy eyebrows adding a touch of demonic charm to features that would otherwise be too fine for a man. And there was a reckless air to him, a carelessness in the way he swung his arms, as if he could break everything in the room and wouldn't care. His suit had once been expensive, I could see that, and he had bothered to shine his shoes. I wondered what Matt had learned from a man like this. It couldn't have been anything good.

"Louisa," he said, "I'm running late. Don't worry, honey, I'll be there real soon. No, don't worry, no gambling." He gave his friends a wink as he said it.

At my questioning look, Matt said with a kind of defiance, "His girlfriend. He lives with her."

I saw then that the money Matt had given his father hadn't come from his mother. It must have been from Matt's salary, probably what he made from his delivery job, the one he was cutting school for. I understood. I too would have done anything to protect Ma, and forgiven her any sin. Perhaps my feelings showed in my eyes because Matt quickly looked away again, as if he couldn't bear to see my pity.

When Matt's father walked back to his seat, where the other men were waiting for him, he seemed to see me for the first time. He turned and waved his cards in front of my face. "What would you play, huh, girlie? Ladies' luck."

The noisy chatter at the table ground to a halt. "Ladies' luck."

"Pa, leave her out of this," Matt said, standing up.

"It's all right," I said to him. I knew luck had nothing to do with it. I would have chosen statistical probabilities over luck any day. Without hesitation, I pointed to the queen of spades and the seven of diamonds.

"Really," said Matt's father thoughtfully. "Strange, strange. But maybe . . . if . . ."

He withdrew those two cards slowly from his hand and threw them on the table. There was a sudden roar from the others and a few of them glared at me. When the upheaval was over, Matt's father scooped up the rest of the money on the table.

He was grinning from ear to ear, revealing a tooth capped with gold. He took a sip of his drink and came over to us again. He reached out and clumsily patted me on the head, as if I were a dog.

"This," he said, "this is a great girl. This is a girl deserving of old Wu's son."

Even though this comment had come from a drunken gambler, I felt like it was a benediction of sorts. Matt seemed proud, but he also shifted his weight from leg to leg, as if he didn't know if we should make a run for it or not before the other men began.

And indeed, the chorus started immediately. "Come sit with us," they said. "We want to do some winning too."

"No, she stays with me." Matt was still only fifteen then, but he stood up in front of me and faced the whole group of gamblers. I was close enough that I could feel him tremble slightly. For the first time, I began to feel afraid, and then someone started to laugh.

"Okay, but bring her again. We can always use some luck."

Matt never took me there again, but I think it was because I had seen what he'd wanted me to see. He had shown me his shameful secret, and I had accepted it. It seemed a kind of turning point for us, a promise of trust and openness, and maybe even love.

This was before the girl started showing up.

TEN

By tenth grade, I was one of the best students, despite my continued disadvantage in English. Unlike the other kids, I hid my test scores immediately and never spoke about them.

Annette was my source of information. She told

me on the phone one evening, "You would not believe the things they say about you. I heard Julia Williams telling this other girl that you never sleep and you never study."

It was true that I didn't manage to sleep much, but I couldn't imagine how Julia Williams, a girl with tight golden ringlets, could possibly know that. My only opportunities to do homework at the factory were snatched during the brief breaks and on the subway, and we usually arrived at home after nine o'clock. By the time I got my homework done, I was so exhausted that I dropped straight onto my mattress and went to sleep.

There was a pause on the line and I could hear the low rumbling of static. "How *do* you do it?"

"Do what?"

"The way you are in class. And like that last history test—I know you hardly studied for it. I mean, the day before the test, you hadn't even read the chapters yet."

I stared down at my hands. "I don't know. It's like being born with an extra head or something."

But in a way, now that my English was fairly fluent, I didn't find my academic achievements to be so remarkable. I simply did what the teachers assigned as best I could and regurgitated what I had learned on the tests. Sometimes I had to do all the preparation at the last moment because I had no choice, but I always got it done. School was my only ticket out and just being in this privileged school wasn't enough; I still needed to win a full scholarship to a prestigious college, and to excel there enough to get a good job.

In tenth grade, I enrolled in AP classes, even though they were generally for juniors and seniors. Later, at the end of the year, I would receive the top score, a 5, on all of my exams. For this kind of thing, the other Harrison kids looked at me with mingled respect and jealousy, but not with what I longed for, which was friendship. Despite Annette's presence, I was lonely. I wanted to be a part of things, but I didn't know how.

My skin was now clear and Ma had finally let me grow my hair out. I was a perfect size six and I could take samples from the factory, which made my attire less noticeably inadequate. But my obligations to Ma and the factory didn't allow room for social ambitions. And even if they had, I was perceived as—or I really was—too serious. I never went to parties or dances.

On the rare occasions when I was invited somewhere, I made excuses without even trying to ask Ma for permission. I kept a deliberate distance from the other girls because I knew it would inevitably lead to an invitation to their house, and I wouldn't be able to go. I already snuck off once in a while to see Annette; I couldn't fit anyone else in.

And at least I had Annette, who understood and accepted the things I couldn't do, even if she had no idea of the true details of my life. She often came to the library when I was working there and had become a great admirer of Mr. Jamali. In private, she'd go on and on to me about how incredibly wise and beautiful he was. Annette's likes were always intense. Her crushes were fleeting and left no real imprint upon her heart. She'd even had an interest in Curt, who had broken up with Sheryl over the summer. For a period of about two weeks, Annette had raved about how artistic he was, how creative and free. Sometime in the last year, he had stopped wearing his neat designer clothes and now went around in worn cotton trousers and old T-shirts underneath his blue blazer. But a few months after the crush began, she found him boring because too many other girls liked him too. All of this happened without any actual interaction with Curt himself, of course. For Annette, a crush was an activity more than a feeling, and she liked it best when I pretended to like the same boy she did so we could talk about him together, much the way other kids shared a passion for a hobby like baseball.

I didn't mind. I enjoyed pretending to have more of a normal life when I talked to Annette. It allowed me the luxury of imagining I was richer and better off than I actually was. It was also too hard to tell someone how we lived when there was so little chance of change. We had long ago given up the idea that Aunt Paula would do anything to improve our situation. We were still paying off our debt to her, which left little money to spare. We could barely afford the things I needed to buy, like new shoes when I grew out of my old ones. Our only hope was when the building would actually be condemned and she would have to move us out.

In my other life, I could feel the buzz of Matt's presence whenever he was at the steamers, whenever he went to take a break. He seemed to walk around in a halo of light. It was as if every excruciating detail of his face, his hands, his clothing was imprinted upon my mind.

I once made the mistake of saying to him, "Your pants look different."

"What are you talking about?" he asked.

"I don't know, something about the way they fit," I faltered, realizing I was getting onto unstable ground.

He looked at me strangely, then said, "Actually, if you have to know, it's probably because I'm not wearing any underwear today."

I laughed awkwardly, as if it were a joke and I were the sort of girl who could laugh casually at such things, but the truth was, I was secretly an expert on Matt's ass and I'm quite sure he was telling the truth. I never did dare to ask the reason for the omission, although I imagine it was because he'd run out of clean underwear.

On the rare occasions when Park, Matt and I had

some extra time, we would gather for a few precious moments outside. One day, when I came downstairs, I saw Park fixing the chain on Matt's cargo bike while Matt watched.

Matt shrugged. "What can I say, I've got slippery hands." Clumsy ones. He hastened to add, "My body has heavenly skills, though."

These half-flirtatious remarks of Matt's thrilled me, but they also made me even more uncomfortable around him than I already was. I pretended I hadn't heard his comment about his body and bent over the wheel next to Park. Park had good hand skills, dexterous hands, and he refitted and tightened the chain in a very short time.

"Will you teach me how to do that sometime?" I asked Park.

As usual, Park didn't meet my eyes, but he nodded. I smiled and patted his arm.

"If you two mechanics are finished," Matt said, "can I have my bike back before the pizza place goes out of business? It's hard enough for a bunch of Italians in Chinatown anyway."

In many ways, I had an easier relationship with Park than with Matt. On the surface, Matt and I were friends and I lived for the moments when we could talk or laugh, no matter how briefly. My feelings were so intense that I associated being close to him with a tightness in my breathing. I was always careful to preserve the space between us, as if he were something forbidden, from which

I needed to keep my distance. When he brushed against me, I would move my entire body away as if I'd been stung and what made it worse was that Matt seemed to enjoy touching me, often laying a hand on my back or arm. In a way, I think I was afraid that if the distance between us were bridged, I would be swept away from all I had worked for, everything that I was.

I was a fool. I should have grabbed him when I could have had him all to myself, snatched him up like a ripe mango at the market. But how was I to know that this was what love felt like?

One day, she was there, waiting for Matt outside the factory, and she was everything I was not. It was the flirtatious skirts and the perfect finger-nails, the melting look in the eyes that said, "Save me." It was the flick of her glossy black hair that tossed the scent of wildflowers into the wind. Ah, her hair was short but it only lengthened her graceful neck, swept forward to point at her perfect lips. Even now, I want to remember her as a femi-nine doll, manipulating him with her weakness, but the truth is that Vivian used to smile with gen-uine warmth whenever she saw me, even though other girls sneered at my cheap clothes. Let me be even more honest: when I say she was everything I was not, I mean that she possessed whatever virtues I may have had and more.

I made it my business to find out how they'd

met. According to the gossip at the factory, her father was a tailor from Singapore, one of the best, and he owned a small shop, specializing in custom-made, expensive clothes, down the street from Matt's apartment. Vivian helped out there and somehow, she'd been standing outside often enough when Matt passed by that they'd gotten to know each other. Of course, I suspected her of planting herself in his path on purpose, but who can blame her?

At the beginning, she was an inch or two taller than Matt. With the passage of time, she dwindled as he grew, until he stood over her with his new broad body and large hands, an arm slung protectively over her delicate shoulder. Matt was as kind to me as he'd ever been, but there was a new absentmindedness to him, as if a part of him was always with her. I would watch them walking away together, away from me, and ache with regret.

Curt broke his left leg skiing in January of tenth grade, when I had just turned sixteen. He had to have surgery before he could fly back and was stuck in Austria for several weeks. We'd hardly spoken after that incident with Tammy in eighth grade, when he'd defended me to Dr. Copeland, although we did continue to have some classes together. Curt had been much too busy being cool, as he began to fulfill his promise of becoming someone special. He made paintings and polished wooden sculptures that our Art department made a great deal of fuss over. Last year, he'd been featured in the Visual Arts Festival. And he was attractive, even I had to admit that, with a smoldering quality in the way he moved. I had seen even our Latin teacher blushing when she spoke to him.

One evening that winter, our phone at home rang. It was close to nine-thirty p.m. and I was sure it was Annette, but when I picked up, it turned out to be Curt. His voice was deep. I was so surprised he had called me that I didn't even ask him how his leg was.

"Listen, Kimberly, I'm back in the U.S. but I'm not even allowed to get out of bed for another month. The truth is, I'm on the verge of flunking out anyway, and now that I can't come to school at all for a while, I'm sunk unless you help me."

"I didn't think you were doing that badly."

"My grades are borderline, but then I've had a few other scrapes as well. Remember the fire alarm someone pulled, right before Christmas break?"

"Was that you?" It had caused a huge commotion: the buildings evacuated, fire engines and squad cars on campus, all classes canceled, students and faculty standing shivering outside for hours.

"Yeah. They were ready to kick me out but my

255

parents did their best. I had to write a letter of apology and swear to maintain a B minus average and be a good boy from now on. Which I'm trying to do, but now my neck's on the line."

I asked him the question that had been on my mind since the phone call had begun. "Why me? Anybody would be glad to help you."

"Come on, Kimberly. No one's smarter than you. I need serious help here. My folks are already threatening to send me to boarding school."

I agreed to give him my notes from the classes we shared, couriered daily by his little brother. They were copied and I got them back the next day. I saw other kids delivering notes to his brother too, probably for his classes in math and science. Once in a while, Curt phoned me with questions about any of his subjects. I don't know if he ever tried calling earlier in the evening, but the calls I received came quite late at night, as if he'd been waiting for me to be home. He never asked me what I'd been doing earlier in the day, which I appreciated. Even though I was a few years ahead of him in science and math, I remembered the material and could explain the topics he was doing.

Although he could have, he didn't keep me private. When he finally returned to school on crutches, there was a rush to sign his cast, but he saved the most central spot for me. He openly sat next to me whenever he could, and in a way, I was brought into his sacred circle. I don't know if he did this mainly out of good manners or genuine appreciation. The end result was that I became accepted by the popular group, though still not liked. I had a kind of power that made other girls want to be seen with me but they were careful around me, tentative and distant. Nothing like Annette, who, amused by my sudden rise in status, remained my one true friend.

With my pseudo-popularity, there seemed to come a new awareness of me by the boys at school. Not every guy, of course. There were plenty who thought I was beneath their notice, but there were also always a handful who seemed to like being with me. I felt strangely relaxed with them. Now that Matt was gone from my life as a romantic interest, it was as if he had been the single repository of all my shyness, and with other boys, I was liberated.

The popular girls at school eyed the cheap factory samples I wore, and any warmth they showed me was far from genuine, but every weekend, after we got home from the factory, the phone would ring and it would be a boy. I would lean against the yellowing wall and twirl the long knotted cord around my fingers as we spoke—twirl, untwirl, twirl—and when I finally disentangled the cord from my hands and hung up the phone, it would ring again and it would be another boy. This drove

Ma crazy, especially if they phoned late in the evening. Talking to a boy on the phone was bad enough but doing it in the dark really crossed the line.

Ma's standard way of answering the phone became "Kimberly not home" and then hanging up. She spent her time pacing around me, calling loudly, "Dinnertime! Dinnertime!" which was pretty much the only other word she had learned in English. Ma was particularly anxious because she couldn't understand what the boys and I were talking about, but she needn't have worried. The calls were all about inconsequential things like homework, motorcycles, mean teachers.

I didn't consider myself pretty at all. With time, I had grown too long-limbed and skinny for Chinese tastes, and despite Annette's best efforts, the intricacies of makeup and clothing remained incomprehensible to me. I was not beautiful and I was not funny, nor was I a good buddy or a particularly good listener. I was none of the things that girls think they need to be for boys to love them. Mostly, I stayed on the call with my eyes closed, listening to the thrum of the phone line underneath our words. I knew what these boys really wanted—freedom. Freedom from their parents, from their own unsurprising selves, from the heavy weight of the expectations that had been placed upon them. I knew because it was what I wanted too. Boys weren't my enemy, they were co-conspirators in a mission to flee. My secret was acceptance.

At school during my free periods, I spent a lot of time taking walks hand in hand with boys. We would walk and we would make out. This was exactly what Ma had warned me not to do with boys, which only made it more fun. I was forced to be responsible in so many other ways that I was glad to have the freedom over my own body. I could only go so far—there's only so much you can do in fifty minutes on school property—but the boys didn't seem to mind much.

"I don't know how you stay so detached," said Annette. "Don't you ever fall in love?"

The fact was, I didn't worry about these boys the way other girls did. The details of whether a particular boy called or not, of an invitation to a dance or a party or a movie, didn't matter to me. Despite my own strange access to the popular crowd, I didn't care if a boy was popular or not, a good athlete or not. Of course, I did have a slight preference for a smart boy, sometimes a handsome boy, but I could also be won over by a certain shy way of smiling or even the shape of their hands. The boys at Harrison Prep were merely a dream to me: delightful and delicious but evanescent. The blistering reality was the deafening thunder of sewing machines at the factory, the fierce sting of cold against my skin in our unheated apartment. And Matt. Despite Vivian, Matt was real too.

• • •

Even though Curt was now back at school, we still met once a week for me to tutor him in whatever he needed. The subject was usually math, at which he was atrocious. The school scholarship program counted this as working time for me, so I was initially glad to do it. As Curt emerged from the immediate danger of failing out, however, he reverted to his old ways. Sometimes he came to our sessions with a joint in his hand. And stoned or not, he never missed an opportunity to flirt with me. I didn't take him seriously because I'd seen him doing the same with other girls. I understood he was just practicing.

There was quite a bit of swooning over his eyes, which were a startling dark blue with a glimpse of white in their depths, but I found them to be too empty to be intriguing. He was not interested in math or most of his other subjects at all, and was hardly ever prepared when we met, which annoyed me. A few times, he was late or didn't come at all. I learned that when he was working on a piece of sculpture, he forgot about the time. Curt had taken over a corner of the enormous room used for Shop and he had a pile of wood pieces there that he worked on endlessly.

Finally I asked him, "Why do you bother coming, Curt?"

He raised his eyebrows flirtatiously. "Don't you know?"

"Maybe another tutor would be better for you. Someone stricter." I hated feeling like I was wasting my time.

Now he looked alarmed. "No. I like you. Sometimes I even understand stuff after you talk about it."

"It should not be sometimes, it should be all the time. You don't listen very well."

"Yes, I do. And for me, sometimes is really good."

"All you do is flirt with me. I would like it more if you just do your homework."

"Sorry about that. It's kind of a habit. And you have such great legs."

I glared at him and he immediately added, "Oops, did it again. I'll try, okay?"

After our talk, Curt did improve. He stopped coming stoned and he was usually punctual. Most of the time, he still hadn't done his homework but at least he seemed to make a real effort to listen more. I realized that he was intelligent; it was only that he didn't care for school. He was my complete opposite.

I found that he was more present in his workspace and I started trying to have more of our meetings there. He made abstract carvings out of separate pieces of wood that he glued together and then polished. I was walking around one piece that looked almost like the simplified Chinese character for water, a vertical stroke in the middle with two wings on the sides.

"This is beautiful, but why do you not ever sculpt something from real life?" I asked.

He wiggled his eyebrows at me. "If you'd pose for me, maybe I would."

He saw my annoyed expression and sighed. "Believe it or not, some girls like it when I say things like that." Then his face turned serious. "Because when something is not realistic, it becomes a container for whatever you want it to be. Like a word or a symbol or a vase. You can pour anything you want into it."

I hated the idea of so much choice. "But that means it's empty by itself."

"That's the beauty of it. There doesn't have to be any meaning."

"I cannot live a life without a purpose."

He looked at me. "You don't care about superficial things, do you?"

"Like what?"

"Money, clothing."

I had to laugh. "Yes, I do. I need to."

"No, you don't, not really. I've been watching you—you don't even notice what the other girls are doing."

"You think that because my clothing is different from theirs. It is actually only because I do not understand what they are doing." It felt good to admit this to someone. "I wish I could look like them!" An image of the lovely Vivian flashed across my mind. "But I don't know how."

"Because you don't really care. Even if you could, tell me you would really spend your free time in front of a mirror trying to make your eyelashes look longer?"

I was silent.

He continued. "You'd be too busy inventing something to save the world."

"Just because I am better at math than you are does not make me into a paragon of virtue."

"That's what I mean."

"What?"

"Where did you learn that—I mean, did you hear someone say 'paragon of virtue' at home or something?"

I paused. "I memorized it from a book."

"See?"

"Don't they talk like that at your home?"

"Actually, they do. I'm the son of two editors—my parents talk like that all the time, God help me."

"So how come you didn't think they'd do that at my home?"

"Do they?"

I looked away. "No." To change the subject, I started talking about his sculptures again. "But I do wonder if you could make something real. It is very difficult."

Curt didn't answer but the next week, he had made a small carving of a swallow. I immediately saw it lying next to his usual sculptures.

"This is wonderful," I said.

"You like it?" His eyes were a bright, warm blue. "You can have it, if you want."

"Oh no," I said quickly. I had been trained by Ma not to be beholden to anyone. "Someday this will be worth a lot of money. I cannot take it."

The light in his eyes was quenched then but it was already time for us to start our tutoring session anyway.

In eleventh grade, Annette fell in love with the theater. It started when she was at the library, visiting me, and talking about Simone de Beauvoir.

"She's writing about how women are excluded when they're seen as the mysterious Other and how that has led to our male-dominated society. People from different races and cultures can also be classified that way and it has always been done by the group in power." Annette gestured with her hands, as she always did when she was passionate about something.

Mr. Jamali had come up behind me. "Look at her, her gestures. Everything is so big, so dramatic. You should be onstage."

"Really?" Annette put her hands on her hips, thinking. "I never thought about it."

"Tryouts are in two weeks. You could explore

your relationship with otherness by being yourself and yet not-you in a role."

That was enough to pique Annette's interest. Although she only started in small roles, I saw that Mr. Jamali was right: she did have a certain flair onstage. Her flamboyant hair and her passionate, questioning nature combined to make her compelling under the spotlight. Mr. Jamali said she had a great deal of talent but it needed to be channeled and refined.

He was always there in his beautiful embroidered tunics, saying, "Very good, that was almost perfect. Now, shall we see it again, with just a bit more restraint, yet losing none of our intensity?"

I was filled with pride when I sat in the darkened theater and watched Annette rehearsing. Since the actual performances were often in the late afternoons or evenings, I never got to see her perform otherwise.

Nelson was on the debate team of his school, and since he was sure to be so good in competition, we'd been invited to come admire him as well. We were all crammed into their minivan together. Ma and I sat in the rear-most row of seats, but we could hear everything that was going on in the front of the car.

"It's my nicest shirt," Uncle Bob said. He'd put on a silk shirt for the occasion. "I brought it back from China. I was just trying to—"

"You're going to embarrass me in front of my friends," Nelson said.

"Yeah," Godfrey, who was now thirteen, piped up. "What a stupid shirt."

"You look gay," Nelson said. "You look like a pimp."

Finally, we had to turn the car around and go home so Uncle Bob could change. Nelson also made Aunt Paula take off her gold jewelry because he said gold was tacky, especially Chinese twenty-four-carat gold.

"Ah, the children develop their own taste," Aunt Paula said. "What about you, Kimberly? You must have many extracurricular activities too?"

"I don't have time," I said.

"What a pity. They're so important for colleges."

Aunt Paula still believed that I was doing as badly as I had been at the beginning of Harrison Prep. Ma and I had never corrected this impression, since it seemed to lessen Aunt Paula's anger and jealousy.

"And how are you doing on your standardized tests?"

"Fine." I was doing well but Ma, on the other hand, had failed the naturalization exam, as we'd both known she would.

Before we left their apartment again, Nelson looked Ma's simple clothes up and down. He opened his mouth to comment.

I stood in front of her and said in English, "Don't even think about it, Nelson."

"What?" he said.

"Just don't." And he didn't.

I saw that his private school on Staten Island was much smaller than Harrison. Nelson seemed to shrink once he was onstage, becoming a red-faced, shy boy. His debating team lost.

It should have been obvious that the oven wouldn't be able to take the constant abuse of being on morning and night, winter after winter, but it was still a great shock when it finally broke. The cold crept in over the floor, freezing the water in the toilet, thickening the layer of ice over the inside of the windows. Ma and I huddled together on her mattress for warmth the whole night long, with everything we owned heaped on top of us.

Ma called a man recommended by one of the button-sewing ladies. He was cheap, he worked under the table, and the lady said he had some kind of certification for his work from China, which told me he didn't have any here.

The man's dirty shirt and overalls were too big for him, as if they'd been stolen. He dragged his toolbox across the floor, leaving a mark on the vinyl. I winced when I saw him bang on the control valve with his hammer. I knew it was a delicate piece of equipment. After a great deal of noise, which I believe was designed mainly to impress us with his exertion, he emerged from behind the oven to tell us that it was unfixable and his visit would cost us a hundred dollars.

"I don't have that much money here," Ma said, lifting her hand to her cheek.

At this, I spoke up. "You've made it much worse than it was! You are trying to beat on our leg bones!" He was trying to take advantage of us. Indeed, the stove had been dismembered and some of its entrails now rested in the kitchen sink.

He loomed over me. His accent was from the north of China. "I spent my time here, I want my money."

Ma tried to push me aside. "Let me handle this, Kimberly."

"Get away, kid," he said.

I was afraid Ma would cave in and agree to pay him later. I was sixteen and I had the confidence then of a teenager who'd had to act like an adult for too long. I didn't know enough to be afraid but I did know that I helped earn our money and I wasn't going to give it up so easily. A hundred dollars was 10,000 skirts, a fortune.

"You want your money, you show me your papers first," I said.

"For what?"

"Your passport, please."

At this, my implied threat, he seemed to swell up like a blowfish. "You want my papers?!"

I was standing close to the phone on the wall of

the kitchen and I strode over and grabbed the receiver. I started to dial Annette's number.

"Who are you calling?"

"The police."

His eyes were very still, wondering what he should do. I heard Annette's little brother pick up the phone on the other end.

"Hello," I said in English. "Could you please send someone over to house number—"

At this, the man grabbed his things and ran down the stairs, though not without one last baleful look at me. Time seemed suspended until we heard the door slam downstairs. Ma slumped into one of the chairs in relief.

"Wrong number," I said rapidly, and hung up, hoping Annette's brother hadn't recognized my voice.

"What a thief's head and thief's brain he had," Ma said weakly.

"With a wolf's heart and a dog's lungs." Untrustworthy and vicious. My heart was still leaping about like a frog in my chest.

At least he was gone. But the stove was still broken and temperatures were expected to be below freezing for the coming days.

ELEVEN

I called Brooklyn Union Gas, and a repairman was sent to our house. He was a heavyset African American man in a blue uniform that covered him from head to toe. The belt cut into his belly, and when he came in through the door, he looked around our apartment with pity in his teddy-bear eyes.

"I'm going to do my best for you folks, all right," he said, "but I can't promise nothing. That last guy really broke this thing up."

"Please," I said. I tried to keep the panic from my voice. "Please do your best." My breath came out in white puffs. I didn't know how we would even get through that night if he couldn't fix the oven. The apartment had grown steadily colder with every day the oven remained broken. It was already getting dark outside and I could hear the wind gusting against the walls.

"I know, honey," he said. "You and your mom just take it easy and I'll try to figure this out."

And he did. With his blunt fingers, he smoothed the pieces back into place and when the stove came to life again with a burst of blue flame, Ma clapped her hands from happiness.

She tried to give him a tip, only a dollar, but he folded the money gently back into her hand.

"You keep that," he said in his slow, deep voice. "You get something nice for yourselves."

I would have liked to have a man like that as my father.

Matt had dropped out of high school so he could work full-time. Now that he was working the entire day, he could often finish his work earlier and got to leave before we did. By then, I'd received special permission to take freshman and premed classes at Polytechnic University in Brooklyn. On the days when I had Polytech classes, which usually ended later in the afternoon, I sometimes saw Vivian waiting for him to leave when I had just arrived.

One spring day when I got to the factory in the early evening, Vivian was standing outside as usual, waiting for Matt to finish work. As was often the case, there was a group of Chinatown teenage boys huddled around her, and I was surprised to see one of them holding a large hanging plant. The acne-faced boy with the plant leaned toward Vivian and I saw the striped leaves sweep against her pretty cowboy boots. Then she murmured something to him and he immediately lifted the plant higher, so its leaves wouldn't brush against the sidewalk. Of course, the plant was hers and he was just holding it for her.

The guys were busy trying to impress Vivian and they paid me no notice. I could hear they were speaking English, to seem cooler.

"Hi, Kimberly," Vivian called as I approached the doorway.

"Hi," I said.

A few of the boys looked up but dismissed me and turned back to her.

The door opened and out stepped Park. Staring at the ground as usual, he didn't see me standing in front of the doorway and bumped into me behind. This set off the whole group of boys laughing. I saw that Park was wearing bright orange pants. His plaid shirt was buttoned wrong and it bunched up where it met his neck.

"Are you all right?" Vivian asked Park.

He didn't reply and just tried to walk on, past the group.

One of the teenage boys, who was wearing a red bandanna on his head, stepped out in front of him. Like an imitation of a gangster in a bad movie, the boy said in accented English, "Lady asked you a question." Then he switched into Chinese. "You, white disease."

"Don't call him that," I said.

"Who made you his keeper?" Red Bandanna said.

"It's not a problem," Vivian said to him. She had a smile plastered to her face. She seemed unsure of what to do.

The boy pushed Park again, no doubt thinking that this would win him points with her. "Say a word."

"Stop it," I said.

He kept shoving Park. "C'mon. The lady asked you something, now you answer her. C'mon." He punctuated each word with a push. Park's eyes were looking in every direction, bewildered and disoriented.

Vivian just stood there, frozen.

I stood in front of Red Bandanna. "Stop it!" I reached up and pulled the cloth off his head. His hair tumbled out in matted locks. "Least he's not so ugly that he's made of essence of monkey."

The whole gang laughed.

Underneath the wild strands of hair, he was red with fury. "Give that back!"

I tossed it in his face, then grabbed Park's arm. "Run!"

We'd already taken a few steps. Red Bandanna was just about to race after us when I looked back and saw him get jerked by the scruff of his neck. He was yanked around to face Matt, who had just come outside.

"What are you doing with my little brother when you don't even have a hole in your ass?" With his arms and fists clenched, Matt had swelled to twice his normal size, it seemed. He threw Red Bandanna to the ground, effortlessly.

"That your brother? Sorry, Matt, I didn't recognize him."

Now Matt pulled him off the floor again.

"You knew. You remains of a human being."

There was a chorus now from the other guys. "Take it easy, Matt. He was just starting a child's game, that's all, it was just a prank."

Matt looked like he wanted to hit him but instead, he dropped Red Bandanna abruptly onto the ground. "You're not worth planting." Matt meant he wasn't worth the effort.

Red Bandanna scrambled up off the floor and the whole group fled, leaving Vivian standing there, still looking apologetic.

By this time, Park and I had come back within a safe distance.

"You guys all right?" Matt bent down and picked up one of my barrettes, which had fallen onto the sidewalk when Park and I had tried to escape. Gently, he clipped it back in my hair. It seemed to me that his hand lingered a moment longer than was necessary. His look to Vivian was cool. I saw she was almost in tears.

"Vivian tried to get them to stop too," I said.

"Sure," Matt said. He was still breathing heavily; I could almost feel the adrenaline draining from his body. He glanced at the plant, which had been abandoned on the ground, and turned to Vivian. "Your admirer took off without giving you your plant back."

"Matt . . ." she said.

"Forget it," he said. He picked up the plant and swung an arm around her. "Come on," he said to Park, and the three of them left together.

Through the tall windows, the spring rain fell onto the trees in the distance. I was still tutoring Curt. Many of the kids were nervous about the upcoming standardized tests at the end of eleventh grade, and had already been enrolled in outside test courses for months. Curt's parents had pressured him to do the same, but he'd gotten them to agree to extra tutoring by me in his school subjects instead. My own preparation for the tests was going to consist of filling in a few sample exercises in the booklets I received with my registration form, since I didn't even have a book with practice tests.

We often met in the Art studio, where he spent so much time that the teachers allowed him to leave some of his work in the back. I'd gotten there early this lesson and was thinking about the upcoming SATs while I waited for him to be ready. I looked down at the studio floor, which was covered in paint splotches and wood shavings. I had to be careful not to step on the electric saw and sanding machine, which Curt often left lying around on the floor, still plugged in. The studio was filled with the smell of rain and cut wood and wallpaper glue.

Curt was using a paintbrush to smear a few pieces of wood with glue before our lesson started. He started telling me about a pair of shoes he'd found in the trash, which he was delighted to be wearing now.

"It is proof that serendipity does exist. They showed up just when I needed them." He fit the pieces of wood together carefully and used a clamp to hold them in place.

I studied the shoes, peeking out from under his faded jeans. They were brown work boots, heels worn down. "Did you clean them first?"

"Nope."

"It is not as fun to be poor as you think."

"I'm trying to cast off the trappings of a wasted life."

"Was it wasted? That your parents gave you a secure home?"

"They were both born with money. Trust-fund kid one marries trust-fund kid two."

"I always thought editors were smart and thoughtful."

"Nah. Well, maybe a little. What about your folks?"

"They married for love."

I was wandering around and I noticed he'd thrown his jacket carelessly onto an easel. A sleeve lay on the floor. I picked up the jacket and felt the fine weaving with my finger, then turned it over and stroked the paisley silk lining. I hung it so that it wasn't dragging on the floor.

Curt hadn't even noticed. He was washing his hands at a small sink in the corner, then wiped them on his shirt. "So, thanks to my smart and thoughtful parents, I'm giving a party. Can you come?"

"I don't think so," I said automatically. This was what I always said to these kinds of invitations, or whenever the boys I kissed tried to see me outside of school. "I'm very busy."

"Well, the party's a bit because of you. My parents are so happy I haven't flunked out yet. The party is meant to be positive psychological reinforcement before all the big tests hit."

"I don't know."

"I couldn't have done it without you. It's almost your party. You can think of it as an extra-long tutoring session."

I laughed. I was tempted. I'd never been to a party or a dance and this gave me an excuse for going. "Let me think about it."

I found Annette at the theater. In addition to her small role, she was also pitching in as the stage manager for the current production. She was on the stage, walking toward a sofa set with a cane in her hand.

"I need a longer one," she called to someone off-stage. She had tied her puffy hair back with a blue ribbon.

"Annette." I stood by the edge of the stage, feeling self-conscious under the bright lights.

"Hey!" She came forward and knelt by me so we could talk.

"Curt's invited me to a party. What should I do?"

Her eyebrows seemed to shoot up to her hair-line. "Are you thinking about going? Why? You never do!"

I started twisting the button on my blazer around. "I know. But I could. Not all the time. Just once."

"Oh, you like him!" Her voice was loud in the theater.

"Shh! No! He's just a friend. I guess it's a bad idea."

"No, I think it's great for you to go to a party! You need to get out more." Then she frowned. "But you never come to my plays or parties."

"I know." I sighed. I knew I was a difficult friend for Annette sometimes. This was why I always said no, because if I said yes once, I didn't know how I would handle any of the invitations after-ward. I could possibly convince Ma to let me go out at night once but not much more than that. It was just on impulse that I'd wanted to accept this invitation, and because he'd said that the party had something to do with me.

"Will you come to something of mine too?"

"I promise."

Annette and I made our plans. Ma would never let me go to a party given by a boy. I would tell Ma I was sleeping over at Annette's and then Annette and I would go together. I was sure it would be okay if she tagged along. I just needed to convince Ma.

Ma frowned. "Why do you suddenly want to sleep over at Annette's house?"

"Ma, I've always wanted to. The other kids— you don't know all the things they do, the freedom they have. I don't ask, because you always say no."

Ma studied me. "I know, it's not easy for you."

"We've known Annette for so long now. And you even met her family."

"That's true." It had been a long time since my graduation from elementary school, but for Ma, it was important that she'd actually seen them once. Since then, Annette had been a constant presence only on the phone. "All right, but just this one time. Otherwise, she'll want to . . ."

"She'll want to come over here too," I finished for her, but I was overjoyed. I would finally have a night of freedom.

"The inspectors are coming! The inspectors are coming!" Aunt Paula looked as flustered as I'd ever seen her.

She and Uncle Bob hurried through the factory as if they'd been caught in a hurricane. They swept clothing off counters, wielded brooms and dusting rags, but most important, they herded the children in front of them and swept them into small, secret places.

"Everyone under eighteen, out of sight!"

Aunt Paula grabbed me by the back of my shirt and practically threw me into one of the men's rooms. She slammed the door behind me as I landed against someone's shoulder. We both recoiled from the shock and then I realized it was Matt.

"Hey," he said. "You okay?"

Before I could answer, the door opened again and three other kids were crammed in with us before the door banged shut again. They were much younger than we were.

The little boy had his head wedged into my underarm. The men's room was filthy, with only a toilet and a washbasin. We knew we had to keep the lights out. Matt was jammed in between the washbasin and the wall. The rest of us all did our best to avoid the open toilet in the middle of the bathroom, which didn't even have a seat or cover. To combat my usual painful sensitivity to Matt, I allowed a small girl to squeeze in between us.

Even with the girl there, Matt was still too close. If he moved his arm a bit, it would almost be as if he could touch me, but the other kids were also there, and now the little boy stuck next to the toilet was staring at it, riveted by its proximity.

"Don't even think about it." I heard Matt hiss above my head. "Hold it."

The little boy pressed his legs together, his eyes wide. His clothes were matted with fabric dust. I reached out and brushed his hair with my hand. "It'll be all right," I murmured. "This will be over before you know it."

A taller girl suddenly hissed: "There's a roach moving in the sink!"

Matt and I both jumped a mile. He leaped away from the washbasin so fast that in a second he had switched places with the little boy on the other side of me, probably in an instinctive reaction to get to the door. I giggled to myself, realizing that he was as scared of insects as I was. The boy was now wedged next to the little girl, both of them jammed against the washbasin. He gave both Matt and me a disdainful look, then took a bit of paper out of his pocket and crushed the roach in the sink.

I sagged with relief now that it was dead. I kept my eyes closed. Matt smelled of sweat and after-shave and his chest was hard. I thought I could feel the thud of his heart underneath his thin T-shirt. They must have yanked him away from the steamers. Yet now that I had no choice but to stand there pressed against him, I could feel myself beginning to relax.

Suddenly, he gave a strangled cry, and I looked up. In the shadows, that child was dangling the piece of paper in front of us. I thought I could see the roach antennae waving above the tissue and the boy was grinning like a maniac. Caught by surprise, I screamed. Despite my daily exposure to roaches in our apartment, I was still as terrified of them as I had been at the beginning, probably even more so.

There was immediate thumping on the door. It was Uncle Bob's voice. "Shut up in there! They're almost in this area!"

At this, we all froze. Outside, we heard obsequious voices and even the hum of the machines seemed more subdued than usual. I could tell they were speaking English, though I couldn't make out the words. We didn't dare breathe for fear that we would be found out. Everyone knew the way Chinatown worked. Money had probably already changed hands to ensure a casual inspection, but we were still as afraid of being found out as the owners. If the factory was closed down, who would fill our rice bowls then?

My heart was now pounding as hard as Matt's. The other children were squirming around, but I could only think about how his warm breath felt against my hair. Right in front of my eyes was the contrast of his rough cotton shirt and the smooth skin of his shoulder.

The murmur of English went on outside the door for what seemed to be a long time and then there were the usual factory noises. Finally, the door was opened and the other three kids toppled out and ran off.

Reluctantly, I recovered my own balance and swayed away from Matt, but then his hand was on my wrist.

"Wait," he said. He reached out with his other arm and shut the door behind him. Then he pulled me toward him and I rested my forehead against his chest a moment. The familiar pain receded again, to be replaced by something languid and inexorable, as if I were riding the extended exhalation of a breath I hadn't known I'd been holding. His fingertips were entwined in my hair, I could feel the warmth of them against my scalp, and then I was looking up at him. A shaft of light from the window in the door fell on his soft hair. His golden eyes were luminous in the half-dark, and finally, we were kissing in one long heat of melting, and the lush afternoon dissolved into yearning for Matt and Matt alone.

And when we were done with that kiss, there was another and then another, before Matt broke off to say, in a husky voice I'd never heard from him, "They'll be looking for me."

"Me too," I breathed.

Then we kissed again and again before I made myself remember that he had a girlfriend and she wasn't me. I wanted to be the one to end this. I pulled myself away. "All right, see you then."

It took him a moment before his eyes focused again, as if he too were waking up from a dream, and then he said, "See you."

He had his hand on the doorknob, then hesitated. Without meeting my eyes, he said, "Kimberly, my climbing can't reach your heights." Then he ducked his head and left.

I stood in the bathroom alone, with my hand supporting myself against the washbasin, shattered. I had made him think he wasn't good enough for me, when in truth it was I who couldn't compete for him.

After work that day, Vivian was waiting in her usual spot outside the factory. I'm ashamed to say I had trailed him downstairs, and I saw him go up to her and kiss her on the lips. When he glanced at me, quickly, guiltily, I knew he was conscious I was there. Then they left.

It may not seem like much—a few kisses in the dark—but it was enough to burn a hole like an ulcer in my heart.

I had nothing else, but I always had my pride. I was as kind to Park as I ever was, but I made a point of flirting with the other boys at the factory, especially when Matt could see. Matt himself, I treated with a cool friendliness. I pictured myself packed in a layer of ice so thick that nothing he did could reach me. Perhaps I imagined it, but I believe that Matt's eyes often followed me during our work at the factory, that he horsed around more than usual when I was around, dropping down on the floor to do one-handed push-ups and the like, while I ignored him. Whatever he may have done, the bottom line was this: he'd chosen Vivian over me, and none of the little things he did to show me he cared about me could stack up high enough against this one fact.

I knew that Vivian was still waiting, every day after work. Fortunately, our staggered schedules meant that I didn't always have to see her, but what I saw was enough. And to make things worse, I did like her. She seemed kind and thoughtful. It wasn't her fault she was so gorgeous. How many images of them I have filed away in my soul: Matt with a package of treats—dried candied lotus seeds— hidden behind his back for her; the two of them seen from a distance, arms around each other's waists, going into the herbal medicine store; once, I'd even caught sight of them together at temple, lighting incense sticks by the flame of the oil lamp and then kneeling next to each other to pray. How many ways can you be tortured by love?

I had finally confided in Annette, my eternal adviser, and she said, "What a relationship looks like on the outside isn't the same as what it's like on the inside. You can be more in love with someone in your mind than with the person you see every day."

She was the only one who knew about my pain, but in a way, she understood it as something smaller than it was, Annette who was always hope- lessly in love herself. But she urged me to move on and forget, which was exactly what I needed to hear.

* * *

The evening of Curt's party, I went to Annette's house early. I felt guilty about leaving Ma alone at the factory but I wanted to have some fun for once, like the other kids my own age.

Mrs. Avery kissed me on the cheek. "It's so nice to see you again."

I smiled. She was one of my favorite people, even though I hardly ever saw her.

Annette lent me an old outfit of hers that she'd outgrown. Although the cream-colored dress fit me well, it was shorter than anything I'd ever worn. It felt quite daring to have it swish above my bare knees. Luckily we were the same shoe size, so I could borrow a pair of her pumps. Then Annette did my makeup, but she'd practiced a lot since the movie theater. After she put gloss in my hair, I hardly recognized myself in the mirror.

"You're gorgeous," she said.

I turned around and hugged her. "You're a great friend."

Annette was wearing a hip dress with a multicolored print and a leather handbag of her mom's.

I braided the front part of her hair back off her face. "You look beautiful too."

Mrs. Avery drove us to Curt's apartment, which was in the city, all the way east in the Seventies. A doorman came and opened our car door so Annette and I could get out. The air was warm, but a cool breeze swept in off the river. We waved good-bye to Mrs. Avery as we went into the revolving door. The doorman stood outside and pushed it for us so we didn't have to do anything ourselves. Another doorman, behind the counter, told us how to get to Curt's apartment when we were inside.

I tried not to gawk but Annette strode with her head held high, swinging her handbag on her arm like a lady. The elevators were next to an enormous display of flowers. I reached out a hand to feel a petal and realized they were all real.

"What do they do when the flowers fade?" I asked Annette.

"They get new ones, of course."

What an expense that must be. When we got to Curt's apartment and rang the doorbell, Curt opened the door. A blast of throbbing music filled the hallway.

"Hey, you made it." His eyes stopped on me. "Wow." It was different from his usual flirtatious look. He was staring at me as intensely as if I were a piece of sculpture.

I looked down at the rust-colored carpet, pleased. "Thanks. Annette helped."

Behind me, Annette giggled.

"Come in. Throw anything you don't want to carry in my parents' bedroom." Curt disappeared through a doorway.

So this was a party. All of the regular lights were out. I peered into the living room, where Curt had gone. Even in the darkness, I could tell their apartment was enormous, because the windows were so far away from where we were standing in the hallway. I could see the illumination from the city and lights on the East River in the distance.

There were already a lot of kids there. In one corner of the living room, a disco ball was spinning from the ceiling and some people were dancing, but everywhere else, it was dark except for small clusters of tea lights scattered around the room. I'd thought his parents might give a little speech about Curt, but there was no sign of them or any other adults.

"I think that's someone from theater club," Annette said, pointing at one of the dancing figures.

"Go ahead," I said to Annette, speaking loudly to be heard over the music. "Give me your bag, I'll put it away for you."

She passed me her handbag, then went over to her friend. I felt my way down the hallway and opened the bedroom door. I flicked on the light. There was a pile of clothing and handbags on the mahogany bed. Suddenly, something shifted. I almost screamed, then realized that it was a boy from my year making out with some girl. He had his hands up her shirt and she was pulling on his hair.

He dragged his lips from hers and glared at me. "Do you mind?"

"Sorry!" I quickly shut off the light, threw Annette's handbag onto the bed and left.

In the disco room, I found Annette chatting with a boy from the school newspaper. They were standing by a long counter that must have been a minibar. Annette made me a gin and tonic from the bottles on the bar, heavy on the tonic. The music was as loud as the machines at the factory. Annette pulled me onto the floor and we started to dance. It was my first time dancing to this kind of music, but I found I had a natural feel for it. A circle of people joined us, and after a while, Annette drifted off somewhere. Spinning around under the disco ball, I felt like a real American teenager.

I felt a hand on my shoulder. Curt. I wondered if he'd been watching me for a while. He took me by the hand and pulled me into the hallway.

"I want to show you something," he said.

He led me to what must have been his bedroom. When he opened the door, a cloud of sweet smoke met us. A group of people were sitting in a circle on the floor around a large cluster of candles. It was much quieter here.

"You guys need to open the window," he said.

"It is open," Sheryl said, from her seat on the floor. I thought she looked surprised to see me, as did a few other people, but no one said anything.

Curt led me to a gap in the circle where we could sit down. One of the boys sitting there was someone I'd kissed a while back. The boy's face lit up when he saw me, but Curt noticed as well and he seemed to deliberately place himself in between the two of us.

They were passing around a huge Chinese water pipe. It was about two feet high and I could see I'd need both hands to wrap around the diameter of the shaft. From the smell, I knew they weren't smoking tobacco.

Annette popped her head in the door. "Kimberly, are you in here?"

"Hey," I said.

Annette realized what was going on. "Are you okay?"

"I'm fine. You want to come in?" I was filled with curiosity and recklessness this evening. Other kids had the choice of giving in to temptation in the moment or waiting for the next opportunity. For me, there was no later. If I didn't try this now, I might never get the chance again.

Annette made a face. "Yuck. No, thanks. I'll see you." And she closed the door again.

"That water pipe's Chinese," I whispered to Curt.

"I know."

"Where did you get it?"

"I swiped it from my dad's office. One of his authors in China sent it to him as a gift. Poor guy probably didn't know what we use *bons* for here. My dad's got so much stuff in there, I don't think he ever missed it."

When the water pipe came to me, I ran my finger

over its intricate carvings. Everyone was looking at me from under their eyelashes, probably to watch the newcomer cough and not know how to take a hit. But I had seen plenty of men smoking water pipes in cafés in Hong Kong.

I put my mouth inside the wide shaft, so tightly that I created an airtight seal, held a lighter to the small metal bowl attached to the main shaft and inhaled through my mouth. I could hear the water bubbling as the smoke was pulled through it and then up into my mouth. I was prepared for the burn of the smoke and I held it in my lungs while I passed the pipe to Curt.

He was laughing. "You're a natural. You should give up being a brain and become a pothead, like me."

The pipe came around several times and I smoked and exhaled until I felt I had blown the memory of Matt into the distance. I lay back across the floor, my head spinning. I didn't know where everyone else had gone, or perhaps they were still in the room. The prickle of the carpet against the back of my hair was extremely pleasant.

"You've never had a real kiss until you've been kissed stoned," Curt said.

"All right," I said, already having a great deal of fun turning my head from side to side.

Slowly, I felt Curt lean over me and capture my head in between his large hands. I felt his hair brush my face. Instead of giving me a quick kiss on the lips as I'd expected, he started by kissing my neck, the tender places underneath the jaw and behind the ear. My world was filled with the touch of his mouth, the scent of his hair. He started gently sucking on my earlobe.

"Mmmmm," I murmured. "Does this still fall under 'kissing'?"

In answer, he kissed me full on the lips, leisurely, as if he were savoring every moment. His kiss was soft and full: like a butterfly, it fluttered against the closed door of my heart and then was still.

Over the years, Uncle Bob's leg had started bothering him more, and we saw him at the factory only now and then. Aunt Paula had taken over most of his duties. To keep up face, because it is so important for the man to appear to be the breadwinner, Aunt Paula told everyone he was working from home. At the factory, though, his office had become in practice Aunt Paula's office.

All of our mail still went through Aunt Paula since that was the official address the school had for me. The first time she brought me one of my score reports, I knew she was hoping my scores would be low.

"I'm sure you did well, such a clever girl," she said with seeming kindness. "Why don't you open it?"

Fortunately, Ma happened to be in the bathroom

then and I said, "I want to wait for Ma. I'll do it later."

Even though I was dying to open the envelope too, I turned and busied myself with some blouses until Aunt Paula reluctantly walked away. When Ma finally returned, I tore the envelope open and removed the thin piece of paper inside.

"Well, what did you get?" Ma asked.

Strangely enough, I couldn't find my results. I held the small square of paper up to the light. "I don't know. They must have made a mistake. There isn't anything here. It just has the scores that are possible on the test."

Suddenly, I heard Aunt Paula's voice. She must have followed Ma back to our work area. "That's ridiculous. Give it to me."

She snatched the sheet of paper from my hand and stared at it. Slowly, a rash of red rose up her neck. "Stupid girl, those ARE your scores!"

"Oh." I took the letter from her. I slowly realized I must have gotten perfect scores on the test. I hadn't been able to find my results because my scores were a duplicate of the top scores possible.

I was still confused by the whole thing, and I said honestly, "I'm sorry I made your eyes red, Aunt Paula."

Both she and Ma breathed in sharply.

"What!" Aunt Paula gave a shrill laugh. "Why would I be jealous because my niece does so well? What type of human being do you think I am?"

"No, I didn't mean that. I, um . . . ." I had made such a blunder I had to anesthetize my face.

"You crazy girl! I'm very proud of you!" She clasped her arm around my shoulders so hard it hurt.

"We're both very proud," Ma said, her eyes aglow.

TWELVE

When senior year began, Curt and I fooled around more, much more. People began to whisper we were going out. The more we told them we were just friends, the more convinced they were that something was going on. Although I knew it wasn't true, I enjoyed having other people think this.

Once, I heard Sheryl hiss behind me: "What in the world can he possibly see in her? Look at her clothes!"

With my newfound confidence, I turned around and smiled. She stopped short, startled I had over-heard her.

"Brains are beautiful," I said.

For me, Curt was a regular inoculation against Matt. With the physical delights Curt was teaching me, I could harden my heart against the daily hurt of seeing Matt with Vivian.

It was a brilliant autumn day, cold for that time of year, and Curt and I were sitting huddled together under the bleachers of the stadium. After the first time, I didn't get stoned with him again, because I didn't like being so dazed in my normal life. My cheap jacket was much thinner than his and he'd wrapped his long cashmere coat around the both of us like a tent. I was rubbing my finger against his bottom lip.

In between little kisses placed on my fingertip, he asked, as casually as always, "How come you're not in love with me?"

I didn't want to hurt him. "Curt, just about every girl in school's in love with you."

He held my finger still and started sucking on it. In contrast to the chilly air, the warmth of his mouth was incredible. "Except you."

"True," I sighed, closing my eyes with pleasure.

"Is it because of before?"

"What do you mean?"

"Because I went along with Greg teasing you. In seventh grade. You remember."

I opened my eyes and looked at him then. "That wasn't very nice."

"I know. I was a little shit. I'm sorry."

"It's been a long time. People change."

"So you're not still holding that against me?"

"No. And you stood up for me with that Tammy incident."

"So, what is it, then?"

An image of Matt drifted into my head but I pushed it away. "I guess I'm only in love with your body."

Curt burst out laughing. "Well, I guess that'll have to be good enough."

And we left it at that.

Dr. Weston, the guidance counselor and psychiatrist for the school, called me into her office.

"Where would you like to go for college?" she asked.

I responded without hesitation. "Yale." Annette and I had talked about colleges. Unlike me, she had ordered dozens of catalogs and read thick books of college guides. In the end, she'd chosen Wesleyan as her top choice. My selection was much more random. I knew Yale was a top school and I loved the photos of Yale in her catalog.

"Good. Let me see your application before you send it in and I'll give you my comments."

"Do you think I really have a chance?"

Dr. Weston stared at me with her little eyes. "Kimberly Chang, if you're not the type of student who gets into Yale, then who is?"

I typed out my application on the typewriter at the library, and Dr. Weston hardly made any changes to it. I asked her if it would be possible to waive the application fee. She wanted to see a copy of our tax return to see if I qualified, and when she took a quick glance at it, her face became still. Then she'd immediately given me the waiver.

When I told Ma what I had done, she was appalled. "Why didn't you pay the fee?"

"It's a lot of money." This was the same month that we had finally managed to pay off our old debts to Aunt Paula. Our financial situation was much better than it'd ever been, especially since I was still working extra hours at the library. But if we were ever going to move, ever going to change our lives, we needed to continue to save every cent we could. I understood this. Even without debt payments, our income was paltry.

"But maybe they won't consider your application. Why would they read it when you didn't give them money for it?"

The next day, Ma brought home a stack of cheap china plates she'd bought.

"Here, throw these on the floor," she said.

"Why?"

"Breaking china brings good luck. It will help you get into college."

I didn't believe in these superstitions but I broke them anyway. If I didn't get into a college with a need-blind financial aid policy, I wouldn't be able to go at all. We couldn't even afford a state school.

I began to worry even more when I heard about what other students had put in their applications. Julia Williams's family kept a Steinway in a soundproof practice room for her. Julia practiced five hours a day and had competed in international piano competitions since she turned sixteen.

Chelsea Brown sang in the Metropolitan Opera Children's Chorus.

The jocks were a group unto themselves. "Speedy Spenser," as he was called, won every race with his long spider legs, and Harrison's field hockey team took the title in our region. Alicia Collins qualified for the Junior Olympics in gymnastics. Once, when a few of the football guys challenged her, she'd dropped to the floor and matched them in one-handed push-ups until the guys fell off in exhaustion. The jocks were just as serious as I was.

Most of the kids had had lessons in something, like dance or violin, since they were seven. If their standardized test scores needed a bit of boosting, they received private tutoring. They could write their college essays about picking grapes in Italy, bike tours of Holland, sketching in the Louvre. Often, their parents were also alumni of the schools they were applying to.

What were my chances? I was just a poor girl whose main practical skill was bagging skirts faster than normal. Dr. Weston's confidence in me gave me some hope but not much. I was good at school but so were many of the other kids, most of whom had been groomed since birth to get into the right college. No matter how well I did in my classes or how well I managed to fake belonging to the cool circle, I knew I was not one of them. A part of me believed the colleges would sense this and shut me out.

Mr. Jamali thought Annette had learned enough to be cast as Emily, the lead in *Our Town*.

"I can't believe it!" Annette couldn't seem to stop jumping up and down. "You have to come see the play the day it opens."

"I will!" I clasped her hands in mine.

"You swear?"

"I do. No matter what, I will be there."

But later, when she told me the date of the opening and I checked my schedule, I saw there was a problem.

I told her in the cafeteria. "Annette, I have my naturalization exam that afternoon."

She bit her lip. "No. But you promised."

"I know. I'm so sorry. I can't do anything about this. If I don't get U.S. citizenship, I won't qualify for most financial aid."

"Why can't you take it on another date?"

"This is the first time I can take it after I turn eighteen. So I can't take it any earlier. And if I take it later, I won't be able to say I'm an American citizen on the financial aid forms for colleges. I'll come see your play the very next show."

"I know." Annette's eyes were still downcast.

"What's the matter, then?"

Now she looked at me. "Kimberly, I don't mind if this is really true, but is it just another one of your excuses?"

I'd given her so many false explanations over the

years, I couldn't blame her for doubting me. "Of course it's true."

Annette said no more about it.

Every time Aunt Paula gave us one of my score reports, she would come by a day or two later to complain about some aspect of our work. We were careful not to let her know how good my results were, but she must have guessed anyway. If we hadn't done something at the factory perfectly, we had to redo it. If a shipment was going out, she would come days in advance to harass us about completing everything on time.

"If you send this out late, I cannot be responsible for the consequences," she said one day.

"We've always been on time," Ma had answered quietly, but I saw the sorrow in her eyes that her sister was treating us like this.

Aunt Paula pushed past Matt at his steamer and then was gone.

He walked over to me. His hair was spiked and dripping wet from the steamers. "What kind of a problem does she have?"

"Jealousy," I said.

"Why?"

"I think I'm doing better at school than her son is."

Matt nodded, then started to turn around to go back to work.

To keep him there just a moment longer, I asked,

"Where's your ma and Park? I hardly see them anymore."

"Ma doesn't feel so well these days, and when she stays home, she keeps Park with her. I can take care of them now." He was obviously proud he could be the breadwinner of the family.

It still tore at my heart to have him so close. "You're doing really well, Matt."

He looked at me intently, then he finally spoke. "I miss you."

Heat rushed to my eyes. So that he wouldn't see my sudden emotion, I turned away. "You have Vivian." When I finally looked up, he was gone.

Sometimes Curt told me stories that made me realize how different we were. Once, he was talking about his meal at an Italian restaurant with a few friends.

"We waited but that arrogant waiter still didn't come with the bill, so we just left. I looked back as we walked out the door and you should have seen his face! Like he was going to have to pick up our tab himself."

"He probably did have to," I said.

"Really? Well, serves him right." Curt looked a bit shamefaced.

I didn't say anything more, but I thought about the fathers and brothers of the kids at the factory who worked as waiters, "standing by tables," as we called it. What would they have done if they'd had to pay for such an expensive meal out of their tips? Many of them weren't paid anything but their tips. This was something Matt would never do. Curt had no comprehension of what it was like to bc working class.

But he was also surprisingly sweet sometimes.

Once I was sitting with him in the art studio when he said, "I just went to the junkyard this past weekend. You can find the most incredible things there. I brought you back something."

I thought about where I lived. "I, um, already have much junk."

Curt reached into a garbage bag and pulled out the skeleton of an umbrella, but he had put in metal supports, twisted and twirled the metal prongs so that it looked just like a flower. The silver links shone, as if he'd polished it.

"Beautiful," I said, caressing an intertwined petal.

He lifted an eyebrow. "I can assure you that this will never be worth a lot of money, so you can feel free to accept it."

"This is now my favorite piece of junk."

The day of the naturalization test was in the middle of January. I was at home when I was surprised by a knock at the apartment door. The thick door downstairs hadn't been closing properly lately, and I'd hurried upstairs after school that day, probably without getting it to latch. Earlier that year, Ma had failed the examination yet again, but I was eighteen now and could take it myself. Though I expected to pass easily, I still wanted to do a bit of last-minute studying before going to the naturalization office later that afternoon.

When I opened the door, Annette was standing there in her lumberjack jacket and her L.L. Bean boots. She looked over my shoulder to stare at the cracked walls and open oven; then her gaze found the stuffed-animal vest I was wearing. Her mouth fell open, but when she saw the white clouds from her breath, she snorted in disbelief.

Instead of pity or embarrassment, there was pure anger on her face. "You should have told me," she said.

I faltered for an answer. "I didn't know how."

Now her face became blotchy and she looked like she was going to cry. "I knew you didn't have a lot of money but this is ridiculous. No one in America lives like this."

I stated the obvious. "Actually, they do."

The words poured out of her. "This is the stupidest place I've ever been. I spent years wondering why you never let me see your apartment. I told myself I shouldn't do something you didn't want me to do. I had theory after theory: that you were hiding your father here, that it was some kind of Chinese secret, that your mom was incredibly sick and you were taking care of her. When the show got canceled today, I just wondered if you were telling me the truth about the test and why I never got to come here, so I decided to visit."

I pointed at the naturalization book on the table.

She nodded, acknowledging the book. "I couldn't stand it anymore. But if I hadn't come here, you'd never have told me. You would have lived here all these years and you would never have asked me for help."

At this, the idea that she would have helped me, I reached out and hugged her. She didn't pull away.

I said, "There was no use. Look, once I get a bit older, I'll be able to get us out of here."

"I don't want you to stay here one day longer." Annette gave me a quick squeeze and started walking around the apartment. She glanced down at the kitchen table and recoiled. "Your soy sauce has iced over! And there's a roach drinking from it!"

I had been in the middle of putting the food away when she knocked. I ran over and banged on the table to scare the roach away, then hurriedly dumped the saucer in the kitchen sink. I had to wash it right away so as not to attract any other creatures, and Annette continued her own tour of the apartment.

"Why did your show get canceled?" I asked.

"There's some kind of electrical problem with

the lights, and the whole system blew out during dress rehearsal yesterday. They still haven't been able to fix it."

She called over her shoulder, "Good thing you're so smart."

"I'm lucky."

She was back now and she crinkled her nose. "I wouldn't say that. You need to report your landlord. This isn't legal."

"I can't. It's complicated."

"Well, you can't stay here any longer. We have to talk to my mom."

"No, I don't want anyone to know. Annette, don't tell."

"Kimberly, you remember my mom's a real estate agent. I bet she could help you."

"We don't have any money." Now that it was so obvious, I could say it.

"Please, let me ask her and see if she can figure it out."

"I don't want her to know." The utter shame of it burst upon me now, like a garden hose turned on full blast.

"I won't tell her. I'll just say that you're looking for something dirt cheap." At my look, she added, "I mean, not expensive."

"Take it from me, Kimberly, life in the suburbs is hell on earth." Curt and I were taking a break from his tutoring session. He lay sprawled across the

floor of the classroom we had borrowed, leaning on his right elbow, the math book closed in front of him. A few other books were scattered around him in a semicircle.

Life in the factory is hell, I thought, although aloud I said, "It doesn't sound too bad to me."

"You only say that because you've never been there."

"How would you know?"

"Well, have you?"

I was stumped. "No. But when have you ever lived there?"

"Actually, never. But aside from this"—he tapped the paperback cover of *Rabbit, Run* by John Updike, which he was reading for English class—"I've seen movies about it, which naturally makes me an expert. Life in a suit, nine-to-five job, that's not living."

"What do you want, then?"

He was silent, and then he let himself fall backward on the floor. The mane of his hair spread gold across the dark carpet. "Greatness. To exalt myself. And to be free." He sat up again and stared at me with his sapphire eyes. "No one can live an extraordinary life in the suburbs."

"I don't need to have such a special life."

"You could never be ordinary. That's why I like you." He leaned over and kissed me.

I pulled away to answer. "I wish I were. That's my dream: a satisfying career, with a nice husband, in a clean home, a kid or two. To achieve that, that would be extraordinary enough for me."

"I'll come visit you in the suburbs, then."

A month later, Annette's mother invited me to her office. As the thick glass door shut behind me, I felt out of place in my shoddy jacket. I saw Mrs. Avery at her desk and there was a woman in a camel-colored suit sitting in front of her. Mrs. Avery looked up and smiled at me, then gestured for me to take a seat in the large waiting area.

Finally, it was my turn. Mrs. Avery stood up and shook hands with me as if I were a grown-up. She didn't ask where my mother was.

"So I may have something for you. It's in Queens, in quite a green area."

My heart beat a little faster. In New York in those days, most Chinese immigrants lived in Chinatown, a few were scattered in places like Brooklyn like us, and the ones that really became successful moved to Queens. It was considered to be even nicer than Staten Island, where Aunt Paula lived.

Mrs. Avery continued. "I don't normally get apartments at such a price, but I'll be honest with you, the place has been rented for a long time so it's not in optimal condition. Most of my other clients wouldn't even want to see it."

I began to get worried. "Does it have heat?"

She looked startled. "Do you mean central heating?"

"Yes, does it have radiators that work?"

"Of course it does. I mean, don't worry, the heat works great." She blinked and hurried on. "It comes fully furnished, with all of the normal appliances: washing machine, dryer, refrigerator, oven, you name it."

A washing machine and dryer in your own apartment! We would no longer have to wash everything by hand and hang our clothes out to dry. The simple idea of a warm, heated apartment was like heaven to me. I knew I was giving myself away with my questions but I had to know before I could be disappointed again. "Are there insects in the apartment?"

She didn't flinch this time. She was prepared. "You mean like ants and roaches? No."

"Rats?"

"No."

"Then why did you say it was not in optimal condition?"

"Well, it's not very big. And the paint's peeling off the wall in a few places—not a lot, you understand, just a bit—and the carpet is wearing thin. That kind of thing."

"That's okay." I couldn't believe how good it sounded, but I still braced myself for disappointment. Now came the crucial question. "How much is the rent?"

She wrote it down for me on a piece of paper. To my surprise, it wasn't much more than what we were already paying if you included the amount we'd had to put in each month to pay off our plane tickets and visas for Aunt Paula, plus the interest she'd added. I was glad we'd just paid off our debt to her a few months before. My face must have brightened, because Mrs. Avery raised a warning finger.

"Wait, Kimberly. It's not that easy. They want to make sure that the new renters are reliable people. They want a deposit and some paperwork. We'll need a salary slip or some proof of employment, and a character reference."

My mind ticked away. For the first time, Ma and I had a bit of financial breathing room, especially with the extra hours I was working at the library. We'd be able to manage the deposit if we were given a bit more time. But where would we get the reference?

As if she'd read my mind, Mrs. Avery said, "Maybe one of your teachers at school could write you the character reference?"

"They've never even met my mother."

"That's true. Let me think about it, but I'm sure we can work that out."

"We have some money in savings, but it will be easier if we have a few more weeks to finish saving the money for the deposit. Also, the salary slip, well, it's not very much."

"That's okay. They just want to make sure that your mother can work, that's all. Maybe you could also include your own salary slip from your work at school. If they see from your character reference that you're dependable people, that will be enough."

"Will someone else get the apartment before we do?"

"I'll talk to the owners and tell them I have someone very reliable in mind for it."

"I will give you the salary slips and other paperwork as soon as possible, so they know we are serious."

When I told Ma later that evening, her entire face glowed. "*Ah*-Kim, another place to live!"

We had been trapped in that apartment for so long that we'd stopped daring to dream of fleeing. But our escape still relied on getting that character reference for Ma.

It was March, and Curt and I had taken to holding hands in public. I felt safe with him, knowing that he wasn't going to demand anything from me I didn't want to give. I don't know how things might have progressed with us, taking step after step down the road of love, or at least acting as if we were, if events hadn't unfolded as they did.

We'd just left Milton Hall together. Curt had stolen one of my pens and I was trying to get it back from him. I had him by the arm and was playfully batting him on the shoulder when I caught sight of a tall figure standing in front of the shrubbery of the main hall.

"Matt." I couldn't imagine what he would be doing here at Harrison. He was as poorly dressed as usual, in workman's slacks and a thin wrinkled jacket, but girls walking by still turned their heads at the way he stood there, proud as a young dragon.

Matt had seen us by now and the shock in his eyes was swiftly eclipsed by pain and jealousy. He shook his head as if to clear his vision and then strode away as fast as he could. At first, I felt sorrow at his hurt, then anger because I knew exactly what that pang felt like, had felt it every day.

Curt too had frozen. "Now I get it."

"I have to go," I said, and without a backward glance, I hurried after Matt.

It was raining and I almost slipped on the slick sidewalk as I chased him. I could just make him out through the rain, a blur in the distance, but then he grew closer and closer until I realized he'd turned around and was now coming toward me.

Then his hands were on my elbows and he gripped me, hard. "That your boyfriend?" he yelled.

"What about your girlfriend?" I screamed back. My hair and face were soaked.

He stopped moving, then seemed to deflate. He let me go. "I know. I'm sorry. I'm made of stupid material."

I saw then that his face was wet not only from the rain. His eyes were swollen and bloodshot. He'd been crying.

"Did you and Vivian break up?" I asked, more gently.

"My mother died," he said. He gave a hopeless little shrug.

I took him by the hand and I led him into my arms. He bowed his head and started to weep, great shuddering sobs. I held him like that, on the sidewalk of the Harrison Prep campus, and let the rain come down.

Then I got us both into the subway and took him home with me.

We hardly said a word to each other until we arrived at my apartment. We were filled with so much emotion that there was nothing but complete recklessness left to us. His quick eyes took in the garbage bags over the windows, the roaches on the countertop and the plaster falling off the walls. If anything, the apartment was in even worse shape than it had been in when we moved there, because it was now seven years older. It still held the chill of winter. Our clothes were wet and I got the two thin towels from the bathroom.

I handed one to Matt, but instead of starting to dry himself off, he took it and wiped it gently over my face. I stood there, motionless, while he lifted my hair and dried the base of my neck with the towel. He unzipped my jacket and pushed it off my shoulders. It fell on the floor.

His lips were all I could look at, and I abruptly disengaged myself and started walking toward the kitchen.

"I better find another towel," I said, knowing we didn't have any other towels.

But he'd caught me by my sleeve and his hands were pulling me back. I closed my eyes. I felt his arms go around me and before I knew it, his hands were under my shirt, stroking and tantalizing. He kissed me and I stopped breathing. He was filled with need, he seemed unable to control himself.

"Please," I whispered. "Wait."

He already had my shirt off. We fell back on the pile of stuffed-animal blankets. He pinned me to the mattress, his weight was delicious, and now he was moving his lips against mine, agonizing and luscious, the brush of stubble against my temples, the sweep of his hair. I felt I couldn't breathe, I couldn't move, I was his and he was mine. I could feel the heat of him burning through his wet clothes. He was a man possessed, by grief and passion together.

Finally, I made myself say, very clearly, "We have to use a condom."

With some embarrassment, he regained control of himself. He took a deep, shuddering breath, then said, "I have a couple in my wallet."

"Let's use two," I said. "Just to be sure."

"Okay."

But once he started to kiss me again, the taste and smell of him overwhelmed me and I became frantic to get his clothes off too. I felt hypnotized, as if I were in a dream, and I kept thinking, *This is Matt, he's mine now, mine, at last.* I looked at him up close and he was more beautiful than I'd ever imagined, the shimmer of his lashes, the thin white scar that ran across his collarbone, the darkened hollow of his throat. Despite all of my experimentation, I'd never been naked with a man before, and Matt's skin felt warm and rough. He must have taken care of the condoms somehow and then suddenly he was inside me. I gasped, but it hadn't hurt as much as I'd expected it to and then I couldn't think at all anymore.

When he finally came, he started to cry again. I held him tenderly in my arms. We lay there together, both breathing hard, returning to ourselves.

"I have to take care of Park now," he said. "The view in front is very foggy." He was talking about how unpredictable their future was now.

"You'll be all right," I said. I had his hand in both of mine and I squeezed it. "What about your pa? Is he going to—"

"No."

"Where is he?"

"I don't know." He laughed a little to himself, bitterly. "My heart is so wounded that I'm vomiting blood. And he disappears, as usual, with another new girlfriend. My whole life, he's never been around, never helped my ma out. I always had to be the man of the family, for Park, for Ma." His voice cracked. "I can tell you, I am never going to be like him. I'll be there for my own wife and kids through everything."

That reminded me of his other responsibility. Although it jabbed my heart, I tried to sound non-chalant. "What about Vivian?"

"I never even told her he was alive."

"No. I meant, what about Vivian and you?"

He gently stroked my temple. "No more Vivian. The moment Ma collapsed from her heart attack, I immediately knew that all I wanted was you. I had to see you. It's always been you."

I couldn't keep the resentment from my voice. "It seemed to be Vivian for a long time."

He turned away from me and stared at the cracked ceiling. "It was nice not to be treated like I had chicken pox for a change."

I said stiffly, "That was only because I liked you."

Now, in profile, I saw him smile. "Really? Sometimes I allowed myself to believe that. But all you did after we . . . umm, you know, in the bathroom that time . . . was ignore me."

"You had a girlfriend, remember?"

"Well, it didn't really help me get less confused. I'm not like you, Kimberly. I'm just a stupid guy.

I'm not some hero from a kung fu movie come to save you from your life."

"You don't need to rescue us. I'm going to do it."

He laughed. "I know, and you will too. Hey, and what about that wave-player you were with?" Hc meant the playboy, someone who frolics in the waves. At this, his nostrils flared. "If you let him touch you again, I'm going to twist his head all the way around."

"Let's keep things simple," I said. "Just the two of us from now on."

After he'd gone and I was trying to get the stains out of the blankets so Ma wouldn't suspect anything when she came home, I stopped short, my hands flying to my mouth. There were the condoms. I should have known. The two condoms had rubbed against each other and they'd both torn. What a stupid idea of mine it'd been. Neither of us had even noticed.

THIRTEEN

Ma and I had been waiting for the decisions from the colleges to come, so we weren't surprised when Aunt Paula called us into her office again. Her face was still and white underneath the foundation and powder. On the table in front of her were two fat envelopes from Yale. I stopped breathing for a moment. A rejection letter would be thin. One white business envelope was stuffed with documents and it was accompanied by a large yellow manila envelope, also from Yale.

"How is this possible?" Aunt Paula asked quietly.

"What?" Ma and I asked together.

"That Kimberly applied to Yeah-loo without my knowledge and permission." "Yeah-loo" is the Cantonese pronunciation of "Yale."

"Your permission?" I echoed, incredulous.

"I signed a legal document guaranteeing the both of you when I brought you here. I am responsible for you, and you are living in one of my apartments and working at my factory. You are not supposed to take one step without telling me."

Despite my resolve to stay calm, my voice sounded furious. "Are you saying that you would have helped me if you'd known? Like you would have helped me with Harrison?"

"Of course! Everything I do is in your best interest."

Ma tried to calm us both down. "Older sister, we don't even know if Kimberly got in or not. Let's not get overwrought."

"Open that letter," Aunt Paula said.

I would have defied her but I was desperate to know what was in it as well. I slit open the white business envelope. It contained a few forms and a cover letter. I read the letter aloud, simultaneously translating it into Chinese for Ma. My voice had a quaver in it. " 'Congratulations. You have been accepted . . .' "

Ma sat down abruptly in the chair across from Aunt Paula.

"You cannot go to Yeah-loo! I do not allow it!" Aunt Paula burst out.

I ignored her and opened the other envelope as well. It contained the financial aid documents. They'd given me a full financial aid package.

I clutched both envelopes to me, my cheeks burning like I had a fever. "Ma."

She had her hands across her mouth, trying to contain both laughter and tears of joy. She got up and took me in her arms. I couldn't stop hopping up and down, I was so excited.

Ma squeezed me tightly. "You did it. I always said you were special."

"If people saw this display of sentimentality, their flesh would feel as if it'd been anesthetized." Aunt Paula's voice brought us back to reality. She meant it was embarrassing to see us acting this way.

Ma released me and turned to face her. "*Ah*-Kim has the right to go to whichever school she wants to. She's earned it."

Aunt Paula looked stunned; then she said, "Your hearts have no roots." She meant we were ungrateful. To my astonishment, she started to sob. "I made myself an abandoned animal to open up the route to America for us."

318

Ma walked around the desk to Aunt Paula and laid a hand on her shoulder. Aunt Paula shook Ma off. Her face, although still wet, was livid. "You always did whatever made you happy. Happy! How much rice can you earn with happiness? Marrying your principal, shirking your responsibilities. I took up your burden for you! I married Bob!"

"I would never have asked you to do that." Ma's low voice was gentle. "I thought you cared for him."

"What did I know? I was just a young girl." Tears began to run down Aunt Paula's face again. "You don't know how many hardships I've suffered to get to where we are now."

"But that doesn't give you the right to treat us the way you have," I said quietly. I felt compassion for Aunt Paula too, but a calm anger had grown in me the entire time she was speaking and pitying herself.

Ma gasped, but I was no longer under her control. I was still drawn along in the wake of emotion of having been accepted by Yale. I had found a new apartment and all of the paperwork had been finalized, except for the character reference for Ma. I knew we could break our ties with Aunt Paula now, and that knowledge allowed me to speak the truth.

Aunt Paula wiped her face with her sleeve, smearing her eyeliner. "Your teeth are sharp and your mouth is keen."

"Fake kindness, fake etiquette is all you've shown us."

"How dare you give me so little face?"

I stared at her. "Face or no face doesn't matter in America. What matters is who you really are."

"America! If I hadn't brought you here, you'd still be in Hong Kong. I even gave you another address so you could go to a better school."

"You did that because it's illegal for us to be living where we are."

Aunt Paula clenched her jaw. She hadn't realized how much I now knew about the way things worked.

Ma tried to intervene. "Older sister, you've helped us a great deal, but maybe it's time we stopped depending on you so much."

I continued as if Ma hadn't spoken. "Just like it's illegal for you to pay us by the piece here at the factory."

"After everything I've done for you, you speak to me like this. You treat the human heart like a dog's lung." But her manner was more regretful than angry, which meant she was getting scared.

I rose to my full height. I wasn't quite as tall as Aunt Paula but I was much taller than Ma by then. "You should be ashamed of yourself for putting us in that apartment all these years. And for making us work here, under these conditions. After we fell down a well, you dropped a boulder on top of us."

Ma had kept her eyes down, but now she looked

up and slowly nodded in agreement. "Older sister, I cannot understand why you have treated us like this."

Aunt Paula was sputtering. "I gave you work and shelter! And this is how you repay my human currency." The currency of humanity is kindness. "I brought you here! That is a life debt, one you can never repay."

"You should think about your own life debt, to the gods," I retorted.

Aunt Paula had had enough and she pulled out her final card. "I wouldn't want to take advantage of you. If you think I've treated you badly, you can leave. Leave the factory and move out of the apartment." She said the words with gravity, then waited for us to beg her to reconsider.

Ma's hands were trembling but she managed to smile. "In fact, *ah*-Kim has found us an apartment, in Queens."

Aunt Paula's eyes popped.

"We've already repaid our debts to you," Ma said. When I heard her words, I knew we were freed of Aunt Paula forever. I met Ma's eyes, and saw she was ready to leave.

I spoke to Aunt Paula. "If you do anything to hinder us in any way, I will report you to the authorities."

And we walked out of there, leaving Aunt Paula gaping in her little office at the factory.

I had a blurred impression of the other workers

staring at our departure as we got our things from the finishing area and then started for the exit. Matt caught my arm as I passed by and I paused for a moment to whisper, "It's all right, come find me later," and then Ma and I were out of the factory and on the street, hurrying toward the subway. A cool breeze blew against my hair.

"Are you all right, Ma?" I had been ready for this step long before. This was what I'd been working toward. I just didn't know how Ma felt about losing her only family except for me.

She sighed. "Yes. I am afraid but I feel light too. Even if Aunt Paula bathed in grapefruit water, she wouldn't be able to wash the guilt off. It is time for us to make our own way."

I squeezed her arm. "Mother and cub."

As soon as we got back to the apartment, I phoned Mrs. Avery and told her we'd had a disagreement with my aunt after I'd been accepted to Yale with a full financial aid package, and we therefore needed to move out of our current apartment as soon as possible.

There was a silence. Then Mrs. Avery spoke. "First of all, a huge congratulations to you, Kimberly! I am sure that the owners will have no problems accepting a tenant who has such a bright future, and I will give you both the character recommendation myself."

Now our greatest worry was how we would

manage to earn the rice until I graduated and had more free time to work for us. If we couldn't find a new source of income quickly, we would lose the apartment.

Later that day, the doorbell rang.

"Who could that be?" Ma asked as I flew downstairs to open the door.

When I walked into our apartment with Matt, Ma's mouth went from a surprised "O" to a calm smile of acceptance.

Matt could look around our apartment more carefully this time. There was no pity on his face, just understanding. He put his arm around me and said, "I could help you put some new glass into the window frames here."

I leaned against him. "We may be leaving soon, but I'll tell you the story later."

He chatted with Ma over a cup of tea. Aside from keeping as far as possible from any places insects could crawl on him, he seemed perfectly at home. I felt I had to be dreaming to have Matt here in our apartment, lighting up the bare kitchen with his beauty.

After chatting for a few minutes with Ma, he asked, "Would it be all right if I took Kimberly to Chinatown for a bowl of a wonton soup? I promise I'll take care of her."

I opened my mouth to protest that I didn't need anyone's care but Ma was already smiling.

"You two go out and get a moon tan," she said teasingly, meaning a stroll under the moonlight.

"Ma," I said, not daring to look at Matt.

"I trust the two of you not to do anything stupid. Don't come back too late."

I couldn't believe I was actually on a date with Matt and that I hadn't had to lie to Ma about it. The moment we got outside, Matt kissed me. Some of the guys on the street hooted.

When Matt pulled back, his eyes were dark. "You have such an effect on me, I'm riding the dizzying waves."

I sighed and laid my cheek against his shoulder.

On the way to Chinatown, I filled him in on most of what had happened with Aunt Paula and the new apartment. I deliberately avoided telling him about Yale, deciding to wait until we were seated somewhere quieter.

The café was packed. Everyone there was Chinese. In those days, the cafés with the best food hadn't been discovered by tourists yet, and if a white person did somehow venture in, the waiter called "Red beard, blue eyes" along with the order so that the cook could adapt the dish for Western tastes.

We stood in a long line of people waiting to be served. A counter ran along the length of the wall beside us, crowded with people who wanted to place take-out orders. Several waitresses behind the counter were packing food in plastic cartons into bags.

"*Ah*-Matt, what are you doing, hiding here?" A short balding waiter was at Matt's elbow, beaming at us. "Get out of there, follow me."

Despite the glares of the other patrons, we were pulled out of line and led to a small table at the end of the restaurant. Another waiter greeted Matt by name, then hurried over to clear off the dishes from our table.

Matt grinned and said, "Thanks, *ah*-Ho. Hey, *ah*-Gong, don't break any plates now."

Our waiter glanced at me, recognizing that I wasn't Vivian, but was too polite to say anything. Our bowls of wonton soup were large and filled with homemade noodles and tender pastry wrapped around meat.

I used my spoon to skim off a few scallions floating on top and poured them into my mouth. "It has been so long since I've had this."

"They're the best in Chinatown," Matt said.

"Do you come here a lot?" I couldn't stop myself from picturing him here with Vivian every night.

"No, I almost never get to eat here. I know these guys because I used to wash dishes here, in the back."

"When was that?"

"A while ago, just to earn a few extra cents when I wasn't at the factory."

"Why didn't you stand by tables?"

"I still looked too young. And then I got the Italian delivery job."

I caught sight of my reflection in the gold-flecked mirror behind him. I was glowing with happiness. I couldn't believe I was sitting with Matt, hearing about his life, and that he belonged to me. I looked down at his hand resting on the tabletop: a square hand with reddened knuckles, a workman's hand, the most special thing I'd ever seen. I took it in both of mine and laid it against my cheek.

He closed his eyes for a moment. "Sometimes, I was out with . . . not with you, and I'd suddenly see your face in front of me or remember something you'd said. But I thought you didn't like me in that way. You were so distant and you went to that fancy private school. I knew you were going places, you weren't just a dumb factory kid like me."

"Is that why you picked Vivian over me?"

"I didn't know you were a choice or I would have picked you for sure. Viv, she really depended on me. I couldn't imagine you needing anyone."

My heart contracted. I forced myself to say the words. "I need you too."

His eyes, shadowed from all his recent grief, lit up. "Really?"

"When I'm with you, I could drink water and I'd be full. So why did you finally come to me?"

"When we kissed in the bathroom at the factory, it gave me hope for the first time. But then you just ignored me again and I couldn't figure it out. I told myself it'd been a one-time thing, that your heart was somewhere else. But when . . ." He paused, not wanting to say the words about his mother's death. ". . . I didn't care if you liked me or not anymore. I feel terrible about it but I didn't care about Vivian either. I just had to see you."

"You told me your climbing couldn't reach my heights."

He stared at his soup. "It's true. I can't compare to you."

"I took that to mean you didn't want to be with me, that you wanted to stay with Vivian instead."

"You thought it was an excuse?"

"Yes."

"I just needed more time to figure it out. When I'm with you, I can't think, especially after I've been kissing you. But I did feel guilty about Vivian too. I don't want to be like my pa. And you are too good for me."

I couldn't bear it any longer. "I've just been accepted to Yeah-loo."

He took a sharp breath. "Wow. Really? Congratulations." He looked genuinely happy for me, but confused as well. "What does this mean? Are you going to move out of New York?"

The words came out in a rush. "If you want, you and Park can come with me. It may take me some time, but someday I'll take you away from all of this."

He was quiet, looking at me. "How about if I don't want to be rescued?"

I leaned on one elbow and stared at him. "You want to live out the rest of your life in Chinatown?"

"Why not? I like it here—great food, low rent . . ."

"Great roaches . . ."

"Ugh. But look, you don't need money to love someone, and you don't need success to have kids and make a life together. Isn't that what counts?"

"I'm only eighteen! How can I even think about having kids now?"

"You'd be a great mother."

"I'd be a great surgeon."

"Okay." He sat back. "That too. But see, that's what I mean. Like now, I'm wondering when you're going to leave me for bigger and better things."

"Never," I said, and I leaned across the table, pulled him toward me and kissed him.

His golden eyes were warm again. "I'd go any-where with you, Kimberly. But I want to be the one taking care of you."

The weeks that followed formed the happiest period of my life. Within a few days, Mrs. Avery had arranged for us to move into the new apartment by the beginning of the next month, May. Ma went to the jewelry factory in Chinatown that Matt had told us about years before, and came home with a large sack of beads and wires and tools. We were paid very little for the work, but until the end of the school year, we had the extra hours I worked at the library to supplement our income. I knew, though, that it would be difficult to live on this jewelry-making alone.

"Thank goodness we're moving," Ma said. "Our hands would get much too cold to be able to do this kind of handwork in the winter."

"As soon as I graduate, I'll be free to work much more for us, Ma," I said. I could type very quickly by then and I thought I would be able to get some office work at least.

"You just worry about your studies. Now that we don't have those debts to Aunt Paula anymore, we'll manage."

The college admissions news created quite a stir at Harrison. I was a part of the blessed circle of kids who'd gotten into the best schools. Dr. Copeland congratulated me in the hallway when she passed me. Other kids turned to look when I walked by. Annette had been accepted to Wesleyan and Curt was going to RISD.

"I'll be in Connecticut too!" Annette said, nearly choking me with her arms around my neck. "We'll be able to see each other all the time!"

After Curt had seen Matt at Harrison, I'd only

had to tell him I couldn't meet him that week for tutoring.

"I told you I understood," he said, avoiding my gaze. His clothes were disheveled and his eyes were shadowed. We didn't meet again after that.

Matt fit into every aspect of my life. Some Sundays, he came over and helped us finish our new jewelry work. It was funny to see such a large man bent over feminine jewelry, especially with his clumsy hands. He still did his best and Ma appreciated his help. Whenever Matt and I could, we snuck away to his apartment, where we could have some privacy. It was hard to imagine how he, Park and his ma had lived in such a small space. The studio apartment was so tiny that they had to put their mattresses and bedding in the closet every day so they had enough room to eat and walk around. Matt and I were so frantic for each other we could hardly wait to get the mattresses out of the closet before we started touching each other.

Matt quit his job at the factory and soon started working for a moving company. He always liked jobs that got him into even better shape than he was already in. The money was good and he knew exactly what he'd be earning each month.

"You didn't have to leave the factory for me," I said.

"I've wanted to go for a long time anyway. I only stayed so I could help my ma sometimes and to keep an eye on Park."

Park withdrew almost completely into himself after his mother's death. He became so regressive, I feared for our ability ever to reach him again. He started peeing in his pants like a baby. He didn't react at all to anything, not to speech, not to gestures. Matt practically had to feed him to get him to eat and Park became alarmingly thin. He stayed alone in their apartment or with their elderly neighbor who had always taken care of him when Matt and his ma needed to be somewhere else. Sometimes Park hung around the garage of the moving company where Matt worked.

"The guys there are all right," Matt said. "They don't mind Park being there. They know he's okay."

I knew that meant Matt was popular there, as he had been at the factory, and that the guys put up with Park because he was Matt's brother.

I had learned Matt was friends with everyone in Chinatown. We never had to wait in line anywhere. Once, we needed to buy some groceries for Ma. The fishmonger saw Matt and asked us for our order immediately, despite all the customers who'd been waiting before us.

I whispered to Matt, "So you used to scale fish here too?"

He looked embarrassed and said, "Nah. I've lived in Chinatown a long time, you get to know everyone."

Ma commented later that she had never gotten such fresh sea bass, and so much of it too.

When we passed the guy at the newspaper stand, Matt would call out, "Hey, you need a break? I'll take the stand for you while you take a leak."

"No, Matt, but thanks."

"How about I get you a cup of coffee, then?" Matt would look at me and say, "You mind? Poor man's cooped up in there all day."

I never minded. It only made me love him more.

I wanted Annette to meet him and she came to Chinatown to join us for a cup of tea. She was the only white person in the café and she insisted on having the most Chinese drink we could think of, which was red bean ice. It was also one of my favorites: cooked red beans and shaved ice mixed together with sweetened condensed milk.

"Are they going to give it to me the Chinese way?" she asked. "Did the waiter tell the cook it's for a white person?"

Ever since I'd mentioned how some Chinese restaurants did that, Annette had worried about not getting authentic food.

"I already asked the waiter to give us everything without change," Matt said. It was strange for me to hear him speak English, with a slight Chinese accent. A lock of his hair fell over his eyes and he smoothed it back with his hand.

"Thanks." Annette grinned at me. "Now I see

why you never fell in love with any of those guys at Harrison."

I stepped on her foot under the table but it was already too late.

"Which guys?" Matt asked.

"Nothing," I said.

Annette giggled. "Kimberly, promise me we'll see each other all the time next year."

"I don't know if I want to see a person who is so indiscreet." I wrinkled my nose at her to show her I was kidding.

"I want to know about the guys," Matt said.

"Oh look, the drinks are here," I said.

One time, when Matt and I were walking down the street, I caught sight of Vivian in a flower shop we passed. If possible, she was even more beautiful than ever in her sorrow, with limpid eyes that looked as if the world had drowned in them. She happened to look up. When she saw us, she seemed heartbroken, her grief so complete that it left no room for anger. I thought, *I never want to love someone like that, not even Matt, so much that there would be no room left for myself, so much that I wouldn't be able to survive if he left me.*

We were lying on his mattress in their apartment when Matt said to me, "Let's just stay in Chinatown together."

"What? You mean, not go to Yeah-loo?"

"School's not that important anyway. Everything's perfect now. We're so happy. Stay with me. I'm earning enough. Step by step, we could build up a whole life together."

There was no question: I wanted to be with Matt every day of the rest of my life. My heart ached for him whenever he wasn't by my side. But it wasn't that simple. Annette had given me her Yale catalog after I was accepted and I'd lingered on the photographs of their laboratories for a long time. They even had an astronomy observatory that any student could operate, simply by showing a Yale ID. Their professors were some of the most brilliant thinkers of our time. What would I be capable of after I had access to a place like this?

"Matt, I can't give Yale up. Come with me. We could get an apartment close to school. You could get a job there, I'm sure. And later, I'll become a professor or a doctor, and we can do the most exciting things together. Travel. Have adventures. It'll take time but eventually maybe you wouldn't even have to work."

His face fell and I knew I'd said too much. He shook his head slowly, looking at his rough hands. "I want to take care of you, Kimberly, not the other way around. That's how it should be."

"In the old days!" I tried to keep my voice light. "Why does it matter who earns more or less? It's like you said, what's important is that we build up a good life together."

"I guess what I really hate is the idea that you'll

be in your classes next to those wave-players like that one you had, and they'll all be chasing you."

"What?" This had never occurred to me and I had to laugh. "We'll be studying. No one is going to notice me in that way."

"You have no idea. I know what men are like, trust me."

"You sound worse than Ma. Even if they did try anything, I wouldn't care because I already have you."

He took me in his arms and kissed me hard. "I can't help being jealous of any guy who gets to be near you for any reason. I've never been this bad before. It's new for me to feel like this about someone."

In those days, I wanted to believe our love was something tangible and permanent, like a good luck charm I could always wear around my neck. Now I know that it was more like the wisp of smoke trailing off a stick of incense: most of what I could hold on to was the memory of the burning, the aftermath of its scent.

In a way, I had known from the moment I saw the broken condoms. And strangely enough, the first person I told was Curt. He must have known something was wrong when I asked to meet him again. He was waiting for me at our old spot under the bleachers, but he didn't try to touch me when I sat down.

"You okay?" he asked.

We sat there in silence a moment and then I started to cry. Curt wrapped his arm around me and held me against his shoulder. We sat like that for some time, with his cheek against the top of my head while I sobbed. Finally, I wiped my eyes on my sleeve.

"Is it that dickhead?" he asked gently.

I nodded. "He's not a—"

"Okay, okay." There was another silence and then Curt said, "Three choices. One, he dumped you. Two, you dumped him. Three, you're knocked up."

At this, my eyes filled with tears again.

He bent his head forward so he could see my face. "Kimberly, you've got to be kidding."

I buried my head in my hands. "I feel so lost. I've never felt like this before. All my hopes, everything I wanted. Gone."

There was a pause, then Curt asked helpfully, "You want me to marry you?"

Despite my tears, I choked out a laugh.

"No, really," he said. "I wouldn't mind too much. And we know we're compatible." He twitched his eyebrows suggestively.

I was more surprised at the thought of carefree Curt getting married than the fact that he'd want to get married to me. "You? What about your fear of the suburbs and a stable life?"

"We wouldn't have to do all that. I could be free

with you, Kimberly." He looked away. "I missed you, when you were . . . occupied."

Now I looked at his lowered eyelashes, which were the same sandy gold as his hair. He was serious, more than he sounded. He continued. "We could start again, completely fresh."

"Curt, I love you." I paused. "But not like that. And you don't love me that way either. Actually, we're friends. Friends who fool around."

He closed his eyes for a moment, then sighed. "Yeah. You want me to give you some money?"

"You're the sweetest guy there is." I put my hand against his unshaven face. "It's not that I don't need it, but I can't take it from you."

"C'mon, Kimberly. If you want, you can borrow it and pay me back whenever you can. Baby costs lots of dough, you know."

At this, the panic reared in me and threatened to take over. I struggled to stay in control. I managed to smile. "I've already used you for your body. I draw the line at using you for your money."

He whistled. "How can you be so ethical at a time like this?"

I frowned. "Ethical. If you knew the things that were going through my head . . . Oh, Curt, what am I going to do?"

"Have you told the dickhead yet?"

"He's not a . . . No."

"Are you going to tell him?"

"I don't know."

337

When it was time for me to go, Curt bent over to kiss me on the lips. I held his face in my hands, then turned so that his kiss landed on my cheek, to the side of my mouth.

With my eyes closed, I said, "Thanks for listening."

"Lucky dickhead."

In between classes, I met Annette in the bathroom. Since I'd just cried so much with Curt, I managed to keep my composure when I told her.

For once, Annette didn't say anything. She just held me in an incredibly tight grip.

Then she spoke. "I'm here for you."

I took a deep breath. "What do you think?"

"You need to tell him."

"I can't."

"Why not? He has the right to know."

I rubbed my eyes. "He does. But if I tell him, he'll never let me . . . you know. He'll want to keep it and get married. He'll want us to stay in Chinatown."

"I guess there are worse things than being an incredibly young mother and living with a hunk the rest of your life."

"I don't want to force him to be with me. I don't even know if I can make him happy in the long run. What kind of wife would I be for him? Poor, stressed, frustrated, with all my potential unfulfilled." I started to yank at my hair.

"Don't do that, you'll hurt yourself. You know what the easiest thing to do is. It's to get rid of it and be with him and just never tell him. But you can't do that. Probably the most likely thing is that you break up."

I must have looked devastated, because she quickly added, "I'm sorry. And if you have the baby, it will mean your life will be harder, much harder, but it won't mean it's over."

"If I'm lucky."

"You've got something better than luck, you're brilliant."

"I wish I were so sure."

Like a small child, I waited for Ma to come home from dropping work off at the jewelry factory. Now that I'd told Curt and Annette, the dam holding back my emotions had dissolved and I was overrun. When the apartment door finally opened, I ran to her as I'd done when I was a little girl.

"Ma!"

"*Ah*-Kim! What is it? What is it, my daughter?" She held me close, even though her head reached only to just above my shoulders, and then led me to a chair in the kitchen.

I couldn't stop heaving, as if I were having convulsions. I had no tears left.

She waited for me to stop and then she said, "You have the big stomach." She knew I was pregnant.

I couldn't answer.

Her eyes were squeezed tight as she held me. Her head must have been spinning. Finally, in a low voice, she asked, "What did he say?"

"I can't tell him."

Now she lifted her head and stared at me. "You're not thinking about dropping the fetus." Having an abortion.

I could hear how dead my voice sounded. "What else can I do? How could I ever take care of you and Park and Matt and the baby?"

She laid a hand on my shoulder. "We'll manage."

With some anger, I brushed it off. "Like we've managed so far?" I let my gaze run through the dirty apartment. I thought about the woman and baby who used to live next door to us, in Mr. Al's building. "I promised I would make a better life for you, Ma. I'm sorry I was so stupid."

Ma's voice broke. "My little girl, you've had to do everything for us. I am the one who is sorry, sorry I couldn't do more to help you." She held my head in her arms.

"Ma? Did you ever wonder about marrying Pa?"

"When I chose your pa over Bob, I never imagined Aunt Paula would still bring us to America. She told me when she left Hong Kong that I would die there. I thought I was giving up my future for him. But if I'd married Bob instead, I would have regretted it the rest of my life. I've never stopped loving your pa, even now that he's been gone for so many years."

"But Pa made the decision to be with you forever of his own free will. I dreamed of Matt and me choosing a life together step by step. Tying him to me with a baby isn't a part of that."

"You may need to change your dreams. My little heart, listen." Ma took me by the shoulders. "When you and Matt finally got together, it was something no one could fight. I've seen you love each other for years. When you were younger, I told you not to get too close to the other kids. I was afraid he would lead you down the wrong path. I understood later, however, that no one could lead you astray. I'm so proud of you. But sometimes our fate is different from the one we imagined for ourselves."

TWELVE
YEARS LATER

FOURTEEN

Pete, six years old, had hidden himself under the low blue table and was hanging on to one of its legs, refusing to come out.

"I thought he just had high blood pressure. I don't understand why he needs surgery. Can't he just take some pills?" The man's tone was frustrated. He was short and bald, with a belly that hung over his pants.

"Mr. Ho, I'm afraid it's more serious than that. Pete has coarctation of the aorta, which is a congenital heart defect." I pulled over the large plastic model of a heart that I kept on my desk. I saw the boy under the table watching us as well.

Mr. Ho was blinking at me. Even though we were speaking Chinese, I could tell he hadn't understood a word.

"It's something that Pete was born with. You see this?" I gestured toward the aorta. "This is the main artery that takes blood from the heart to the body. This part is not wide enough." I pulled out the echocardiogram of his heart. I smiled at the child. "Pete, would you like to see a picture of your heart?"

Slowly, he climbed out from under the table and got into his father's lap. I turned the echocardiogram around so that they could see it more clearly. "You have a very good heart but because this part is too narrow, your entire heart must work harder. There's especially too much pressure here, in the left pumping chamber. This can really hurt your heart muscle later and lead to a lot of other problems."

"Like what?" Mr. Ho asked.

I answered again. "High blood pressure or heart failure."

His face fell. I knew he'd been hoping that surgery wouldn't be necessary.

"This is a curative operation," I told him, "which means he would be cured afterwards. Obviously with follow-up care and a cardiac rehabilitation program."

They both looked happier at this.

With a glance at me, Pete asked, "Will the pretty doctor be there for the operation, Pa?"

His father sighed and nodded. "She'll be the boss."

Impressed, the boy addressed me directly. "Really?"

"I'm your surgeon," I said to him. "I'll be there with you the whole time."

Now I looked at Mr. Ho more carefully. He seemed familiar, like someone from long ago. Where had I heard that name before? An idea occurred to me and I couldn't stop myself from asking, "You wouldn't know a Matt Wu?"

The man looked at me in surprise. "*Ah*-Matt. Of course." Now he examined me more carefully as well. "Are you a friend of his? I didn't know *ah-*Matt was acquainted with such important people!"

"You probably don't remember. Matt and I used to come have wonton soup sometimes." I couldn't help smiling at the old memories. This was the waiter who'd always pulled us to the front of the line.

"Oh," he looked at me vaguely, clearly trying to remember, trying to see me as someone other than his child's doctor. "Yes, sure." Mr. Ho nodded without meeting my eyes, and I knew he was only pretending. He remembered only Vivian.

I tried to sound as casual as possible. "Do you still see him sometimes?"

"Sure, Matt's always around."

I took a deep breath. This was my chance. I held out a copy of my card. "Would you give him this for me?" Pete took it and started scraping it across his cheek. "Tell him . . ."

Mr. Ho waited, expectant.

"Tell him I said hi."

He plucked my card out of Pete's hands and put it in his wallet. "I will."

In my imagination, I'd run into Matt hundreds of times over the years: on the bus, at the bank, in New Haven, in Cambridge; I had fantasies of him being a patient at the hospital, school, university, wherever I was. Perhaps it was also for this reason that I'd taken the position at the hospital close to

Chinatown when we'd finally come back to New York. I'd imagined that he would walk in through the door one day, but of course, he never had—not to the pediatric cardiac surgery department, anyway. Finally, I'd gone looking for him in Chinatown. I knew the places he used to hang around and made excuses for myself to frequent them. I saw that the nameplate for his old apartment had changed, so he'd moved. I didn't dare face him directly anyway, not after what I'd done to him, and I tried not to be noticed as I wandered around.

Then, I actually saw him once. It was late in the evening, and through the crowd, I suddenly caught a glimpse of him, just a few feet away, going into a bridal shop. It was only for a second, and I'd seen him from the back, but I knew it was him. I had to follow. I heard a woman's voice greet him, then I stepped up to the lit window. There was a little girl, about five years old, sitting underneath a mannequin. Was she his? I could remember now the reason I'd lied to Matt all those years before: to avoid dooming our child to this lovely little girl's fate. But who was I to say that she, too, wouldn't take her future into her own hands? This was the reason Vivian had been given a whole life to spend, every day of every year, with my Matt.

And then there he was, in the doorway. The little girl jumped up, ran to him and he caught her in his arms, laughing. I quickly stepped out of sight. I was afraid to linger, I felt as if I had no more strength in my legs. I left him there and didn't dare return to disrupt his happy life.

It was early on Saturday morning and I hadn't even changed out of my motorcycle gear, because I'd come in only to check the status of one small patient of mine: a newborn who'd come out of surgery with me the evening before. She'd made it through the night. I said a few words to the parents, who were waiting in Intensive Care.

Even after all these years, I am still filled with awe each time I hold the knife in my hand. My patients are often small, so small that some have breathed our common air for only a few days, and here they lie under the scalpel. Every time, I am filled with dread that it is my skill that will determine if my charge shall live or die. I try to believe in fate. I try to tell myself after the failed surgeries that there are times when there is nothing anybody could have done better. Those are the nights when I lie in bed alone, reliving the operation, wondering why this one was chosen to die, wondering if I had made that choice by some error I had made. It is a task that demands constant perfection from me; perhaps that is why I chose this work, to have that unending call of faultlessness deafen me to the call of my own heart.

"Can I have a minute too, Doc?" It was Matt's voice in English that came out of the corridor. He was standing there in a T-shirt and jeans, and at the actual sight of him in the flesh, looking at me with the same golden eyes I'd dreamed about for so long, my heart inflated at such a speed that I thought I would die of joy right there.

I saw him take me in. A smile began to light up his face. "Kimberly."

A wave of happiness rose from my chest to my face and I looked down to hide my sudden flush. I shifted the motorcycle helmet to my other hand. I snuck another look at him and saw he really was older: instead of the young guy I'd known, this was a man. The muscles of his shoulders and arms were hard from a lifetime of physical labor, and the strength of his gaze seemed to say that he knew who he was.

Now he spoke in Chinese. "I wasn't sure I'd find you here today."

"Actually, I'm off duty. I just came to see one patient. Come on. Let's go to my office."

The walk through the hospital hallways felt electric with Matt by my side. I didn't know what to say, and I took care not to bump into him by accident, but I couldn't stop myself from smiling at the simple fact that he was here with me.

When we stepped inside my office, he took his time walking along the walls, looking at all my diplomas and awards. "You've come real far, factory girl."

I went to my desk, to flip over the only photo I

keep there. "Thanks," I said, trying to sound casual.

He noticed, of course, and came over to me. "You don't need to do that. I don't want to see the love of your life anyway."

I took a breath. "How's Park? And Vivian?"

He didn't seem surprised by my knowledge that he was with her again. He must have figured I would have found out. "Both fine. He's helping out at UPS, where I work, doing some odd jobs in the garage. Vivian's got a job at a bridal shop."

So Matt was working as a UPS guy. "What happened to her father's place?"

"Closed down. Bad economy. She's doing good too, the boss says she'll become the manager someday."

"Great," I said. I'd heard that one before and I knew Matt didn't believe it himself either. "I thought I saw her in a magazine years ago."

"Yeah, it probably was her. She did some modeling for a while but then she quit."

"Why?"

"Her husband got too jealous." He ran his fingers through his hair, seeming embarrassed. "Stupid guy, huh?"

I felt as if he'd struck me. He did love her, of course he did. They'd had years of loving each other and caring for each other. After I broke up with him, I found out that he'd gone back to her very soon afterward. I'd just been a short break in between Vivian and Vivian.

"And how are you?" I managed to ask.

He flicked his gaze across my large office, then shrugged, a bit defensively. "I make a good living."

"Yes." I looked up at him and I couldn't stop myself anymore. Slowly, I reached up, laid a hand against his cheek. I wished I could keep him safe the rest of his life. I took a deep breath. "I have to tell you—"

"I know."

"No, you don't."

"I'm not as dumb as I look. I was there too, remember, when we made the baby?"

I was speechless.

His voice cracked. "When you broke up with me, you shattered my heart. At first, I believed you that we were too different. 'A bamboo door needs a bamboo door and a metal door needs a metal door.' I'll never forget you saying those words. I always knew you were better than me, but I couldn't figure it out either, how you could be so cold all of a sudden. And then I counted the days and I knew."

I took him in my arms then and he let me. He still smelled the same, of aftershave and sandalwood soap. I pressed my cheek against his shoulder and whispered, "I'm sorry."

"That's why I never came after you. That's why I went back to Vivian."

"You already knew then?" I could hardly recognize my own voice. "You got back together with her because you hated me?"

"It broke me, Kimberly. You never asked me. You never gave me a chance. We could have made it. Maybe not with all those fancy degrees of yours, but we could have been together and we could have had our baby." Now his eyes were clotted with unshed tears.

"I can't tell you how much I regret what I did. I was never better than you, and I'm not now. In those days, our financial situation was so unsteady, I felt as if we were all hanging on to a tiny piece of flotsam that could never take all of our weight. You, me, Park, Ma, the baby. I had to cut you loose." I paused for a moment. "And I didn't think I could make you happy."

"What?"

"I know, we were so happy then. But I didn't think it was fair to tie you to me with a baby. Could you have lived with this? A pediatric cardiac surgeon for a wife? I often work eighty hours a week. I'm on call weekends and nights. It would have been different if you could have chosen freely, day by day, to be with me, but with the baby, you would have had no choice."

"What about you? You didn't have to become a surgeon. You could have stayed home. Are you happy now? I would have taken care of you."

My answer was soft. "I had an obligation to my ma and to myself. I couldn't have changed who I was. I wish I could have. Sometimes, I wish I had." I stopped and walked a few steps away. He was watching me. "But I wouldn't have been happy on your journey, and I know you wouldn't have been happy on mine."

"And our baby paid the price." His eyes were filled with emotion. "You don't know what it means to love a child."

I parted my lips to speak, ready to change everything now, but then he said, abruptly, "Vivian's pregnant again."

I was blinded as all the tears I'd been holding back rushed into my eyes. Despite all of my logical reasoning, despite knowing we could never really have a life together, I realized now I had hoped that if he knew the full story, our fate would somehow change. I turned away and wiped my face with the back of my hands. I felt his arms go around me.

He whispered into my hair, "It's always been you, Kimberly, from head to tail. But Vivian needs me."

My voice was quiet. "I know. Your family needs you. Matt, why did you come back here today?"

For a long moment, he held me. "For the same reason you sent me your card. To say good-bye."

I closed my eyes. "I'll give you a ride home."

Matt gave a long whistle when he saw the Ducati. Sleek and powerful, it was everything I had dreamed of in a motorcycle.

I'll never forget that ride with Matt. His arms were around me, the smell of leather was everywhere and the scenery of New York blurred and turned liquid as we raced by. I felt as if we were traveling through a time warp, back to that first bike ride when Matt was working as a pizza delivery boy. I wished we could go back to then and through all the years that we had missed together. He was wrapped close around me, my hair streaming back onto his neck. What I would have given to have that ride last forever.

I stopped the bike. He slowly let his arms drop away from me, as if he too were reluctant to let me go. I had parked the Ducati a short distance away from his current apartment building. They lived next to the FDR Drive. The roar of the highway must have been deafening in their apartment, and the ground seemed to tremble as we walked toward their place. I stopped around the corner from the entrance. I didn't want anyone to see us.

I swallowed. "That's it, I guess. Ride's over."

He didn't say anything. He just looked at me, his eyes sadder than anything I'd ever seen.

I saw the glint of gold around his neck, under his T-shirt, and I reached out a finger and touched it. "I remember this."

I pulled him down by the necklace around his neck. Slowly, we kissed. I was engulfed by the softness of his lips, the delicious taste of him. I had lived all these years for this kiss, so that I could be here, on this morning, with him. I would have given anything to be able to go home with him, go to our life together, with our children and no one else. Had I made the right decision? Could I have chosen the life he'd wanted for us? I hadn't had a choice, it was simply who I was.

Then we pulled away.

There was a long moment when he looked at me with his golden eyes. Again, I drew breath and he put his finger on my lips. "Kimberly, please don't say anything."

He slowly lifted his necklace with the Kuan Yin pendant over his head and poured it into my hand, as he'd done so long before by the steamers at the factory.

"Take this," he said. "Keep it. Stay safe."

"What will you tell Vivian?"

He gazed at me steadily. "I'm going to lie and tell her I lost it."

I knew I should have refused, given it back, but I wanted it too much. "I miss you, Matt. I will always miss you."

Despite his sadness, he shook his head with a hint of a wry grin. "One thing I know about you, Kimberly Chang, is that you'll always be all right."

"Good-bye, Matt."

He turned and walked into his apartment building, without looking back at me again.

I walked back to my bike. I don't know how long I stood there, staring at the building that contained their apartment, cherishing the knowledge that

Matt was inside. Then I started to ride away but my mind and heart were so filled with him that I couldn't help myself, and I pulled over to take one last look back.

One of the windows on the upper floors had just opened, as if that inhabitant also had too many thoughts on his mind, and someone climbed out onto one of the fire escapes. I knew it was Matt. I parked the bike on the side of the street and got off. It should have been obvious that that one was his apartment. It was crowded with plants and flowers: beautiful, that tiny fire escape filled with living things, a gentle protest against the highway and the city.

Vivian should have had my garden now. I was overwhelmed by the sheer size of that thing. Ma had taken it over for me, planting plot after plot filled with squash and winter melons, as if we were in danger of starvation. Then she would go to our bewildered neighbors with her extra vegetables in a little basket, still speaking almost no English.

"For you," Ma said.

At first, our neighbors had either refused or tried to pay her until they realized that she lived in one of the nicer houses on their street.

"Eccentric," they now whispered among themselves.

I got off my bike and walked a little closer. Matt stood there in the morning light, glorious in a thin T-shirt he'd changed into. He leaned on the railing while the highway rumbled behind him and the smog rose into the air. He was the most beautiful thing I'd ever seen.

And then she came out.

Her hair was long now, and it blew backward in the wind. Her shoulders and arms were thin in contrast to her swollen belly. She touched his shoulder, and whatever thoughts he may have been having dissipated and he was back there, with her, his lovely wife and mother of his children. He pulled her in front of him, wrapped his arms around her, and they stood there, looking out into their future.

It started to rain as I rode, the drops beating down on my helmet like a funeral drum. It was all so much. I could let go of my past with Matt. But what really hurt was the reanimation of a dream I'd thought I'd let go of. A future of lying with him every night in our bed, raising a family together, wavered against the reflection of my headlights on the tar and disappeared into the air like smoke from a fire.

I kept his necklace inside my glove during the whole ride home. It seemed longer than usual. My mind and heart were filled with Matt, the smell of him, the feel of him. How would I ever get him out of my head again? But in the end, my emotions quieted themselves and by the time I turned onto the long driveway of our house in Westchester, I knew that someday, I would be able to fully accept it all. In a bittersweet way, I was glad I had given him his happiness with Vivian.

I parked the Ducati in front of the garage, then composed myself before walking across the lawn. As I approached the entrance, my twelve-year-old boy hurtled out the door, his gym bag in tow.

"Hey, where are you going?" I asked in Chinese.

"I've got baseball practice! Mom, I'm going to be late." His Chinese, although not quite as perfect as his English, was excellent. Jason's face was so similar to his father's, Matt would have recognized him in a moment had he seen that photo in my office: the golden eyes, the bushy eyebrows, even the lock of hair that always fell in his face.

He was already getting his bicycle from the bike rack but I called, "Jason."

"I have to go."

"You forgot our special good-bye."

He paused, then ran back to me. "I'm too old for this."

"Come on." I put down my helmet and gloves and slipped Matt's necklace into my jacket pocket.

Then we both switched into English and chanted together, "I love you, give me a whack." We gave each other a high five. "Have a great day, and I'll be back."

He gave me a big hug and kissed me on the cheek. As he rode away down the street, he waved to me and called, "See you later, alligator."

● ● ●

In our spacious living room, Ma was wiping off her piano. The dust motes hung in the sunlit air. In her mid-fifties now, she was still beautiful. I paused in the entryway to watch her.

Without glancing at me, Ma said, "The animal doctor called again. He must worry about the cat. Although the cat doesn't seem to be sick." Now she looked up and raised her eyebrows, challenging me to give her more information. Andy, the gray tiger cat in question, was sitting in one of the Palladian windows behind Ma, licking his white paws.

I chose not to respond to this. I'd been surprised when Tim, our vet, slipped in an invitation to an art opening with his last bill. We'd gone out a few times since then, and I liked him because he was gentle and patient. I'd stopped telling Ma about any of the men I dated because she always wanted me to marry them. "I'm feeling a bit tired. I want to lie down."

Ma knew something had happened. She crossed over to me. "Are you all right?"

"Yes." I managed to smile.

I went upstairs and shut myself in my bedroom. I closed the shutters to darken the room, then slipped the CD from Bellini's *Norma,* which I'd seen at the Met with Ma, into the stereo. I lay on the bed with Matt's necklace in my hand and let it all wash over me.

Ma and Annette had both come with me for the

abortion, both sat outside in the waiting room as I was being prepped. Before they could do anything, the doctors needed to confirm the length of the pregnancy by means of an ultrasound. A mere technicality, I'd thought. The technician smeared a viscous gel across my stomach. I had goose bumps on my skin. I felt I would die from the cold. She kept my hospital gown open so she could use the ultrasound wand to locate the fetus.

I expected a clump of cells attached to the uterine wall. I kept my mind carefully blank but without warning, an image of the fetus sprang onto the screen and I gasped. I shifted so abruptly that I dislodged her wand. The technician gave me an irritated look, which I registered in the back of my mind, but I ignored her injunction to stay still. I was riveted by the monitor.

He was doing gymnastics. A small tadpole-like figure, he pushed himself against the thick uterine walls and toppled over, swayed from side to side, swam in that enormous space with complete joy. He was defiant and playful, I imagined he was laughing. In that moment, I started to love him, Matt's child. And mine forever.

If his father had been another man, I think I may still have gone through with it. But he was Matt's. As soon as I saw him, I had no choice, even though our journey afterward was not easy. If it hadn't been for my talent for school, we would all have gone under.

When I didn't go through with the abortion, I did wonder if my relationship with Matt could possibly recover. I'd even gone to look for him, and seen him with Vivian again. How that had hurt. I didn't know he'd already figured out what I'd done, what I'd intended to do. I could have broken them up again, I knew that. But the pain had given me more time to think, and I realized the baby didn't actually change anything: much as it wounded me to admit it, I had to face the fact that in the end, I would have made Matt unhappy.

Ma and I brought Jason up carefully, the two women who were his only parents. He loved me so much. I was away for much of the time he was growing up. From when he was just a little boy, he noticed the rare occasions I bought something new for myself. "Pretty Mommy," he would say. Before his round childish eyes, I truly felt beautiful. How he cried every time I had to leave, even though Ma, his grandmother, was always there for him. I would come home deep in the night to find him clutching his grandmother in his sleep, in a chair before the front door, where he'd waited for me to come home until they both fell asleep again.

The first apartment he lived in was that one in Queens, a paradise compared to the old one in Brooklyn, which he never saw. I remember Ma would run her hands over the surfaces of the furniture, the walls, the kitchen appliances in a sort of dazed surprise. I too was amazed that the walls and floor were clean and intact, that when we were all in the living room together there were still other rooms in the apartment, empty of people and insects.

I deferred Yale for a year to have him. Those were the hardest times, when Ma and I worked on sacks of jewelry at home to keep the pregnancy hidden. With both of us working as hard as we could, we could barely make the rent and bills. Then soon after Jason was born, I took double shifts sorting mail at night at the post office so I could be with him as much as possible when he was awake. At the beginning of the following school year, we all moved together to New Haven, to a little apartment close to the university. Once I was under Yale's protection, things got a bit easier.

We got by on scholarships and loans. I worked four jobs at a time while I was a student, but I still graduated with honors and then moved on to Harvard Medical School. In those debt-ridden years before I finished medical school, I called upon any and every talent I had to become the best surgeon I could.

I gave Matt this: his life with Vivian and his family, his simple happiness. At the same time, I took away his life with us. I owed Jason a great debt, one I could never repay. I kept him from his father all these years. When I gave Matt up, I forced Jason to do the same. For my attempt at nobility, our son paid the price. He was still young enough not to ask me too much about the topic I didn't want to talk about: his father. I knew there would be a time when he would want to know the whole truth. What would I tell him? How could I know what the truth was, so long ago, when I knew so little myself?

I sat up as the lyrics of "Sola, furtiva, al tempio" filled the room:

> *I break the sacred bonds.*
> *May you live happy, forever,*
> *Close to the one you love.*

Then I took a deep breath, got off the bed and opened the door.

ACKNOWLEDGMENTS

I would like to thank first my mother, Shuet King Kwok, who taught me the meaning of kindness and courage, and my late father, Shun Kwok, who always led the way for my family.

With the publication of this debut novel, I've stepped into unfamiliar territory. Fortunately, my agent, Suzanne Gluck of William Morris Endeavor Entertainment, knows every pathway of all the worlds I need to navigate. I have complete admiration for my entire team there, especially my international agents, Tracy Fisher and Raffaella De Angelis, and Suzanne Gluck's assistants: Elizabeth Tingue, Caroline Donofrio and, most especially, Sarah Ceglarski.

Every single person at Riverhead has been phenomenal. With her unfailing intelligence and sensitivity, my editor, Sarah McGrath, has the ability to step inside the text. She's the ideal reader and editor I've always imagined. Special thanks to Marilyn Ducksworth, Stephanie Sorensen, and Sarah McGrath's assistant, the insightful Sarah Stein. My foreign publishers have also been wonderful, especially Juliet Annan and Maaike le Noble.

Lois Rosenthal, editor in chief of the now defunct *Story* magazine, was the first to pluck me out of the slush pile and teach me what fierce editing was all about. The Columbia MFA program showed me how to become a professional: in particular, Helen Schulman and Rebecca Goldstein made all the difference to me. I'm also grateful to the people who included me in the Holt textbook *Elements of Literature: Third Course:* Karen Peterfreund, Mary Monaco and Ann Farrar.

These are the professionals who assured me the road ahead was safe: author Pete Jordan and especially author Patricia Wood, who has been so generous in sharing her knowledge and experience with a person who e-mailed her out of the blue (me). Most of all, I'm grateful to Lisa Friedman of the Amsterdam Writing Workshops for her tremendous kindness and wisdom.

Special thanks to readers and friends Hans and Henriet Omloo, and the great Dutch poets and writers Leo and Tineke Vroman. Thanks also to other talented writers, readers and friends: Erica Bilder and Jill Whittaker (both of whom gave me helpful feedback at a critical moment), Shelley Anderson, Kerrie Finch, Kate Simms, Sinead Hewson, Pubudu Sachithanandan, Ingrid Froelich, Chauna Craig and Sari Wilson. Katrina Middelburg-Creswell not only helped me find the title but also showed me the right way to end the book.

My friends are an inspiration: actress/dancer Julie Voshell, artist/puppeteer Alex Kahn and brilliant/indefinable Lisa Donner. Eric Linus

Kaplan first pointed me in the right direction, and Shauna Angel Blue took the earliest professional photo of me. The many students I had at Leiden University and the Delft University of Technology kept me enthusiastic through the years. I'm also indebted to my friends with impeccable taste: Sally O'Keeffe, Shih Hui Liong and Astrid Stikkelorum (thanks for lending me your clothes).

I'm proud of my six older sisters and brothers, who have all come so far: Lai Fong, Kam, Choi, Chow (Joe), York and most especially my genius brother Kwan, who got me my first set of contact lenses and helped me in every possible way. And my nieces and nephews keep me up-to-date on everything cool: Diana, Elaine, Justine, Amanda, Wendy, Ping, David, Eton, Elton, Alex and Jonathan.

My life in Holland would be much less fun without my in-laws, the fabulous rockin'-and-rollin' Kluwer family: Gerard, Betty, Michael and Sander. Special thanks to Betty and Gerard, who have done so much for me and my book.

And finally, I am so grateful to my three guys, Erwin, Stefan and Milan, without whom I would truly be lost.

Center Point Publishing
600 Brooks Road ● PO Box 1
Thorndike ME 04986-0001 USA

(207) 568-3717

US & Canada:
1 800 929-9108
www.centerpointlargeprint.com